Sing Your Heart Out

Crystal Kaswell

ISBN-10: 1942135092
ISBN-13: 978-1942135098

CHAPTER ONE

Between the throbbing house music and the dance floor full of beautiful people grinding, it's difficult to move. It's harder to think.

I need to pee. Now. Waiting in the line snaking around the corner is not an option.

How can there only be one bathroom downstairs? One hundred people plus one bathroom equals far too many tortured bladders.

Kara must know where the bathroom is. Wherever she is.

I push through the crowd, but there's no sign of my best friend.

Someone bumps into me, her hip pressing firmly against my pelvis. Dammit, my bladder is going to explode at this rate.

Screw upstairs being off-limits. This isn't a church. It's some up-and-coming band's Hollywood mansion. I'm not about to pee my pants respecting the sanctity of rock stars' bedrooms.

There's a couple making out on the curving

staircase. I step past them and make my way to the second floor. The sounds of music and conversation fade to a murmur. I'm tempted to hang out here until Kara is ready to go home.

Parties are not my scene. Even my bladder hates them.

I scan the wall, trying to figure out which of the five doors is attached to the smallest room. There. Second on the left. That must be it.

I turn the knob and push the door open.

Not a bathroom.

Definitely not a bathroom.

There are two people on a bed. The woman is on all fours. The man is kneeling behind her.

They're naked.

They're having sex.

Then they're not. The grunting stops. Flesh ceases to smack together.

The man looks at me. There's no sign of embarrassment or awkwardness on his face. He's totally unmoved.

The woman shrieks. She scrambles off the bed, pulling a sheet over her chest. "Miles, you fucker. I told you I don't do threesomes!"

Miles. There's something familiar about him. I try to place him but my thinking abilities are back to zero.

He's tall, broad shoulders and chest, sculpted abs, and below his bellybutton...

He's hard.

He's hard and he's huge.

Save for the condom, he's completely and utterly naked.

A blush spreads across my cheeks. I stammer,

attempting and failing to speak. I've never seen that before. Not in person. In movies, sure. Textbooks, of course.

But never in person.

I can't look away.

The guy, Miles, makes eye contact. His voice is even. Calm. "You mind?"

I take a step backwards. My foot sinks into the plush carpet. I only barely manage to hold my balance. "Excuse me. I thought this was the bathroom."

"Next door on the left."

I know I'm red. Beet red. "Thanks."

I pull the door closed so I'm alone in the hallway. Next door on the left.

I step into the bathroom, lock the door, and die of embarrassment.

It takes twenty minutes for my cheeks to return to a normal color. I slink back to the sprawling main room and do my best to blend in amongst the partygoers.

Every inch of the hardwood floor is packed with beautiful people talking, flirting, or making out.

It's like the up-and-coming models, actors, and musicians are attracted to each other. They have a certain glow that mere mortals lack. And here I thought this was a normal college-students-with-a-keg-and-cheap-vodka kind of shindig.

Kara's friend invited us. He's in a band. Are they really this popular? I can't remember their name, but then it's hard to think of anything but Miles naked on the bed, hard and ready for action.

The lines of his hips and torso are burned into my

brain.

And his…

Dammit, I'm not going there.

I find the closest thing to an empty corner and try to clear my head. I fail. My mind keeps going back to that vivid mental image.

Miles. He was unfazed, like the sex meant nothing to him. Like the girl on his bed meant nothing to him.

The man is a player. He's not the kind of guy I need in my life. He doesn't deserve my thoughts.

This stops. Now.

I scan the room for some better way to stay occupied.

It's no use. He's here. Miles is still effortless and aloof. He's still unaffected.

The guy has already moved on from the blonde in the bedroom. He's flirting with a redhead in a designer dress and stilettos.

She's model gorgeous with perfect hair and makeup. I'm standing here in an H&M skirt and blouse, my brown hair its usual frizzy mess, my black eyeliner doing little to enhance my plain-Jane brown eyes. Liner, mascara, and under-eye concealer are the extent of my makeup knowledge. I think I'm the only woman here who isn't contoured. Hell, I know I'm the only one wearing canvas sneakers.

I don't belong here.

It doesn't make sense that Miles is looking at me instead of the pretty redhead.

But he is. His clear blue eyes are fixed on mine. They're gorgeous. I couldn't see them in the dark but out here, they're practically shining.

Heat spreads across my chest. I'm gawking.

He smiles, reveling in my attention.

I press my eyelids together to temper my out-of-control blushing. It's no help. My head fills with that beautiful image of him in nothing but a condom.

Why did I let Kara talk me into coming to this party?

I push my way through the crowd, trying to get as far from Miles's gaze as possible. A dozen steps and I'm standing in the clean, modern kitchen. It's dark and mostly empty.

"You're not big on respecting people's privacy, huh?"

It's the same voice I heard upstairs. Miles.

I could swear I've heard it before. A lot, even.

I turn so we're face to face. Why does Miles seem so familiar? I don't go to parties. Hell, I've been MIA the last few months.

I wouldn't forget his strong jaw, his messy brown hair, or his gorgeous blue eyes.

Those eyes are fixed on me. He's staring at me, picking me apart.

I don't like the scrutiny. Sure, I'm hiding. But I'm not admitting that to him.

I clear my throat. "No, I'm not big on alcohol. Can't find anything else to drink."

He reaches past me. His hand brushes against my shoulder as he pulls open the fridge. He nods to a row of water bottles on the middle shelf. "Help yourself."

"Thanks."

Miles looks so familiar. And his voice is familiar too. Almost like he...

No. That's not possible.

There's no way this guy is the singer of alternative rock band Sinful Serenade, the guy who sings In

Pieces, the guy who's been haunting my thoughts for the last three months with his breathy, tortured voice. With all the pain in his soulful eyes.

I try to recall the song's music video but my damn brain goes right back to the image of Miles naked on the bed.

Damn. I watched that video a thousand times. It was a massive hit. The song hit the top 40 for a week or two, a rarity for alternative rock in this day and age.

More importantly, the video and the song went right to my soul. The singer was whispering in my ear. He promised that I wasn't alone. He promised that I wasn't the only person who had ever felt this way.

I understood him and he understood me. We were the only two people in the world who knew how badly it hurt, losing everything that mattered.

The man who sings In Pieces is a tortured soul. He doesn't screw one woman, wash up, then move on to flirting with lay number two.

Kara keeps playing down how famous her friend is.

He lives here. I know that much.

This Miles guy seems to live here.

Fuck.

Why didn't Kara warn me her friend was in that band?

Miles clears his throat. "You okay?"

I nod a yes and attempt to hold his gaze. "Don't walk in on casual sex very often."

"Mhmm."

"I was looking for the bathroom."

He laughs. "Is that the best you can do?"

"I was." I take a half-step backwards. "Excuse me. I should go."

His voice drops an octave. "You're not going to let me formally introduce myself?"

"Okay." My stomach flutters. "I'm Meg Smart."

"Miles Webb." He takes my hand with a strong grip. His eyes pass over me like he's trying to place me. "How is it we haven't met before?"

"I don't go to parties."

"Guess that makes this my lucky day." His hand brushes against my wrist. Then it's back at his side. He leans in a little closer, his eyes on mine. "Why'd you decide to come tonight?"

I should be the one asking him that. "My friend convinced me I wouldn't hate it."

"What's the verdict?"

"I still don't like parties." I take a deep breath. "Why'd you come tonight?"

"That was my bedroom you burst into."

Somehow, my cheeks burn hotter.

His eyes rake over me. "Can't blame you for looking. I'd do the same."

My knees go weak at the seductive tone to his voice. That's him, the guy who sings In Pieces, the man who has been haunting my dreams.

That song is the centerpiece of my listen on repeat and fall apart playlist.

I try to formulate some excuse for why I need to leave immediately, but nothing comes. "You're um… you're in the band? The one that is throwing this party?"

"Yeah. Sinful Serenade. I'm the vocalist." His eyes pass over me again. He takes his time, like he's sure I'll be in his bed in thirty minutes flat.

A pang of desire shoots straight to my core. My damn body isn't obeying my commands. It can't help wanting Miles Webb. There's something appealing about the tattoos poking out from under his t-shirt. About the confidence in his eyes.

It's not like me to fall for the bad boy.

Even when he's so tall. Two inches taller than me at least. I'm 5'11', a giant for a women. I tower over most of the men I know.

But not Miles.

I take a deep breath, trying to convince my body it doesn't want him.

He's bad news.

A player.

A rock star even.

But I can't stop staring.

I clear my throat. "I was looking for my friend, Kara. She's tight with some guy in your band. They go way back."

"Oh, yeah, Drew's friend. Heard a lot about her last tour."

"So, I should really find her." I step aside. "And go home. I have to study. You know how it is. Or maybe not, being a rock star and all. But I have a test tomorrow."

I turn and make my way out of the kitchen.

There are footsteps behind me. "Meg?"

I spin, eye to eye with Miles again. Once again, my mind flashes with the image of him kneeling on that bed, his cock hard, the muscles of his thighs and torso taut.

How is it possible that Miles is the guy who has been singing me to sleep? He's not a poet.

He's a manwhore.

"Yes?" I ask.

"Your friend isn't in a state to drive."

He points to Kara, curled up on the couch. Her dark eyes are filled with an expression of drunken excitement. She looks especially short and curvy next to her tall, muscular friend. That must be Drew. His black hair and intense brown eyes are appealing. No wonder she's staring at him like she wants to devour him.

She bounces to her feet and throws her arms around me. "Are you having fun? Please, tell me you aren't completely miserable."

I hug back. "Only partially."

She laughs. "That's a start!"

Good. She still happy. Kara is an endlessly patient friend. She's been dragging me out of mourning for months now. I'm not going to ruin her night.

"I'm about ready to go home," I say. "I'll take a cab."

"No. I can drive. It's getting late," she says.

The dark-haired guy, Drew, butts in. "Kendrick, you are way too drunk to drive. If you even think about getting in your car, I'll throw you over my shoulder, carry you to my room, and strap you to my bed."

Her eyes light up the second he calls her by her last name. "I didn't know you were into that. Do you have rope or handcuffs or what?"

"I'll call you a fucking cab." His voice is equal parts playful and protective.

She nudges him and points to me. "This is my friend Meg, who you are so rudely ignoring in favor of lecturing me."

He pushes off the couch and offers his hand. "Drew Denton. Nice to meet you."

I shake. "Meg Smart."

"Miles giving you a hard time?" Drew asks.

"I can handle myself," I say.

"If you won't listen to reason—" Drew turns back to Kara "—then I will drive you home."

Kara looks Drew in the eyes. "You were drinking too."

"I can." I bite my tongue. Dammit, Kara's car is a stick. I can't drive us home. "Never mind."

Miles butts in. "I'll drive you guys home."

Drew's eyes narrow. He shoots Miles an incredulous look.

"Not letting you drive tonight." Miles throws back a stern look. "You'd do the same."

Slowly, Drew's protective expression melts. He and Miles share a look of understanding.

The cocky singer turns to Kara. "Your keys."

"It's a manual." She digs through her purse.

"That's fine." He smirks. "I know how to handle my stick."

CHAPTER TWO

After three minutes of giving directions, Kara rests her head against the backseat door and falls asleep.

I'm as good as alone with Miles.

I try to think up small talk, but nothing comes to me. So much for that. I should probably give directions. "You want the Wilshire exit off the 405."

"Mhmmm." He turns to me for a moment then his eyes are on the road. "Should be twenty minutes."

"Right."

"Anything else you want to discuss?" he teases.

I clear my throat. "I'm not sure what you mean."

"Yes you are."

I need to set the record straight here. "Kara is my closest friend. I don't know how close you and Drew are or how long you'll be in Los Angeles, but I figure you and I are mutual friends... so how about we agree to never discuss this again?"

A smug smile spreads across his face. "I can't agree to that."

"Why not?"

"You're too cute when you blush."

"I'm not cute." I bite my tongue so I don't snap. Who the hell does he think he is calling me cute? Deep breath. I can be as cool and aloof as he is. "Let's pretend it never happened."

"If it bothers you that much." He stops at a red light. "But it's not a big deal. Nothing you haven't done before."

Right. Because I'm a twenty-one-year-old college senior. And no normal college senior is quite so sexually inexperienced.

"Of course," I say.

A smug smile spreads over his face. His eyes fill with disbelief.

I try my most confident voice. "I've had boyfriends." I hate that look. I'm not an innocent flower. "We did all sorts of stuff." In high school, above the waist, but he doesn't need to know that.

"There's no shame in lacking sexual experience. In being a virgin even."

"I know, but I'm not."

He cocks a brow.

"It's really none of your business."

The light turns green. Miles steps on the gas. Changes gears until he's going way over the speed limit. "What's your favorite sexual position?"

"I'd rather not discuss that with a stranger."

"What happened to us being mutual friends?"

A compelling point. I shrug like I'm as unaffected as he is. "Um… missionary."

He laughs, not at all buying my answer. "Second favorite?"

I try to think up something less obvious than missionary but I draw a blank. What the hell? My brain has no problem imagining me and Miles in the throes of passion—¬him pressing me against the wall, me climbing onto him in the driver's seat, the two of us tangled together on his bed—but it is utterly unable to articular any words.

He stops short at a yellow light. "I can show you a few good ones."

I take a deep breath so I won't turn the color of a tomato. "Excuse me?"

His eyes find mine. His expression is the epitome of confidence. "You do want to fuck me."

"I do not."

He shakes his head. "You've been picturing me naked all night."

"Because I saw you naked. I couldn't help it."

"Mhmm." The light turns green and he slams on the gas. He turns the corner and speeds onto the freeway on-ramp. "And now you're thinking about it."

"I'm not."

"I'm better than whatever you're imagining."

"Did you even know that girl's name?"

"Yeah."

I'm not convinced. "What was it?"

"Stephanie. Pretty sure it was Stephanie." He shrugs. "It's just sex. You'd know if you—"

"My sex life is none of your business."

"Don't have to be defensive about it. Nothing wrong with being a virgin."

I cross my legs. I'm sure Miles never has to be defensive about his sex life. Nobody ever thinks he's uncool or uptight. Nobody looks at him like he's a buzzkill.

He's a stud.

Hell, he's a rising rock star.

I want to explain it, to justify my frustration, but he's still aloof as hell and I'm still rattled. Why bother?

Social lives are overrated.

The weight of the silence spreads through the car. It's too much. I have to turn the radio on. It's tuned to KROQ and, God help me, the station is playing In Pieces.

The vocals are a low moan, a sound meant to express an extreme outpouring of emotion. I can't get past the moan. Is that what Miles sounds like when he's mid orgasm?

I scramble to change the station. Rock. That won't do. I find the oldies station. It's sure to be free of Miles's voice.

He laughs. "You're cute when you're nervous."

I fold my arms over my chest. "Do you have a problem with oldies?"

"That's why you changed the station, just hoping to hear Build Me Up Buttercup?"

"No, I was hoping for Happy Together."

He smiles and looks at me. "You want your first time to be good?"

"I'm not…"

"I'm more than happy to oblige."

What the hell? Is he serious? I take a deep breath. I don't like how rattled I feel. I need it to stop. "I don't need your pity sex."

He raises a brow. "There'd be no pity about it. I want to fuck you, too."

"There's no 'too.' I don't want to… I don't date."

"It's just sex. Might let you buy me breakfast in the morning, but it's not a date."

My mind goes blank. He's direct and confident. He knows exactly what he wants and he just goes for it.

How the hell does he do that?

Words escape me. Talking is overrated.

I turn up the radio, settle into my seat, and watch the sky whiz by outside the windows.

It feels like an eternity passes, but finally we arrive at Kara's apartment.

Miles gets out of the car but stays out of earshot. I walk Kara up the stone staircase and fish through her purse for her keys.

She looks at me with concern. "Thanks for coming out, but Meg—"

"Yeah?"

Her gaze drifts to Miles leaning against the car. "Be careful. Miles is a total whore."

"Drink some water."

She steps into her apartment. "He was flirting with you."

"You were listening?"

She smiles deviously, clearly not as drunk as she let on. "I worry about you. Be careful, okay?"

I nod.

I must look more confident than I feel, because she closes the door without another word.

This night needs to end. Now. I rush down the steps, one at a time. Then the ground. Only it's not the ground. There's another step.

Fuck. I try to steady myself. It doesn't work.

I go down, landing on my hands and knees.

Ow. My wrists are okay but my knee is screaming.

"Hey." Miles's voice is close.

He's a mere foot away. How did he get here so fast?

He kneels next to me. "You mind?"

"I'm fine. I can clean up at home."

"Let me see."

"I don't need your help."

"You're bleeding."

Dammit. He's right. My knee is scrapped and bleeding.

His eyes find mine. He raises a brow as if to ask permission. This time, I nod.

Miles's fingers skim my skin as he inspects my wrists. Then they're on the tops of my knees. The gentle touch sends heat flooding through my body.

I wasn't lying to Miles. I don't date. Everything in my life is arranged around getting into medical school. Between studying and my part-time job, I have barely any time and energy. It's hard enough keeping my life on track without adding a boyfriend to the mix.

I've never met a guy who seemed worth the trouble. I've certainly never had a guy's touch stir this kind of desire.

I want those hands under my clothes.

My heart thuds against my chest. It's terrifying how badly I want those hands under my clothes.

Miles looks up at me. "This is a bad scrape. You have a first aid kit?"

"I can take care of it."

"I bruised plenty of knuckles in my day. I'm bandaging that. Either we do it at your apartment, or we go to a twenty-four-hour pharmacy."

Going back to my place will be faster. I nod fine and follow him to the car.

He slides into the driver's seat. "Where do you live?"

"Sawtelle and Idaho. The complex on the left."

He drives without any need for directions. After a few quick turns, we pull into the garage. But the gate to the underground garage is closed. Damn. The only way to unlock it is by inputting the code and my landlord can't stand tenants giving it out to strangers.

That means I have to lean over Miles to do this.

I motion to the window. "You mind?"

He nods and rolls the window down.

Here goes nothing. I undo my seatbelt and lean over him, planting one hand on the windowsill. It brings my body over his, my chest over his mouth. His soft, slow exhale sends shivers down my spine.

His lips are inches from my chest. I want those inches gone, want my blouse and bra gone. Want his mouth on my skin.

I've never felt like that before.

Ever.

I input the code as quickly as possible. There. The garage door opens. I slide back into my seat and direct him to my open parking spot.

Now there's nothing left to do but lead him to my apartment.

Just me and the rock star playboy, alone in my apartment.

What could possibly go wrong?

Clothes cover the already limited floor space of my tiny studio. The desk is littered with papers and notecards. The kitchenette is no better.

Damn, it looks like a slob lives here. I've been lax about cleaning, about taking care of myself, about everything, really. Ever since Rosie... it's hard to do anything.

I never want anything.

Only I want Miles.

I want him in my bed.

Want us out of these stupid clothes.

I take a deep breath, trying to shake it off. Figures I want something bad for me. It's fitting, really. If I'm not careful, I'll fall down the same rabbit hole that destroyed her.

I kick a pair of underwear out of view and take a seat on the bed.

Miles is close.

There are only two feet between the bed and the wall. There's nowhere else for him to be. The reasonable explanation does nothing to calm my racing heart.

Miles scans the walls, taking in the movie posters breathing life into the otherwise drab room—the Star Wars original trilogy, Jurassic Park, The Matrix, Dark City, and The Terminator.

His lips curl into a smile. "I like your décor."

"I'm sure you've seen plenty of women's apartments with much better décor."

"I still like yours." He sits me on the bed. "First aid kit?"

I point him to the bathroom. He disappears for a moment and returns with a bottle of rubbing alcohol, a bag of cotton balls, and a wide bandage. I don't remember buying any of this. Must have been Rosie's.

I guess she doesn't need them anymore.

"You don't have any antibacterial cream?" he asks.

"Only have the kit."

"Get the cream for next time." He uncaps the rubbing alcohol, presses the cotton ball over it, and tilts the bottle. His eyes find mine. "This will sting."

Miles drops to his knees, kneeling in front of me like he's about to pull off my panties and plant his face between my thighs.

The beautiful mental image dies the moment he presses the cotton ball to my skin. Ow. Ow. Ow. It doesn't just sting. It burns like hell.

"Fuck," I mutter.

"Here." He presses his lips together and blows cool air over the wound.

It lessens the sting but it sets the rest of my body on fire. He pats my skin dry and applies a bandage. There. Fixed. We're done.

Only he's still here, still between my legs.

He looks up at me. His fingertips trail along the inside of my calf as he pulls his hands back to his sides. "Better?"

"I could have handled that." I press my knees together. I want him. I can't deal with that. I need to tell him to leave. "But yes. Thanks."

"My pleasure."

He's still here. I'm still on my bed. It would be easy to remind him of his offer.

Maybe I can be casual and aloof too. Maybe sex is the secret to not feeling like my heart weighs a thousand pounds.

Or maybe I'll go down the same path my sister did.

I clear my throat. "It's getting late. I should go to bed."

"Sure." He pushes himself up to his feet. He plops on the bed next to me, his jean-clad thigh pressed against my bare skin. "You have a cell phone?"

My hands share none of my caution. They dig into my purse and offer him my cell.

He taps the screen for a moment and hands it back. There he is, in my phone: Miles Webb. I have his number, his email, his address even.

He stares at me like he's thinking about how easy it would be to pin me to the bed and pull my panties to my knees.

Or maybe I'm projecting.

His lips curl into a smile. "Let me know if you need anything."

"What would I need?"

"To satisfy your curiosity."

Time to put an end to this flirtation. I clear my throat and throw my shoulders back. I can do confidence too. "Listen, Miles. I'm sure you're a great guy in a lot of ways, and I'm sure I'll see you again, what with our mutual best friends."

"True." His voice is calm, totally unfazed.

"But I'd appreciate it if you'd stop flirting with me."

He nods. "If you stop staring at me like you're thinking about what you want to do to me."

I know what I want to do to him. I want to tell him to go screw himself. I fire up an insult and turn to face Miles. But when our eyes connect, my mouth goes sticky.

He chuckles. "That look, right now, you're thinking about fucking me."

"You're mistaken."

"No, I'm not." He stares into my eyes. "I don't want to make you uncomfortable. If you're not interested, stop undressing me with your eyes, and I'll stop flirting."

I go to stammer an objection but I've got nothing. Are people really this direct? It's unnerving.

An electric current courses through my body, settling between my legs.

What would his hands feel like farther up my

thighs? Under my skirt? Under my panties? My body is begging me to find out.

"I won't stare." I press my palms together, but I'm not at all convincing. I'm staring right now. "I'll work on it."

He pushes himself to his feet. "I really hope you don't."

I'm not interested. I open my mouth to say the words. Nothing. I am interested. I'm unbearably interested.

Shit. I have to say something. "Have a safe ride home."

His lips curl into a cocky smile. "Sweet dreams."

He nods goodbye on his way out the door.

Damn, that was close.

I collapse on the bed. My heart is pounding against my chest. My lungs are totally void of oxygen.

Miles Webb, the gorgeous rock star, singer of the band poised to be the next big thing, wants me. He could have any buxom actress or model he wants, and he wants me. Flat-chested, gawky, wallflower me.

CHAPTER THREE

The buzzing of my cell phone snaps me out of my poetry class¬induced dazed. This is one of the smaller lecture rooms. It fits about a hundred people but there are only fifteen in this class.

I pull my cell phone from the front pocket of my jeans as discreetly as possible.

Miles: How about a picture of your wound?

My palms are slick with sweat. It's not the temperature. It's nerves. Doesn't help that Kara is sitting next to me, sipping a can of black tea, scribbling notes with her purple pen.

She shoots me a knowing look. "Who is that?"

I clear my throat. "Shouldn't you be hungover?"

She certainly doesn't look any worse for wear. Her hair and makeup are perfect. Her wrinkle-free blouse does amazing things to highlight her ample chest.

"Lucky me, my friend reminded me to hydrate." She pulls a can of green tea from her backpack and places it on my desk. "I know how to repay the favor."

Yes, sweet caffeine. I pop open the can and down half of it in one sip. It's a sencha green tea—crisp, nutty, ever so slightly grassy. Damn, it's good. With my next sip, I finish the can.

My eyes meet Kara's. She cocks a brow as if to say don't play dumb.

Okay, I won't play dumb. But I won't admit it either. Kara and I have an unspoken policy of not prying. Or at least we did, before everything with Rosie, before I spent the summer locked in my room with sad songs on repeat.

Now, she asks questions. She makes a point of dragging me out of my misery. I appreciate the concern, I do, but I'm tired of the kid gloves.

I wait until she turns her attention to her notes to text Miles.

Meg: Something tells me sending you pictures is a bad idea.

Miles: Suit yourself. I was going to send you something very nice in return.

Meg: Nice how?

Miles: A picture for a picture.

A blush spreads across my cheeks. He can't mean a picture of that.

Kara clears her throat. "How is Miles?"

I shrug and slide my phone into my lap.

"Sweetie, whatever story you're selling, I'm not buying it." She taps her pen against her paper. "Did he keep flirting after you dropped me off?"

The professor is explaining some poetic device with absolutely no enthusiasm. You'd think a guy who devotes his life to a romantic art form would have a little passion, but no.

"It was a total non-event," I say.

"What happened to your knee?" She points to the bandage on my leg.

"I fell. No big deal."

"Swear he didn't give you a hard time."

If only. The image of him naked on the bed, hard and ready, flashes through my mind. Dammit. I don't think about guys during class. I don't text during class. Medical school is competitive. I'll never make it if I get derailed this easily. That's not an option.

I have to make it. For myself and for Rosie.

I slide my phone into my backpack and turn to Kara. "Miles is fine. He's not going to be my best friend, but I won't cry if you want to do something with him and Drew. Not a double date but—"

"We're just friends." She looks at me carefully, examining me. "You know he's a player."

"I figured." I adjust my t-shirt. "You know I'm twenty-one, right? I can handle being alone with a man."

"He goes through three girls a week."

"I get that he's a slut. I can handle that. I'm not a child."

She shrinks back, wounded. "Just want to help."

"I know. But I'm doing better than I was in June." I look to my notes before the uncertainty in my eyes will give me away. "Would it be so wrong if I did have sex with him?"

"Not wrong, no. But do you really want to—" she lowers her voice to a whisper "—lose your virginity to a manwhore?"

"Maybe."

"If you're sure it's what you want, I can help."

"I'm just thinking out loud."

"Maybe think about it when you're in bed alone

tonight." She winks.

My cheeks flush.

"Did you already?" Her eyes light up. "He is hot. Super hot."

Okay, maybe I did. Masturbation isn't a crime. Last night was the first time I enjoyed myself in a while.

It was the first time I fell asleep thinking about something besides losing my sister.

It's scary, actually, like I'll lose her all over again.

I change the subject to something less embarrassing. "Jurassic Park is playing at the Nuart Friday at midnight."

"I'm there."

All day, my phone burns a hole in my pocket. It taunts me during lunch. It taunts me during my bio test. It taunts me during the lulls of my shift at the ER.

I write a dozen text replies in my head but none of them are right. I can't care what Miles thinks of me. Writing papers, studying, my job—it doesn't pay well but it's great experience—those come before guys.

But when I get home and collapse on my bed, I keep thinking of him.

I want his hard body pressed against mine, his soft lips on my skin.

How the hell does this flirting thing work?

I take a picture of my skinned knee and send it to him.

Meg: Don't complain if you think it's gross.

He replies quickly.

Miles: Right back at you.

There's a picture message attached—the back of

his hand. His knuckles are battered and covered in scar tissue. He got into a lot of fights once upon a time.

Meg: That's not what I thought you'd send.

Miles: Imagining some place a little lower and lot more exciting?

Vividly. I change into my pajamas in an attempt to buy myself time to think.

It's been easy avoiding complications until now. Guys never interested me. School took precedent. Period.

But then I never felt like this. I never craved someone's hands on my body.

I certainly never hoped a guy would send me a naughty picture.

I play with my phone. Maybe it's a good thing that Miles is experienced. He'll know what he's doing. Know how to make sure I enjoy myself.

Or maybe he'll be all aloof and cool and I'll be a nervous, tongue-tied mess.

Dammit, I don't know.

Meg: No, I wouldn't expect you to send a picture like that unless I asked.

Miles: Accurate.

Meg: I'm not going to ask.

Miles: Good. I'd say no. You have to earn that.

Meg: No, I have to go study.

Miles: It's almost eleven.

Meg: Just got off work at the ER. No time to waste.

Miles: You work in an ER?

Meg. Yeah. Why do you ask?

Miles: Your reaction times are a little slow.

Meg: I don't do much in the ER. I'm a scribe.

Means I write down Dr's orders, put information in the computer, that kind of thing. Don't need fast reaction times.

Miles: Uh-huh.

Meg: I have to go. I have a lot of homework to finish before bed. Goodnight.

Phone on silent, I devote my next two hours to my bio textbook. When I'm finally done, my cell is sitting there on my desk, face down, taunting me.

I turn it over.

Miles: Sweet dreams.

That's what he said when he left last night.

Was he thinking about me in bed?

It's too late for me to contemplate this. He's already becoming a complication. Guys are trouble. Rosie was smarter, stronger, and more relationship savvy than I am and that asshole Jared still ruined her life.

I get ready for bed and collapse under the sheets. I repeat my manta mantra—medical school acceptance comes first—but it does nothing to chase away the mental image of Miles naked on my bed, his hand wrapped around his hard cock.

Dammit. I don't know how to handle this. Rosie would. She was so good at this kind of thing.

My heart sinks. My arms and legs are heavy. Hell, the entire world is heavy.

It still feels impossible, doing this without her, doing anything without her.

I didn't think about her last night. I didn't think about her when I was with Miles. Maybe that's worth the risk of the complication.

It can't be worse than this. Nothing is worse than how badly this hurts.

I grab my phone.

Meg: Did you mean what you said in the car? About sleeping with me.

Miles: Is that an invitation?

Meg: Just a hypothetical question.

Miles: Hypothetically, I can be at your apartment in twenty minutes flat.

Meg: Would you really come right now? It's the middle of the night.

Miles: That's the usual time for a booty call.

Damn. He makes it sound simple. Is he really that casual about everything? It doesn't seem possible. The guy who sings In Pieces is tormented. He's hurting. He's committed.

The Miles who's texting me is flirting, sure, but that's as far as his investment goes.

Meg: Nevermind. I should go to bed. Forget I said anything.

Miles: I'll be your first.

Meg: I didn't say I was a virgin.

Miles: You are.

Meg: And you know that how?

Miles: It's cute you're so defensive about it.

Meg: It's not cute.

Miles: Why not admit it?

Meg: What's it matter to you? Trying to hit a quota of "virginities taken"?

Miles: Don't have a fetish for it. But I would like to fuck you, Meg. I'll make sure your first time is good. That it doesn't hurt. That you come. But only if it's what you want.

All week, my phone is silent. There isn't a peep from

Miles. No new texts when I wake up. No new texts when I check my phone at lunch. None during my study break between class and work. None when I get home from a shift at the ER.

His last text sits there, that smooth, confident offer to take my virginity. Like it's no big deal.

To him, it isn't a big deal.

It's not like I've been waiting. It's just that not dating makes it difficult to have sex.

I don't want a boyfriend. I really don't. But I don't want to be a notch in someone's bedpost either.

Miles is a slut. There's nothing wrong with him being a slut, but I don't want to lose my virginity to a guy who goes through three women a week. Not if he's going to forget my name the way he forgot that other girl's name.

The ball is in my court. I keep it there. Miles and I are friends by association. That's all.

Late Thursday night, I get home particularly exhausted. I don't have the energy for homework. I collapse in bed and turn on the radio instead.

KROQ does its usual Nirvana, Smashing Pumpkins, 90s and 00s rock thing. Then it's his song, In Pieces. It still tears me apart. It still presses every single bruise.

Three weeks now.
Can't sleep.
Gaping hole in my chest
shows no signs of recovery.

That word, a joke, you laugh.
"Running away again, kid?"
A minute here

and then you're gone.

I close my eyes, willing my thoughts to go anywhere but that awful memory.

It doesn't work.

I'm in that hospital room, watching doctors try to save my sister. I can see her blue lips, feel her cold hands. They're freezing, no grip, no signs of life at all.

Lights out.
Can't sleep.
Heavy head,
but no one else can see.
(No one ever did).
A lost cause still,
worse than before.
No signs of recovery.

She's dying. I watch her die again and again. The same stupid dream I have every night. The reason why I can't allow myself a single minute of free time. Because my thoughts go back to her and all the ways I failed her.

An opiate overdose.

I had no idea.

How could I have had no idea?

That word, a joke, you laugh.
"Running away again kid?"
A minute here
And then you're gone.

Four weeks now.
That hole, that dread.

I can barely breathe
Anywhere but here.
Anything but this.
I want to take your lead.

She's gone. It's been three months. Just like the song goes, the gaping hole in my chest shows no sign of recovery. I can't sleep. I can't breathe.

How is it possible that Miles went through something like this and came out calm and unaffected?

I try to study but I can't focus. The question eats at my mind. How is it possible that Miles, the cocky player, is the same guy as Miles, the wounded poet?

I have to know.

Meg: Can I ask you something?
Miles: You're up late.
Meg: Always am.
Miles: Shoot.
Meg: Do you write the lyrics for Sinful Serenade?
Miles: All but one song.
Meg: In Pieces?
Miles: Nope. That one is 100% Miles Webb.
Meg: Really?
Miles: You getting at something?
Meg: It's hard to imagine you going through something like that.

He doesn't reply. Five minutes pass. Then ten.

Meg: I only mean, because you're so casual about everything.
Miles: What do you know about how casual I am?
Meg: You're casual about sex.
Miles: And?

Meg: You're aloof and unaffected.

Miles: Says who?

Meg: Says me. The guy that wrote that song. He's affected. He's tortured. He hurts deep down inside.

Miles: And I don't?

Meg: It doesn't seem like it.

Miles: Are you this rude to all your friends or only me?

Meg: We're not really friends.

Miles: Apparently not.

My cheeks flare. That isn't how I mean it.

I stare at my screen. That heaviness is back. I feel awful.

If someone tried to convince me I didn't know what pain felt like, that I wasn't wrecked by losing the person I loved more than anything...

I'd punch him right in the face.

I don't talk to anyone about Rosie, not really. And here Miles went and wrote a whole song about losing someone. He told the whole damn world, and I accused him of making it up.

Meg: I'm sorry. I shouldn't have said that.

Miles: I've heard worse.

Meg: I didn't mean any offense. I swear.

Miles: I'm sure you'll find a way to make it up to me.

CHAPTER FOUR

Miles occupies my thoughts all day Friday. I resist my cell until I'm home alone.

There's no real food here. I make a dinner out of dry cereal. It's not the healthiest option in the world, but it's quick and easy.

Kara: Remember how you want to sleep with Miles?

Meg: I didn't exactly say that.

Kara: I might have mentioned movie night to Drew. He and Miles invited themselves. Do you want me to tell them to get lost or do you want me to help you take him home?

Meg: Neither.

Kara: You sure it's okay?

Meg: Reasonably sure.

My body is already in knots thinking of the proximity to Miles. Thinking of all the things he could do to me in a dark theater.

Kara: So you're not going to cancel on me at 11:59 because you're "too tired"?

She knows me too well.

Meg: I'm not going to let anyone ruin my favorite movie.

Kara: You can have my pick Sunday.

Meg: And next Sunday.

Kara: Deal. Do you really want to use Miles for sex? Because I can make sure you two get a chance to be alone.

Meg: I don't know yet.

Kara: I want it on the record that it's a terrible idea. But he's super fucking hot. Like hotter than the sun. I don't fault you for wanting him.

Meg: It's on the record.

Kara: So?

Meg: I'm leaning towards it.

Kara: OMG! You have to promise details.

Meg: Aren't we a little old for that?

Kara: Not at all, sweetie. I'll make sure it happens. And I am sorry. I should have asked before I soft-invited Drew. But he loves sci-fi as much as you do. I had to mention it.

Meg: It's not because you want him.

Kara: Don't start with that. We're friends and he's never going to think of me that way. I don't want to be reminded that it's never going to happen. I like Drew. He's a good friend. I'm happy to have him as a friend.

Meg: But you do like him?

Kara: Seriously, don't start. It doesn't matter. He'll never see me that way.

Meg: He was looking at you that way at the party.

Kara: He was drunk. Doesn't count. Wear something cute. If you want to sleep with Miles. A skirt. No black. It looks good on you but it puts you in a mood.

Meg: It does not.

Kara: You want to sleep with the hot rock star or not?

Meg: Point taken.

My outfit is plain—a white tank top and a short denim skirt—but Miles is looking at me like I'm wearing the world's finest lingerie.

Like I have the curves to fill out lacy lingerie.

Most of the time, when I stand next to Kara, I feel particularly tall and flat. But right now, I feel like a supermodel. Like I'm the sexiest girl in the room.

I clear my throat. "Hi."

Miles nods a hello. "I like your skirt."

"Thanks."

Drew looks Kara up and down, taking in her snug dress. The girl wears clothes. And it's clear Drew appreciates the way the fabric stretches over her curves.

He is looking at her that way, whatever that means.

He's practically got steam coming out of his ears. It makes me more aware of my desire, of how badly I want to pull off Miles's fitted t-shirt. Damn, I bet his skin would feel good against my hands.

Drew barely manages to pull his eyes away from Kara. He nods hello. "Hope you don't mind us crashing your girls' night out."

"Who could resist the chance to watch Jurassic Park on the big screen?"

My tank top strap slips down my shoulder. I watch Miles's expression for signs of interest. He's not as obvious as his friend, but his interest is clear. His tongue slides over his lips. It sends shivers down my spine, seeing how much he wants me.

I pull my strap up. "Should we get tickets? It's almost midnight."

Kara pulls something from her purse. "Already got 'em."

Miles chimes in. "Meg and I can grab seats. You guys get drinks."

"Sure." I step inside the theater and take the door on the right. The Nuart is a cozy, single-screen theater. It seats about a hundred and fifty people. There are two dozen here tonight.

Miles presses his palm flat against my lower back, guiding me. My body fails to realize what a nonevent this is. Heat spreads from my back to my stomach and thighs.

Why stay through the movie? I should take him up on his offer now. I should take him home now. I need a release from my thoughts. I need a break from school and work.

I need to stop feeling like the weird buzzkill, like I'm the only college student who hasn't had sex.

Like I hurt so much I can't breathe. I want to be as casual and effortless as he is.

I take an aisle seat. Miles plops next to me, hand on the armrest, body turned towards mine. His eyes pass over me slowly. They focus on my bare thighs. "You keep looking at me like you're thinking about throwing me on your bed."

"I do not."

"Mhmm." His gorgeous blue eyes bore into mine. "Any thoughts you'd like to share?"

"This movie, it's all about how men shouldn't fuck with female creatures. It should be a warning to you."

He laughs. "True."

"You like Jurassic Park?"

"Why? Did you also not imagine the guy who wrote In Pieces as liking Jurassic Park?"

"I didn't consider it."

"Guy who's been through that kind of pain. He'd want something dark. Alien," Miles offers. "Maybe Terminator 2."

I let out a deep laugh. It's a full-blown belly laugh. I can feel it in my cheeks, in my sides, all the way to my fingertips.

It's the deepest, fullest laugh I've had since before Rosie died.

My eyes meet Miles's. I'm still not sure what to make of him. He treats everything casually. I don't. And I don't know if I can handle sleeping with someone if the sex means everything to me and nothing to him.

But damn do I want to seize this opportunity. When will I meet another guy who stirs this kind of desire in me? I have four years of medical school then another few of residency in my future. I'm not going to spend the next decade celibate.

Better to start now.

My train of thought is interrupted by Drew.

He steps over us, taking the seat next to Miles. "Kara's in the bathroom." He looks at his friend, shaking his head. "Meg, find me if Miles is giving you trouble. I'll take care of it."

"Next you're supposed to threaten violence." Miles chuckles. "So we all know you're tough."

"You think I won't punch you in the face?" Drew asks.

"You have before." Miles turns to me. "It was over

a riff. I called it derivative and Drew snapped."

"Fuck you. That was an amazing lick." Drew shakes his head. His expression is equal parts teasing and frustrated.

"Not gonna change my mind no matter how many times you hit me," Miles says.

Drew flips Miles off. His expression shifts, sixty-forty teasing to frustrated. "Damn, forgot about my favorite part of this movie, when the T-rex eats the piece-of-shit lawyer."

"I was going to be a lawyer," Miles offers. "Drew is pretty subtle sometimes. He can be hard to understand."

Drew shakes his head. The guys exchange a knowing look. They're up to eighty percent playful. Give or take.

I settle into my seat and try to focus on the screen. I can still feel the heat from Miles's muscular thighs.

I go to adjust my skirt. Instantly, I can feel his eyes on my skin. He's staring. Instead of pulling my skirt down, I let it ride up an inch and watch his reactions.

His blue eyes go wide.

He wants me.

I want him.

Maybe I really can do this.

CHAPTER FIVE

I've never paid less attention to my favorite movie. Somehow, it's less interesting than Miles's fingers grazing my wrist.

That's all it is for the entire movie. He runs his fingertips along my inner wrist.

I order myself to shrink away from his touch, but I can't do it. His hand feels so damn good.

The movie ends with the T-rex attacking the raptors. Credits roll. Lights turn on. Miles pulls his hand back to his lap, no doubt playing nice now that his protective friend is watching.

"Excuse me." I push out of my seat and make my way to the bathroom. I always have to pee after a movie. Today, it's a great moment to regain control of my senses.

I barely know Miles. But I do know he's the only thing that can get my mind off how much I miss my big sister.

It's worth the risk. If I can figure out how to mitigate any complications.

Kara, Drew, and Miles are waiting outside the theater.

Miles taps my shoulder with his. The simple gesture sets my body on fire.

"Why don't you walk Kara home?" Miles says to Drew. "I'll walk Meg."

A defensive look spreads across Drew's face.

Kara throws me a pretty please look.

"Yeah, I was telling Miles about the great boba tea place by my apartment. It's only open till three, so we better hurry," I say.

"Right." Miles catches on immediately. "See you later."

Drew looks at me. Once again, his expression is equal parts playful and protective. "If Miles gives you any trouble, tell me. I'll take care of it."

I try to laugh it off. "It's just bubble tea." I grab Miles by the shirt and pull him in the direction of my apartment.

I take the first right. It's faster to stay on the main road, but I'd rather not risk Drew or Kara getting the idea to come with us.

The side streets are dark. This time of night, the only illumination comes from the moon. I have to concentrate to avoid tripping on the uneven sidewalk.

Miles walks beside me. "You have the same idea I do?"

"I doubt that."

"Your friend and mine. He needs to get laid and he's looking at her the way a dog looks at a bone."

"They're just friends."

Miles shrugs. "Doubt it."

"Why?"

"You didn't notice them eye-fucking?"

"No, I did. Just… she says they're just friends. I don't have any reason to doubt her." I turn at the next intersection. My apartment is about four blocks away. Not a ton of time to figure this out.

"I like your skirt," he says.

"Thanks."

"You wear it for me?"

"In your dreams."

A laugh escapes his lips. "Oh, no, I had a dream about you already, and it was a lot more fun."

My heart pounds against my chest, but I'm not about to show it. "You did not."

"I did. In fact—" he leans even closer "—you were wearing something a lot like that skirt."

I press my knees together.

"Only without any panties."

Deep breath. He's only fucking with me. It's a story. "I don't believe you."

"I didn't save my sticky sheets."

My lungs fail me. They're supposed to be breathing in and out, but they're still. "You didn't...You're just flirting."

"No. We're past that point." He brushes my hair off my shoulders. His voice drops. It's low and sincere. "You want me, and I want you. There's no reason to hide that."

He drags his fingertips over my shoulders. My hips shift. I squeeze my thighs together as he tugs at the straps of my tank top.

The expression in his eyes in earnest.

He's still calm, but he's not entirely casual.

"Okay." I nod. I do want him and I can tell he wants me. "What does that mean?"

Miles stares into my eyes. "It's up to you. I'm not going to push you to do anything you don't want to do."

"Oh."

"If you're not ready, I'll walk you home. That's it."

I follow him to the next corner. Only two blocks now. "And if I am ready?"

"Then I'll make sure you come so hard you forget your name."

The elevator has never felt slower. Or smaller. Miles is three feet away but it feels like three inches. I have to respond to his offer.

I almost jump at the ding. I almost fall when I step into the hallway.

It's fifteen feet to my door.

Ten.

Five.

Zero.

I pull my key from my purse and slide it into the lock.

Miles moves closer, pinning me to the door. His chest is against my back. The warmth of his body sets me on fire.

This is already intense as hell.

Miles runs his fingers over my cheek. "Did you make your decision?"

His fingers trail down my neck and shoulders.

I don't understand it. How can he have such a sweet touch when he acts like he doesn't give a fuck about anything?

He brushes my hair behind my ear. "Turn around."

I release the key and turn. My eyes find his. He's staring at me, into me, through me.

I want him.

I want to do this.

Miles presses his hand into my lower back, pulling

my body into his. Our stomachs, our crotches, our thighs connect. Our lips are six inches apart. Then three.

My eyes close as our lips press together. It's been a long time since I've kissed anyone. I let him lead. It starts soft, a peck, then he's sucking on my lower lip.

Damn, he tastes good. I moan. I melt into his touch, letting him pull my body closer.

His tongue slides into my mouth. He shifts his hips, pinning me against the door.

He's hard.

Heat spreads through me like wildfire. I need to do this. Now.

Miles breaks the kiss and takes a half-step backwards. It gives me room to think, to breathe. But I don't want to think. I want his body against mine again.

I exhale slowly. "I want to do this, but not if I'm going to be some girl who's name you can't remember."

He stares back at me. "I don't do relationships."

"Me either. But... I don't want to be another notch in your bedpost."

His expression softens. "We're friends, right?"

"Something like that."

"Sinful Serenade is gonna be in Los Angeles for the rest of the year. We're recording our new album. It might be nice having something consistent."

"So I'm convenient?"

"No. You're sexy. And different." His eyes pass over me slowly. "Most girls trip over themselves trying to impress me. You don't."

"That's all it takes to win you over?"

He shrugs. "We could be fuck buddies."

"Monogamous?"

He nods.

"But you sleep with a different girl every night."

"Only most nights." He shifts, pressing his hips against me again. "I don't play games, Meg. If you're not interested, tell me."

"No, I am. But I..." My eyes go to the floor. "I haven't ever done it before."

He runs his fingers through my hair. "We can take it slow."

"No. I want to do it."

He chuckles. "You're eager."

"You're hard."

"Accurate." He cups my hip with his palm. "Let me lead. I'll walk you through this."

"Okay." I suck in a deep breath.

It seems impossible, but I'm about to have sex with Miles.

This is happening.

I unlock the door and push it open. "Come in."

Miles locks the door and presses his back against it. His eyes pass over me, undressing me.

Heat collects between my legs. I need to cool down. I need to make sure we're on the same page about this friends-with-benefits thing.

I go to the sink and pour two glasses of water.

Miles is standing next to the bed. Not that there's anywhere else to stand. I hand one glass to him and sip the other.

The lukewarm beverage does nothing to temper the heat racing through me.

Deep breath. I can do this. "I have terms. I'm sure you do too."

He nods. "Shoot."

"I want total honesty. No secrets. No lies. No deception at all."

He takes a long sip. "I don't want you getting the wrong idea here. This isn't going to turn into some boyfriend/girlfriend relationship."

"Good. I don't want a boyfriend. During the week, I barely have time to study. And…" I'm not telling him about Rosie. Not right now. "I don't want that kind of connection to someone." I don't want to trust anyone enough they lead me astray.

He sets his glass of water down and moves closer. His fingertips skim my shoulders. "You seem like a nice girl."

"No, I don't."

He laughs. "Okay. You're a little defensive, and it's awfully rude that you assumed I never hurt." He drags his fingertips over my chin. "I like you. But you're never going to be my confidant. You're never going to be the shoulder I cry on."

"Do you cry?"

His lips curl into a smile. He presses his palm into my lower back. "Honesty, right?"

"From both of us."

"Haven't cried in a while. You?"

"Can't say the same."

His voice softens. He pulls me closer. "I'm not a monster. I don't want to hurt you."

"You won't. Not if you're honest."

Doubt creeps onto his face. He takes a step backwards, pulling his hand to his side. "See, these conditions, they worry me. Make me think you're after more than just a good time."

I press my fingers into my glass. "Now you're the one being presumptuous."

"Fair point." His eyes meet mine. "Okay, I'll agree to total honesty. But I have my own condition. The second you develop feelings for me, this is over."

"What if you develop feelings for me? What if you fall in love with me?" I tug at my skirt. "Isn't that possible?"

His voice is even and calm. "No."

"Whatever." My temper flares. Where does he get the nerve? How can he be so sure he'll never feel anything? "I'll tell you if I develop feelings for you."

"You're cute when you're flustered."

"Fuck off. You're not cute when you're acting like nothing has ever mattered to you."

"It's a compliment."

"Not to me."

He nods. "This, us being on the same page, matters to me."

"Me too."

"We're fuck buddies and we don't lie to each other." He takes my glass from my hands and sets it on the counter. "And you'll tell me if you develop feelings for me."

He offers his hand to shake.

Despite my sweaty palm, I take his hand with a firm grip.

We shake.

And it's done.

Miles is my friend with benefits.

Miles, rock star sex god, is my friend with benefits.

CHAPTER SIX

I'm on fire.

We're in agreement. We're friends with benefits. We're about to have sex.

Why are we still talking?

Why are we still clothed?

Miles is endlessly patient. He moves closer. Until we're pressed together.

His eyes meet mine. The pretenses fade away as he traces the neckline of my tanktop. "Had enough conversation?"

I nod.

"Me too." He pulls the straps of my tank top off my shoulders. Slowly, he rolls the top to my stomach. "Been thinking about this all week."

"You have?"

"Yeah." He traces the outline of my bra. His eyes go wide. "First time I've gone a week without sex in a long time."

My breath hitches. Damn, his touch feels good. "Because of me?"

"Yeah." His voice drops low. "Wouldn't be right

fucking some other girl if I was thinking of you."

He slides his thumb into my bra and uses it to tease my nipple.

I let out a sharp gasp. My back arches. My hands go straight to his shoulders. I have to do something to steady myself.

He makes slow circles with his thumb. They get faster, harder. Every brush of his fingers sends pleasure racing through my body. I've made out with guys before, been felt up before. But it was never even close to this.

I groan. I don't know what to say, how to react here. I look into his eyes so I can take his lead.

The only thing in his eyes is desire. There's no smugness in his expression. He's not cocky, casual, or aloof.

Right now, he's without pretenses.

I try to shake off my impulse to run from the intimacy. My eyelids press together. I nod a yes. I'm not sure what I'm asking for, only that I need it immediately.

Miles unhooks my bra. Slowly he rolls it off my shoulders.

He lets out a low groan. "Your tits are amazing."

I blush, blinking my eyes open so I can stare back at him. His eyes are fixed on my chest, like it's the best thing he's ever seen.

He brings one hand to my hip and pulls my body into his. It feels good, being close to him. It's terrifying how good it feels. Like I'll develop an addiction.

Again, I press my eyelids together. I try not to run from the reactions he's causing. He cups my breast, teasing my nipple with his thumb.

The backs of my legs press against the bed. Desire pools in my core. Damn, that feels amazing. I let out a groan. I lean into his touch.

He keeps teasing my nipple. Just when I think I can't take it anymore, he moves to my other breast.

My fingers dig into his shoulders. Then it's my nails. What am I supposed to do here?

"You're nervous," he whispers.

"It's nothing."

His voice softens. "I'll go slow." He presses his lips against my neck. "I'll walk you through it. Relax."

I nod.

His hands go to my hips. He pushes me onto the bed. I place my palms at my sides, keeping my balance so I can stay upright.

Miles lowers himself onto his knees. It's the same position we were in when he patched me up.

My breath hitches. I want this to go faster. I want his hands under my skirt.

He nudges my knees apart and places himself between them. It's not enough. His hands are on the bed, not on me.

I take a deep breath. He's leading. I can handle that.

He looks up at me, checking in. I nod a yes. A now. A please.

Miles brings his mouth to my nipple.

Fuck. It's soft and wet and warm.

Pleasure overwhelms me. My hands go to his messy brown hair as he sucks on me. Damn, that feels so good I can barely stay upright. I tug at his hair.

His moan reverberates against my skin. He wants this. He wants me.

Miles kisses his way to my lips. His tongue plunges

into my mouth. His hands move to my thighs.

I spread my legs. Arch my back. I'm practically offering myself to him. It's scary how much my body wants his, the way it takes over.

But it feels so fucking good.

He takes the invitation. His hands slide under my skirt. His fingers brush against my panties.

No one has ever touched me before, not here. It's overwhelming. I'm dizzy with lust.

I fall onto my back, relaxing into the bed, relaxing into his touch.

Then he's on the bed. His body is next to mine.

I slide my hand under his t-shirt. Soft skin covers hard muscles. It feels good, touching him. I want more. I want to touch every inch of his skin.

It's terrifying how desperately I want every inch of his skin.

I take my time exploring the lines of his torso. I'm still dizzy. I'm not sure which way is up or down, only that I want him leading.

His lips find mine. He pulls my panties to my knees.

Slowly, my body takes over. My knees slide apart. My hands go to his hips.

My thoughts drift away. For once, nothing hurts. For once, I only feel pleasure.

His fingers tease my nipples, then they're on my stomach, then they're undoing the button of my skirt, sliding it off my hips, past my knees, all the way to my feet.

I'm naked. I'm naked with a man I barely know. And I want so badly to be here.

I'm not shy or worried I'm not good enough.

I'm aflame.

He groans with pleasure as he drags his fingertips over my thigh. Closer. Closer.

There.

His fingers skim my clit.

Fuck yes.

His eyes stay on me, studying my reactions. I nod.

He drags his fingers over me, teasing my sex. "Damn, you're already wet."

I let out a groan.

Miles slides one finger inside me. I take a deep breath. It's intense, but I can handle it.

Then he slides another finger inside me.

I bite my lip. I tug at his hair. He's slow about sliding his fingers deeper. Deeper.

I don't care how much he'll brag when we're finished. This feels too good. I have to groan.

I arch my back to push his fingers deeper. It's different, having his fingers inside me, but it's a very good different.

I want more than his fingers.

I want him inside me.

Miles brings his lips to mine. He kisses with intent. Damn, his kiss is hot, aggressive.

Little by little, he moves deeper, faster, harder.

Pleasure spreads through my thighs. I'm almost there.

But the worst thing imaginable happens.

The phone rings.

It's not my ringtone. It must be him.

He groans with pleasure. "Ignore it."

He slides his thumb over my clit.

Sensation overwhelms me. The knot of pressure is damn intense. It's better than anything I've ever felt before.

But that stupid phone is still ringing.

That voice inside my head is screaming. What if it's important? What if someone needs you and you're too late, again?

My body tenses.

Miles pulls his hand back to his side. His posture changes, as tense as mine. "You okay?"

I shake my head. "The phone. You should get it."

"You're about to come, and you'd prefer I use my hands to answer the phone?"

I nod. "Do you doubt your ability to get me back here?"

"No, but I'm going to scream if I'm not inside you soon."

The air escapes my lungs. God, that sounds amazing. But not if something is wrong. Not if someone needs us.

He pushes off the bed with a heavy sigh. This is as painful for him as it is for me.

He pulls his phone from his pocket and looks at the screen. Shakes his head. Answers. "Yes." His voice is strained. Like he can barely think, much less speak. "Give me an hour." He sighs. "Fine. But I can't teleport. It'll be at least half an hour." He ends the call and places his phone on the kitchen counter. His eyes find mine. "It's nothing you need to worry about. Just some drama at the Hollywood place."

"And you'll be there in half an hour?"

"Around that."

"You really think we're going to...in thirty minutes?"

He shakes his head. "That's not enough time to do this right."

"Oh." Suddenly, I feel cold, exposed, and not at all

right. I'm naked and Miles is still dressed. He never bothered to take off a single article of clothing.

"I guess you're leaving then," I say.

This relationship, arrangement, whatever it is, is already off on the wrong foot.

"I'd really hate to leave without making you come," he says.

His eyes find mine. I squeeze my thighs together and slide back on the bed until I'm pressed against the headboard.

I take a deep breath. Relax, dammit. I can't let him have this much power over me.

I consider asking him to go. I can finish this on my own. It won't be as fun, but it won't leave me in knots either.

His expression is sincere. He seems sorry, truly sorry.

I can handle this.

"You have a serious time crunch there," I say.

He smiles, sits on the bed, and positions his body next to mine. He feels warm, hard to the touch.

His fingertips brush my nipples. I'm hot instantly. Every inch of my skin burns for his touch.

Miles sits up, his back against the headboard, his legs flat on the bed. He pulls my body into his, my knees outside his hips, so I'm straddling him.

Our eyes connect. I don't know what his expression means, only that I like the intensity of it.

I settle into the position. I can feel him through his jeans. He's hard. Damn, I want that.

But this is good too.

He looks up at me. One hand curls around my neck. It guides me into a deep kiss. The other slides between my legs.

This is nothing but him giving me pleasure.

I'm going to enjoy it.

His tongue slides into my mouth as his thumb slides over my clit.

I kiss back, hard. It's a desperate plea for him to continue.

His touch is still patient. Soft. Then harder. Harder. Perfect.

I groan and dig my nails into his shoulders.

He reads me like a book, rubbing me with that same pressure, same speed.

Damn, that feels good.

I moan.

Almost.

I kiss him like this is the only chance I'll ever have to kiss anyone.

The tension between my legs builds to a fever pitch. It's intense. I can barely take it.

Almost.

There.

With his next stroke, I come. Pleasure spreads through my thighs. It's a hell of an orgasm. Different than when I'm on my own. Better.

I dig my hands into his hair. I squeeze my thighs together reflexively. His hand is still between them. His hand is still on me.

He's not stopping.

He strokes me again. Again. His lips stay pressed against mine. I suck on his tongue. I lose track of my body, arching, and squeezing, and melting exactly where I need to.

His touch gets harder. Faster. I'm almost there already.

I cry out loud enough to wake the neighbors.

I come again. All that tension in my body releases in a perfect wave of pleasure. I exhale every ounce of air in my lungs.

I melt into the bed. I'm a puddle. I'm shapeless.

Miles looks up at me. His lips curl into a smile. I'm not sure if it's smug or proud. Hard to say. At the moment, it's hard to say what day or month it is.

He kisses me goodbye. "Fuck, Meg. I guess I don't need to ask if you'll miss me." He slides off the bed. "My cock isn't going to forgive me for leaving."

I stifle a grin.

"I'll make this up to you next time." He collects his things and takes a step towards the door. "Sleep tight."

"You, too. I mean, after you get home."

He waves on his way out the door.

It takes every bit of energy I have left—almost nothing—but I drag myself out of bed to lock the door, brush my teeth, pull on a pair of pajamas, and collapse in bed.

Miles brought me to orgasm. Twice. The two most amazing orgasms of my life. And now, he's on his way home.

I take a deep breath, but the calm I had a moment ago eludes me. We're friends with benefits. Nothing like boyfriend/girlfriend.

No reason why I should miss him.

No reason there should be an uneasy feeling in my stomach.

It's late. I'm tired. I ate almost nothing for dinner.

That's it. That has to be it.

CHAPTER SEVEN

"Sweetie, Futurama movies do not count as movies," Kara says. "I'll let you have it because I love you, but you have to know it's total bullshit."

"You're such a stickler."

"You're the one who came up with the idea of taking turns. I don't give a damn. We can watch sci-fi every week. Anything except Battlestar Galactica."

My phone buzzes. I try to ignore it. It's difficult. I haven't heard a word from Miles since he left my apartment late enough it was technically Saturday morning.

It's been more than twenty-four hours.

I tap my fingers against my cell's screen. "It's not the show's fault everyone called you Starbuck in high school."

She watches my tapping and raises a brow. "You gonna check your phone?"

"It's probably nothing."

"Uh-huh." She shakes her head and moves to the kitchen. "Frosted Flakes or Cocoa Puffs?"

"Both."

Kara and I have a weekly routine. Sunday brunch. It's supposed to be for homework, but mostly we watch movies, eat cereal straight from the box, and drink medically unsound amounts of caffeine.

Last year, our weekly meetings were the only time I wasn't studying. I was so focused on that stupid MCAT. It was the only thing I paid attention to. It's why I let it slide when Rosie told me she was fine, even though that uneasy feeling in my gut screamed that she was lying.

My phone buzzes again.

I know it's Miles. He and Kara are the only two people who text me. But I don't want to be desperate to turn my phone over. I don't want him to have the power to leave me in knots.

My fingers curl around my phone. I want to read his reaction. I need to know what he's saying.

I unlock my cell.

Miles: Any soreness?

Meg: No. I'm good.

Miles: Only good?

Meg: Only good. I'm studying.

Sort of.

Kara plops next to me. She hands me a can of green tea and a bowl of puffed corn coated in sugar and cocoa powder. I pop open my can and take a long sip.

"Earth to Meg?" She taps my shoulder. "Is that who I think it is?"

"We're just talking."

"That is 100 percent grade-A bullshit." Her eyes are sincere. "You have any details to share?"

"I'm working on it."

"What the hell does that mean?"

"It means I can handle it."

She stares me down like she's challenging me to tell the truth.

"If I can't, I'll talk to you," I say.

She plays with her t-shirt. "After what happened with Rosie, I don't want to see you hurting again."

My gaze goes back to my phone. "I'll be okay."

She studies my expression for a long moment before she speaks. "If you're going to text during the whole damn movie, I'm going to put in something I like."

"Okay."

"Something with subtitles."

"Go for it."

She shakes her head like I'm hopeless. But, still, I turn back to my phone.

Miles: We have a show next week. Why don't you come? Then you can come and come and come.

Miles: That was three. But three is the bare minimum.

I turn my phone over and slide it into my pocket. "There's a Sinful Serenade show next weekend?"

Kara taps the remote, starting play on some independent film with stark scenery and a minimalist soundtrack. She raises an eyebrow like she's challenging me to explain. "Friday. Starts while you're at work, but I can wait."

I shake my head. "I'll take the bus."

"You can't take the bus to Hollywood that late. No way in hell. I'll pick you up."

"You'll miss—"

"It's decided," she says. "And you'll text me if you decide to leave with someone?"

"I promise."

My shift at the ER ends at ten on the dot. By 10:05, I'm in Kara's car, in one of her bodycon dresses, applying makeup with an unsteady hand. Black eyeliner, dark lipstick, plenty of blush. One of the upsides of having dramatic features is that I can pull off a lot of makeup.

I run a comb through my messy hair. It doesn't help. Better to return it to a work-appropriate ponytail.

At least the dress is nice. A little short for my long legs, and I certainly don't fill it out well, but it looks better than I'd expect given the ten inches I have on Kara. Or the four cup sizes she has on me.

I scroll past the flirty texts about nothing to get to Miles's promise.

Miles: We have a show next week. Why don't you come? Then you can come and come and come.

Miles: That was three. But three is the bare minimum.

I'm not dreaming. This is really happening.

Kara parks two blocks from the venue at an expired meter. She smiles. "Here goes nothing."

I take a deep breath, pulling in all the confidence I can manage. The walk to the venue nearly undoes me. These aren't even heels. They're wedges, short wedges, but I can barely move in them.

Kara gives our names to the bouncer. We're on the list. I've never been on a list before. I've never been anywhere that needed a list.

I try to channel Miles's cool aloofness but I fail. I'm teetering. My dress is too tight. Do people really go clubbing for fun? I feel hopelessly out of place.

Until I hear his voice.

It's a low moan, not actual words, but I'm still positive that Miles is the guy who is singing. Which means Sinful Serenade is in the middle of a song.

Sound echoes around the high ceilings. It gets louder the further we get into the club. A guitar screams. Drums pound. The bass-line throbs. The energy from the music flows into the room.

There must be three or four hundred people squeezed into a space meant for far, far fewer. Mostly girls, mostly screaming their lungs out.

Everything is dark, almost black, save the bright white stage lights.

Miles stands on the front of the stage, his fingers wrapped around a microphone, his eyes closed as if he's feeling the song so deeply he can't bear to keep them open.

All of my attention is on Miles. His voice is beautiful. Not just beautiful. It's breathy, and throaty, and wounded as all hell. Every word comes out with a thousand pounds of emotional force behind it. It's like his voice is seeping through my skin and bones, all the way into my soul. It's like I can feel whatever it is that made him write this song.

It hurts. Not as badly as In Pieces, but enough.

The songs ends. There's no break. Sinful Serenade transitions right into the next number. This one is faster, harder, louder. It's more upbeat, but there's still an undercurrent of hurt in Miles's voice. I catch a few of the lyrics. They're beautiful wisps of poetry.

Right now, he's not cocky, arrogant, or aloof. His heart is in his words. The ache in his soul is in his words.

My chest is heavy. I'm hurting with him.

I close my eyes and lose myself in his voice. There's so much sound around us—the screaming, the guitar, the bass, the drums—but all I can hear is Miles. It's like he's singing to me.

The song ends. I open my eyes, startled by the quick return to reality. The room feels darker and brighter at once. Miles feels closer and farther away.

The singer smiles at the crowd with that same cocky expression on his face. He waves and blows a kiss. A dozen girls squeal, sure his adoration is meant for them.

He looks back at his bandmates. Can't say that I'm paying much attention to the other guys. They seem to be in some kind of blissful, meditative state. They're all so effortlessly cool.

Miles looks back at the crowd. "I'd like to dedicate this next song to a very special girl. I'm not sure that she thinks much of me, but Meg, I wrote this song, too."

The drummer brings his sticks down hard on his drum kit. "Only the lyrics, Romeo."

Miles sends the drummer a sweet smile then blows him a kiss. Must be some kind of inside joke. The drummer shakes his head, stands, and pulls off his shirt.

The screams are so loud I can't even think. The crowd likes him sans shirt. They like it a lot.

Hard to blame them. He's an attractive man— wavy dirty blond hair, sculpted torso, a tattoo with thick black lines on his chest and snaking down his arm.

Next to me, Kara laughs. She's eying Drew like she hopes the stripping will start some kind of chain reaction. I don't call her on it.

Miles tugs at the bottom of his t-shirt, teasing the crowd to a chorus of cheers. He walks over to the equally handsome dark-haired bassist and hands him the mic.

It's unfair, having four attractive men in such close proximity. There isn't a woman alive who could resist all four of them.

Miles's eyes go back to the crowd. If I didn't know better, I'd swear he's looking at me. I'd swear he's doing this solely for my benefit.

He pulls the shirt higher, higher, higher. And then it's off his head and on the ground.

There's barely an inch of fat on his body. He has a six-pack. And those v-lines. They make it difficult to think. The color tattoos that decorate his chest and arms keep my brain in a damn, he's hot loop.

Miles drags his hands over his sculpted chest like he can't bear how sexy he is.

The cheers are deafening. Mr. Miles Webb is certainly the object of lust. Hard to blame the girls staring at him with their eyes wide and their jaws dropped. No doubt, there will be a dozen pairs of panties on stage by the end of the song.

He could have any woman he wants, and he wants me.

He made me come.

He's going to make me come again. Three times. He promised three times.

Miles takes the microphone back. "Is it hot in here, or is it just me?"

The crowd screams.

"So it's just me?" He winks at the crowd. He points to the guitarist then to the bassist. "Only two songs to go. Think we can get the string jockeys shirtless by the end of the show?"

There's another set of cheers. Every guy in the band has his fans.

Miles smiles that same smug smile. He throws up four fingers and uses them to count down.

The song starts. It's one of their singles. It plays on KROQ but not nearly as often as In Pieces does. It has a slick guitar riff, a throbbing beat, and, of course, a perfect vocal melody.

Kara squeezes my hand. I can't bring myself to look away from Miles to catch her expression. No doubt she's ecstatic, too. I squeeze back. I shift my hips to the music. I scream. Just another fan. Just another girl who wants that sexy boy on stage she'll never have.

Only, I can have him.

I have had him.

The song transitions into the next. The last song, according to Miles's earlier claim. There is something final about it. It's like everyone is playing harder. Miles goes all out with his vocals. He's not in smug mode, not flirting with the crowd. He's there, in the music, in the moment that made him write this song.

It's captivating, sexy, and terrifying at once. There's more to Miles than bad boy rock star. There must be, or he wouldn't be so lost in his words.

The song ends to a chorus of screams and cheers. The Sinful guys wave goodbye. Miles takes a bow. The drummer blows kisses. He even holds his hand up to his ear to make the "call me" motion. They walk offstage, and a roadie collects their discarded t-shirts.

Kara pulls me away from the main crowd. She gives our names to the bouncer guarding the backstage area. He lets us pass.

The small space is crowded with gear. There are other musician types here—must be the opening act—but most of them are busy soaking in groupie adoration. One of them is sucking face against the wall. And oh, God, he's getting a handjob.

I guess they don't call it sex, drugs, and rock-and-roll for nothing.

There's a door marked "Sinful Serenade." It's a lot less busy than the rest of the backstage area. Drew is sitting on the couch alone. The light-haired drummer is surrounded by a cloud of fans. His attention turns to us.

He nods to Drew then to Kara. "Kara, right?"

"You're not sleeping with my friends." Drew waves the guy off. "So why don't you get Aiden to put another one of our songs in a commercial while I'm occupied?"

The drummer offers his hand. "I'm Tom."

"Meg." I shake.

"Nice to meet you. And to see you again, Kara." He looks from Drew to me. "Sometimes, I think I'm the only person in the band who cares about making money." Tom shakes his head with outrage and returns to his cloud of fans.

"Want a drink?" Drew asks. His gaze fixes on something behind me. "Maybe a shirt."

I turn. It's Miles, standing there in his tight jeans, still sans shirt. He shakes his head but he grabs a t-shirt off the couch and pulls it on.

Miles throws Drew a cocky wink. There's no challenge or animosity to it, just mutual understanding. They're teasing each other.

Drew goes to grab Kara's wrist but she pulls it into her chest. He looks at her a little funny. She shrugs like it's nothing.

"Come on, Kendrick. You'll miss the good tequila."

She nods. "Meg, you want something?"

I shake my head. "No, thanks."

She follows Drew to a table in the back, leaving me alone with Miles. Or as good as alone.

He runs his fingertips over my exposed shoulders. I'm hot instantly. It feels good being near him. It will feel better without the audience, without the space between us, without the clothes.

"I like your dress," he says.

"Thanks."

"And the heels, too. Tall girls are usually afraid of them."

My mouth refuses to form words.

"Bet they give you extra leverage when you're pressed against a wall."

A blush spreads across my cheeks. I open my mouth to speak, but it's still not happening.

Dammit, he's effortless again. And I'm nervous and bumbling again.

This is too much, too fast. I need to collect my thoughts. I take a step backwards. "Excuse me. I changed my mind about that drink."

The bar in the corner is mostly booze in every color. There are mixers. Only one interests me. Grapefruit juice. Truly the most under-appreciated fruit in the world—tart, sweet, and sour all at once. I pour myself a large glass and take a sip. It's not fresh squeezed, but it's not bad.

I want Miles. I'm sure of that.

But there are other feelings stirring in my gut. Something besides desire. Something I might not be able to handle.

By the time I'm done with my juice, the room is packed. People bump into me, nod hellos, introduce themselves in breathy voices meant to imply I'm another girl here to hand out blowjobs to anyone with the ability to play a musical instrument.

I slip out of the room. The backstage area is equally slammed. It's a real party scene—people drinking from red cups, flirting, kissing, sharing stories, and laughing at the top of their lungs. I find the closest door and push through it. Air. I need air. And I need to not be here.

The alley-slash-parking lot is an asphalt wasteland. There are a few loners leaning against the wall smoking cigarettes. I copy their position, breathing deep to suck in as much air as possible. Instead, I get a lungful of smoke.

Forget that. I move to the corner of the parking lot.

A girl in a mini-dress and stilettos waves at me. "We don't bite, hun."

She giggles and motions for me to come closer. I do.

There are half a dozen people milling around a parked car.

One of them, a skinny guy in a suit, is tapping white powder out of a baggie onto the back of his cell phone. He drags a credit card across it and rakes it into straight lines.

They're doing cocaine.

My heart races. I can't be around this. That's how it starts. How it started for Rosie. First, it was her jerk boyfriend dragging her to parties where everyone was desperate to be up or down. Then she was trying drugs—Rosie never was the type to back down from a dare.

Then she was gone.

It happened so fast. Just playing along, being one of the cool girls at the party, and then she's gone. Overdosed. Dead.

The skinny guy leans over, bringing his nose to the back of the phone. And just like in a fucking movie, he snorts the line.

He snorts the other line, sits up, and rubs his nose. Then he's back at it, raking another line and passing it around.

My phone buzzes in my purse. I ignore it. I have to watch these people, to see what they're doing, to see why this had so much power over my sister.

They laugh. They stare at each other with the deepest anticipation, like they can't wait to be in the middle of bliss. Another person snorts. The skinny guy taps out another two lines. Snort.

I can't move. I'm a deer and I'm staring straight into the headlights.

There's a sound behind me. Someone else is out here now. Maybe a smoker desperate for an even stronger high.

"Meg."

It's Miles.

His voice booms. "What the fuck do you think you're doing?"

CHAPTER EIGHT

He takes steps towards me, but I'm still stuck in the headlights. Who the hell are these people, and why did my sister throw her life away for this?

He's behind me. I can feel his body, hear his breath. His fingers wrap around my wrist so tightly I lose sensation in my hand.

"Excuse us." He pulls me away from the people, all the way to the sidewalk across the street. "Do you do coke?"

It's dark here. The headlights are finally gone. "No."

"Then what were you doing waiting your turn?"

I have no response.

His grip tightens around my wrist. "You do drugs?"

I dig my heel into the concrete. "That's none of your business."

"We're friends. Makes it my business."

I grit my teeth. "You made it clear we're not confidants."

He takes my hand and tugs me away from the scene. "Look me in the eyes and answer me. Do you do drugs?"

My gaze goes anywhere but his eyes. "No. I don't do drugs." The sky is dark enough that I can see stars. So many stars. "I don't even like being around drugs."

"I'll take you home." He pulls me towards the sidewalk.

I'm the wet blanket again, the girl who can't handle the party, the girl who belongs at home.

I pull my hand free. "That's not necessary."

"You're pale. You're barely breathing." His voice gets serious. "You look like you saw a ghost."

Those people might as well be ghosts. How long until one of them is lying in a hospital bed, heartbeat fading to zero?

I take a deep breath. "It's nothing."

"No lies. That's our deal."

"I just remembered something awful." I hug my purse against my chest to keep the warmth in my body. "I'm not going to talk about it."

He shifts. His expression softens. His eyes brighten like he's trying to lift the mood. "You want to give me some hint what's wrong?"

"Not particularly."

"The sooner you tell me, the sooner we leave, and the sooner you get to fuck me."

My cheeks flush red again. "You're—"

"Don't say dreaming, because we both know what my dreams are like." He leans closer, holding my stare like he's daring me to explain.

I need to not be talking about this or thinking about this. And there's no way I'll be thinking about it if we really do sleep together.

So, fine, I'll tell him as much as it takes to change the subject. "There was someone in my life who went down a bad path with drugs. It still hurts but I'm not going to talk about it."

"Oh." His voice is soft. There's a hint of vulnerability in his eyes. "I'll take you home."

"You have to promise to drop this subject."

"It's dropped." He leads me around the corner. We walk in silence for a few blocks then Miles stops.

In front of a motorcycle.

He pulls two helmets from a compartment and hands one to me. Then he slings a motorcycle jacket around my shoulders. "This might make your thighs a little sore."

I climb on after him and hold on for dear life.

My knuckles are white. My wrists are numb. Every muscle in my body is tense from the vice grip I have around Miles's waist.

The man drives like a Goddamn maniac.

After we park in my garage, I pull the helmet off my head and shove it into his hands. As usual, he's effortlessly cool and I'm trembling. Only known the guy for weeks, and we already have a pattern that gives him all the cards and leaves me with none.

He locks his bike, looking me over like he's trying to read my mind. He shrugs his leather jacket off his shoulders. "You'll want one before you know it."

"Fat chance." I dig my purse out of the bike's tiny trunk. "You've saved the pathetic damsel in distress. You don't have to stay." I turn and step towards the door.

"Meg."

"What?"

"You're wearing my jacket."

Ugh. I am wearing his extra jacket—it's early fall in Los Angeles, but the air is cold when it's whizzing by at eighty miles per hour.

I return the garment without another word.

My stomach is in knots. I want him in my room, in my bed, but not if he's going to treat me like the pathetic girl who can't handle her shit.

Those people… Their eyes were empty. I can't get it out of my head. I need it out of my head. I need to think about something else now.

Miles can deliver on that. Does anything else really matter?

I motion for him to follow and I make my way through the lobby. His calm steps remind me that he is still effortless. I am still clumsy and out of my comfort zone.

I press the button for the elevator. My hands are anything but steady. I press them into my thighs and take deep breaths.

Miles leans closer. His voice is steady, reassuring. "I hope the bike didn't wear out your thighs."

A blush threatens to form on my cheeks. I bite my lip. I can be cool too. I can be calm too. "It didn't."

"Good."

The elevator doors open, and we step inside. Miles hits the button for my floor. He says nothing.

Ding. We're at my floor. Miles moves steadily, his hand pressed gently against my lower back. His touch rekindles the fire inside me. I don't want to banter or fight. I don't want to talk at all.

He needs to be naked in my bed. Now.

Deep breath. I can do this. I unlock my door and

slide it open.

"Is that an invitation?" He drags his fingertips over my back. "I'd really hate to leave without making you come."

The mouth on this guy! He doesn't lack for confidence. "Come in."

He laughs at my choice of words but this time I feel like he's laughing with me, not at me.

Some of the nerves in my stomach settle. This, having sex for the first time, is a big deal. But I can handle it.

Shit. I promised Kara I'd text her if I left. I stop just inside my door and dig through my purse.

Miles looks at me quizzically. "Someone else you'd rather talk to?"

I shake my head. "Kara. It's a girl thing."

"Tell her you're about to have the best sex of your life."

"Not a lot of competition there."

He slides his hands over the hem of my dress. That hand is so, so close to exactly where it needs to be.

I find my phone and tap out a text to Kara.

Meg: Went home early. Everything is fine. See you Sunday.

Miles plucks my phone from my hand and slides it into his pocket. He shifts, pinning me to the wall.

I close my eyes and soak in the weight of his body. God, he feels so good. We're almost there.

When his lips connect with mine, every bit of ugliness fades. My awful memories fade. The outside world fades. Every moment that isn't this one fades.

The kiss breaks. My body is buzzing. I'm desperate, but I can't let it show. I channel Miles's aloof confidence. I'm cool, calm, collected. No problem.

His eyes pass over me again. "You look amazing in that dress."

"I know."

"You're supposed to compliment me after that."

"I know that, too."

His lips curl into a smile. "You've got to butter me up a little if you want me naked."

Damn, the man is a mind reader. Or maybe he's used to women wanting him naked. Doesn't matter. Right now, I need him naked.

I press my thigh into his. "You have tattoos, right?"

"Several."

"And you got them just so you'd have a reason to take off your shirt."

"You caught me." He laughs. "You sure you weren't drinking at the show?"

I run my fingers over the hem of his t-shirt. "Positive."

He moves my hand gently and pulls his t-shirt over his head. Damn. He's even more attractive up close. His chest and shoulders are strong. I run my fingers over his sculpted abs and trace those v-lines at the top of his hips. They're like an arrow pointing to a prize.

A prize I need desperately.

But I don't want to rush. This feels good. It's the only thing that feels good. I'm going to savor it.

His tattoos are just as sexy as his muscles. Somehow, the ink makes him hotter. It's like his songs— his soul is on his skin for anyone to see. It's obvious and mysterious at once.

What does it mean, the Chinese-style dragon

adorning his shoulder and bicep? The rose and thorns on his chest? The words above the flower: Be Brave, Live?

I wish I was brave enough to draw my soul on my skin. To offer up my pain in a song for the whole world to see.

I trace the words with my fingers. "When did you get that one?"

"About a year ago."

"No women's names?"

"Love is temporary. Ink is forever."

His chest and shoulders are strong. Not an ounce of fat to cover a perfect six-pack. I run my finger down his torso to that sexy v-line guys get.

I look back into his eyes. "You won't fall in love, or you won't fall in love with me?"

"I won't fall in love."

"How can you be so sure?"

"I am."

"But how?"

"Because I know."

I press my hand against his stomach to remind myself why I invited him in. "That's not an answer."

"I'll make you a deal. You accept my answer and—"

"You can believe whatever you want." Even if it doesn't make sense. The Miles in that song, the Miles who tattoos a mantra on his chest—that Miles is committed, passionate, vulnerable.

The one sitting next to me… If I didn't know better, I'd be sure that nothing had ever hurt him.

Miles ignores my objection. "If I ever do fall in love, I'll add her name to my collection."

"Whatever makes you happy."

He digs his hand through my hair. "This makes me happy."

A blush spreads across my cheeks. He's in control again, and I'm the prey again. I need to do something to affect him, too.

I brush my hand against the waist of his jeans.

"Doing some more investigative work there?" he asks.

I nod.

His breath gets heavy. "What are you hoping to find?"

I tilt my head so my lips are inches from his. "The reason why you're so arrogant."

"You already saw me naked."

"It was too dark. I didn't get a good look."

I cup the bulge in his jeans. Words flee my brain at an alarming rate. My body takes over. It knows one thing: it needs to touch him.

I rub him over his jeans.

His kiss starts slowly. He sucks on my lips. Then he's scraping his teeth against them. He tastes amazing, like salt, sweat, and Miles.

I push him onto the bed and position my body on top of his, straddling him. His thighs are between mine. His crotch is against mine. I can feel him through his jeans. He's hard. And he's warm. And damn do I want these stupid clothes out of the way so I can feel him properly.

Anticipation spreads through my thighs and pelvis. I sink into his body, grinding my crotch against his. My nerves slip away. There's no room for nerves in my brain. There's no room for anything but the overwhelming desire to touch Miles and have him touch me.

It feels so fucking good, being in this moment, thinking about nothing but this moment.

His voice is heavy. "I've been dying to get my hands under that dress all night."

He needs this too. It relaxes me, makes me forget he holds all the cards.

Miles pulls the straps off my shoulders, exposing my breasts. No bra tonight. I don't need a bra in a dress that hugs me as tightly as this one does.

His eyes go wide. His pupils dilate. "Damn." The pad of his thumb brushes against my nipple. "Better than I remembered."

I swallow hard. He was thinking about me when he was alone?

"What do you remember?" I ask.

"The taste of your skin." He pulls me closer and presses his tongue against my nipple.

Damn, that feels good. I dig my fingers into his shoulders. He groans against my skin as he teases my nipple with his tongue.

I barely manage to form words. "Is that all you remember?"

He swirls his tongue around my nipple. Sensation overwhelms me. Every flick of his tongue sends pleasure straight to my core. He can take as long as he wants to respond if he keeps doing this.

Hell, he can give up words forever if he keeps doing this.

His teeth scrape against my nipple. I gasp reflexively. It hurts just enough to feel amazing.

He pulls his mouth away and replaces it with his fingers. "And that sound you make."

"You like it?"

"No. I love hearing you groan. Want to hear it

every fucking day."

He pinches my nipple, just hard enough that it barely hurts. Desire shoots through me. I groan. His pupils dilate. His lips press together. He does love it.

I love it.

Finally, we can really agree on something.

This is far too much thinking.

I need to stop thinking.

I grind against Miles. He groans as he brings his mouth back to my chest. He sucks on my nipple. Soft then hard then soft again.

My body floods with pleasure. He's too good at this.

Miles pulls my dress up, over my hips, stomach, chest. I lift my arms to help him. Then the garment is a heap on the floor.

I'm in nothing but panties.

He shifts our bodies. I'm flat on my back. He's on top of me, his hips pressed against mine, pinning me to the bed. His cock is against my clit. Only there's all this fabric in the way.

I've always hated fashion. Right now, I loathe it. He shouldn't be allowed to wear clothes. At least not in my apartment.

I reach for the button of his jeans. "You're wearing too many clothes."

He smiles. I'm not sure if it's smug or playful or confident. All three maybe. Right now, I feel at ease. Like he's not pushing or prodding me. Like he wants me comfortable, wants my pleasure. After all, he thinks about my breasts and the sounds I make when he touches me.

He wants me to feel good. Sexually. But that's something.

That's a lot.

Miles drags his lips over my neck. He shifts to his side, unzips, and slides off his jeans. It's all effortless. He's smooth, in control. I must seem like a desperate mess.

This is almost happening.

We're going to have sex.

He's going to be inside me.

Miles slides his fingers over my stomach. "You're nervous again."

I shake my head, but I can feel the trembling in my hands. I have almost no experience, and Miles is clearly some kind of sex god.

He's staring at me, his eyes filled with sincerity. He really is concerned about me.

"You are," he says.

Still, I shake my head.

His lips curl into a smile. "It's cute that you don't want to admit it."

I don't want to be cute. I want to be sexy. I want to be making him as needy as I feel.

Confidence. I can do that. I drag my fingers over his torso. "Don't you have a better use for your mouth?"

"Oh." His voice gets low. "You mean this." He trails his lips against my chest, stopping to draw circles around my nipple with his tongue.

"Yes. That." Pleasure surges through me.

His hand slides between my thighs. "You don't have to hide how badly you want this. I mean, it's cute and all—"

"I'm not cute."

"Try adorable."

"Didn't we discuss the appropriate uses for your

mouth?"

He nods and presses his lips into mine. It's a hard kiss, possessive even. "How's that?"

I struggle through a breath. That is amazing. "It's a start."

He smiles, takes my hand, and places it on the waistband of his boxers.

I pull the damn things to his knees and wrap my fingers around him. He places his hand over mine, guiding me. I stroke him harder. Faster.

His lips find mine. It's fast and hard and messy. I kiss him back, sucking on his tongue, scraping my teeth against his lips.

He groans into my mouth.

He wants me. Miles, the sex god, wants me.

My heartbeat picks up. We're really doing this.

I watch him fish a condom from the pocket of his jeans. My palms get sweaty. Nerves rise up in my stomach. What if it hurts? What if I'm not good enough?

Miles places his body next to mine. He drags his hand up my leg and strokes my inner thigh. "Relax. You won't do it wrong."

"Okay," I breathe.

He pulls my panties off and presses his lips to my neck.

I groan as his fingers skim my clit.

He scrapes his teeth against my neck. His voice is low, hungry. "Don't hold back. I like you groaning. I like you loud. Turns me on to know it's good for you."

I have no control over my vocalizations. Taking in this experience is about all I can handle.

He sucks on my skin as he moves his fingers

closer. Closer. They slide over my sex.

It feels good. We're close to doing this.

Nerves fade away as he rubs me. I take a deep breath and look into his gorgeous blue eyes.

His expression is heavy with need, but it's attentive too. Somehow, I trust him to guide me through this.

I let my eyelids press together and I sink into the bed. Slowly, he slides a finger inside me. He warms me up then it's two fingers. Three. I gasp.

That's intense. It hurts. I dig my nails into his shoulders.

"More?" he asks.

I nod.

He takes his time speeding up, going deeper. The discomfort fades to pleasure. Then it's a lot of pleasure.

Then his thumb is on my clit, stroking me. I groan as my sex clenches. That feels amazing. And the pleasure is building so quickly. With a few more strokes I'm at the edge. About to come.

Then I'm there. All the tension in my sex builds to a fever pitch then it's unwinding, spilling through me. I scream his name as I come.

It takes a moment to catch my breath. I blink my eyes open and stare into Miles's. He's still attentive, but he looks even needier. Like he's desperate to be inside me.

I want that.

I press my hand into his chest. "I want to do this. I'm ready."

He groans something that resembles a yes as he unwraps the condom and slides it on.

No more waiting.

This is happening.

He grabs my hip, pressing me against the bed, shifting my position so his cock brushes against my clit. I thrust my hips forward, and his tip strains against me.

Every nerve in my body is turned on, and they're all screaming the same thing. I need him inside me. Now.

I shift my hips to push him a little bit deeper. Deeper.

It's intense. There's pain but there's pleasure too. I dig my nails into his back until there's more pleasure than anything else.

I shift my hips to push him deeper. I can feel how my sex stretches to take him.

Miles goes slow. His eyes are on mine, watching my reactions. There's no sign of that arrogant, aloof guy. He's here, in this moment, committed to my pleasure.

He goes deeper. Deeper. It hurts but I don't want him to stop.

I tug at his hair. "Don't stop."

I kiss him like the ship is going down.

His hands curl around my back. Our bodies press together. It's intimate, the way he's holding me, the way he's kissing me, the way he's sliding inside me.

Then he's there. I'm full. It still hurts, but the pleasure far outweighs the pain.

My body takes over. I rock my hips to match his steady rhythm. It's slow. A good slow. A hell of an intense slow.

Pressure builds inside me. It's such sweet, perfect pressure.

I close my eyes and surrender to the feeling of Miles inside me.

I groan as loudly as I can. Something to let him know how much he's affecting me, how fucking good he's making me feel.

After a few more thrusts, I'm there. My sex clenches. Tighter and tighter. So tight I can barely take it.

Then I'm coming. I groan his name as an orgasm washes over me. It's different than before. More intense. Deeper.

Miles grabs my wrists and pulls my hands over my head. Then his lips are on mine. He thrusts into me so hard it hurts.

He groans into my mouth. It feels good in a different way, knowing he's close, feeling his pleasure.

His posture changes. His eyes close. His breath gets heavy.

I have to bite my lip to contain myself. It's still intense. It still hurts. But I don't want him to stop. There's something about hearing his groans and feeling his muscles tense.

It's hot as hell.

I want to feel him come.

His teeth sink into my neck. That, too, hurts just enough to feel good.

A few more thrusts and he's there, groaning against my skin as he comes.

He holds me for a moment. Our bodies are pressed together. It's intimate in a different way, overwhelming in a different way.

I take deep breaths, trying to process the experience. I had sex with Miles. Lost my virginity to him.

It's real. Adult. Dangerous.

He presses his lips to mine then untangles our

bodies and takes care of the condom.

I sink into the bed. I had sex with Miles. It really happened.

The weight on the bed shifts as he brings his body next to mine. He slides his arms around me and pulls me close.

This still feels intimate.

There are no pretenses. I can't remember the last time I spent this long with my guard down.

His lips press against my neck and I lose track of conscious thought.

It's not really safe, his arms, but it feels like it. It's comfortable.

A few more minutes and I'll figure this out. A few more minutes and I'll get into my pajamas. Just a few minutes…

CHAPTER NINE

The shower in the bathroom turns on. Light streams through the curtains. It's bright. I can barely keep my eyes open.

I drag myself out of bed. The room is messy—comforter and clothing in a heap on the floor. Miles was here last night. Miles is still here. He's in my shower.

We had sex—my first time—and it was amazing.

I pick his t-shirt up off the floor and pull it over my head. There's something enticing about it. It's soft, and it smells like him.

I knock on the bathroom door.

He shouts something, but it's muffled by the water.

"Can I come in?"

The water turns off. "Door's open."

I turn the handle. So it is. I step inside the bathroom.

And there's Miles, behind the glass door of my shower, naked.

85

He pulls the door open. "Good morning."

I nod, mumbling something that isn't technically a word.

Damn, what a view. Light is streaming through the room, surrounding him with a soft glow. He looked amazing last night, but I couldn't see him with this kind of detail.

He's chiseled, like he's made out of stone. Water drips off his broad shoulders and chest, rolling down his six-pack, all the way to that perfect V.

Miles clears his throat. "You don't have to make it so obvious that you want me."

"It's not obvious."

He smirks and turns the water back on. I do my best not to stare at him while I brush my teeth. His reflection—right in the middle of the mirror—makes it difficult.

Miles is, without a doubt, the most beautiful man I've ever seen. And he's naked in my bathroom.

He catches me staring at him, and he smiles that same smug smile. His gaze passes over me, resting on my ass.

He pulls the shower door open a few inches. "I know you want me, Meg, but you don't have to come in here half-naked."

"I want nothing but caffeine."

"I don't believe you."

I rinse off my toothbrush and replace it. "What do you believe?"

"You fell asleep last night."

My cheeks flush. "You wore me out."

He motions come here. His eyes light up. "I still owe you one."

"What?"

"Three orgasms." He makes that same come here motion. "A promise is a promise. Though I'm thinking I'll go for four."

I bite my lip. I'm thinking that will send me into a coma. No medical basis for such a theory, but I'm holding to it. "Total or right now?"

"Only one way to find out."

There's a naked rock star in my bathroom threatening me with orgasms. What the hell happened to my normal life?

His eyes meet mine. "Do me a favor and grab one of those condoms."

He motions to the medicine cabinet, now stocked with a long row of condoms. He brought all these with him. The man is ambitious.

Deep breath. Here goes nothing. I pull my t-shirt over my head, grab a condom, and step into the shower. Miles's arms go to my hips, holding me steady. He leans closer. Our foreheads touch.

There's this look in his eyes—a desperate, needy look. He wants this as much as I do.

He pulls the shower door shut and presses me against the tile wall in one fell swoop. It's cold and hard, but I can't say that I mind.

His hands slide to my ass. He holds me in place as he presses his body into mine. First his hips, then his stomach, his chest, his lips.

It's an aggressive kiss, but there's still something patient about it. I open my mouth to make room for his tongue. Heat rushes right to my core. He's slick from the shower, and his skin feels so good against mine.

I kiss back, exploring his mouth with my tongue. His grip around my hips tightens. He shifts into me, pinning me against the wall.

I'm a little sore from my night—my thighs and my sex—but I want him too much for that to matter.

He breaks the kiss. His eyes find mine. He brushes my hair behind my ears. Runs his fingertips over my neck and shoulders. "You really are unbelievably sexy."

"Thank you."

His lips curl into a smile. "This shower is a little small. Might be tricky."

"Show me."

"Turn around."

I do. It puts me right under the showerhead. Water pounds over my hair, shoulders, and neck. Within a few seconds, I'm soaking wet. As slick and slippery as he is.

Miles unwraps the condom and slips it on. Then all his attention is on me.

He positions himself behind me, his crotch against my ass, his chest against my back. He places my hands on the tile wall, one at a time. His head settles between my shoulder and my neck. He really is the perfect height. Our bodies really do fit together nicely.

He drags his fingertips down my chest and stomach. With all the water, there's only the slightest hint of friction. It's smooth and seamless.

He's so damn good at this.

I press my eyes closed, but it only makes it harder to balance. Okay. I take a deep breath and try to get a grip on the tile wall. This seems awfully complicated, but for some reason, I trust him to guide me through it.

"We haven't even gotten started." He sucks on my

earlobe. "Relax."

I nod. "Make me."

"Is that a challenge?"

I use my most confident voice. "Yeah."

He laughs. "I like the way you think."

He holds me against him with one hand. The other draws circles over my thighs. It starts at my knees and works its way up. The closer he gets, the more my body buzzes. You'd think electricity and water would be a dangerous combination, but they're only better together.

There. His fingertips slide over my clit. It's smooth, seamless. I shudder, immediately struck with a wave of bliss. He really is good at this.

He sucks on my neck as he strokes me. Little by little, my taut muscles relax.

Pleasure builds in my sex. Every touch of his fingertips is magic. I allow my eyes to close.He holds me tighter. No doubt about it, if it weren't for his grip, I'd be a puddle on the floor. I'm already halfway there. Upper hand. Who cares? As long as he keeps touching me like this, he can have every ounce of control.

It's just sex.

It's just pleasure. Things can feel good. I can feel good. The world can be good.

In this moment, it's obvious. In this moment, nothing can hurt me.

This is fun. I'm going to have fun. I'm going to enjoy every single moment.

Miles plants kisses along my neck and shoulders. His touch gets faster. Harder. When it's perfect, I groan. My eyes blink open. The water is pounding against my chest, melting my body into his. Warmth spreads through me.

Almost.

I shift my hips to match his movements. My ass presses against his crotch. He's hard.

God, do I love the way that feels.

I lose control of my breath. I reach back for Miles, grabbing onto his thighs. Those are such amazing, muscular thighs. Slick from the shower, but that won't stop me. I dig my nails into his skin as he strokes me.

The tension builds, and builds, and builds. It's such a wonderful ache, and he's the only thing that can soothe it. I moan, digging my nails into his skin until his breath gets heavy. He sucks on my earlobe, hard, like it's the only thing he can do to contain himself.

One more brush of his fingers and I'm there. At the edge. His breath sends me over, tumbling into an intense orgasm. It's this heavy ache of pleasure, spreading out from my sex to my stomach and chest and lips. Every part of me feels so damn good.

Sex.

Fun.

That's all this has to be.

Miles groans. He brushes his lips against my neck. "Time to go for four."

I press my ass against his crotch. Yes. He's still hard, and now that's mine.

"How's your balance?" he asks.

"Could be better." I hold y body into his. "I'm awfully distracted."

His lips trail over my shoulders. "I'll make it quick."

I plant my hands on the tile without provocation.

He doesn't waste any time. His hands go to my hips, tilting me so I'm in position. I feel his cock straining against my sex.

He shifts, entering me. I let out a heavy exhale. It's intense and a little painful but it's damn good.

Miles holds me steady as he thrusts into me. His breath is heavy already. Desperate already. His hand goes to my chest. He rubs my nipple with his thumb, toying with me until I'm groaning so loudly I can't hear the water. Then he moves to my other breast and does it again.

He's more gifted than any person should be.

Every inch of my body is humming with pleasure. It's crying out for more. He's inside me, holding me, touching me, and still I want more.

I throw my head back, so my cheek is pressed against his. His hand goes to the back of my head, and he turns me until our lips connect.

It's a perfect spark. That buzz of pleasure goes straight to my core. I slide my tongue over his. I suck on his lips until I can feel his moan in my mouth.

He releases me, shifting me back into place. No more patience. He moves faster. Harder. His hands tighten around my hips. His breath gets heavier, heavier, heavier.

I arch my hips to match his movements. It doesn't hurt today. It only feels good.

I'm almost there. It's like Miles can sense it. He slides one hand down my stomach and over my clit, stroking me to another orgasm.

It happens so quickly this time. The tension builds to a fever pitch. It's almost too much to take. And then he thrusts into me. I scream out in pleasure, my sex pulsing as I come. Pleasure spreads through me in waves. My hands slip off the tile. My legs go weak. All the energy in my body is focused on this perfect sensation.

But he hasn't come yet. This isn't done yet.

Miles pulls me upright. "Come on."

He turns off the shower and pulls the door open. His arms slide under me. He lifts me, holding me against his chest, and carries me to the bed.

He sets me down on my back. I'm still dripping wet. The cotton sheets cling to my soaked skin. I shake them off, spreading my legs in invitation.

Miles positions himself on the bed. His body sinks into mine. He's wet, warm, hard.

He grabs my ass and shifts me until we're aligned again.

Then he's inside me.

I gasp in pleasure. God, he feels good.

Miles's eyes find mine. I can't explain his expression. Lust, yes, but there's affection, too. If he didn't feel so damn good, I'd ask him to explain it. But things being what they are...

I close my eyes.

Fun.

Sex.

That's all this is.

He thrusts into me, hard and fast. His body is shaking, his breath is frantic. He's about to come. I can feel it, and my God, do I love the feeling. I wrap my legs around him. I dig my hands into his wet hair.

He groans. This perfect low groan. Pure animal. Pure need.

There. I can feel his orgasm, not just in my sex, but in the tensing muscles in his back. I open my eyes to watch the pleasure spread across his face. It's amazing. So much so that I can barely breathe.

He shifts into me one last time, groaning as he comes.

His eyes flutter open. He presses his lips against mine and collapses on the bed next to me.

"Better than caffeine?"

A blush threatens to form on my cheeks. Sex and fun I can understand. Talking afterwards is a lot more complicated. "Better."

"You still want your caffeine?" He rolls onto his elbow. His fingertips trail over my chest. "I'll buy you breakfast."

"I should really study."

"Meg, I expect better from you." He smirks like he's teasing. "You can't use me for sex then send me home without feeding me."

"Would you even let me buy you breakfast?"

"Of course not." He shifts off the bed. "It's on me."

CHAPTER TEN

It's twenty minutes on the death bike. Riding on the streets isn't quite as terrifying as racing over the freeway, but it's still plenty scary.

After parking on a side street in Venice Beach, Miles leads me to an out-of-the-way restaurant. It's a repurposed house, blue with white shutters and wide windows.

Miles opens the door for me. He pulls out my chair for me. Like he's a perfect gentleman. Like we're on a real date.

It's a tiny table. A little wood laminate thing with barely enough room for two plates and two glasses. I sit on the edge of my chair, my legs crossed. Miles leans back in his chair, his knees wide open.

His eyes connect with mine. "Should we do the usual first date conversation?"

"Is this a first date?"

He shakes his head. "It's not a date. We're friends."

"But it is our first time out together."

He raises his eyebrow like he's challenging me. "Okay. Let's try it. What do you do?"

"I go to UCLA, premed. I work as an ER scribe from six to ten Monday through Friday. It's a lot of grunt work but it's great experience. And you?"

"I went to Stanford. Poli-sci."

"That right?"

He smirks. "You don't believe I went to Stanford?"

Somehow, I do believe it. Miles is handsome and charismatic. I can see him just about anywhere.

"And now?" I ask.

"I work in the entertainment industry."

"Is that the line you normally use?"

He shrugs. "Most women either know who I am or they don't care."

"Are you that famous?"

"Depends on how recently we dropped a music video, how well it's doing. We have a handful of diehard fans but we're not famous enough that everybody knows our names. It's been different since In Pieces. More people stop me on the street. It was our first hit. Our only top 100 song so far."

"Have you made a lot of money?" I ask.

He laughs. "I like that you asked that. Most people would think it's impolite."

I copy his effortlessly cool shrug.

He smiles. "Good amount. We're poised to make a great amount. But we're not there yet." His eyes go to the window. "Money isn't an issue for me. I inherited a lot. I could quit the band tomorrow, never work again, and still be okay."

"That is a lot."

He nods. "It's a shitty way to become a millionaire."

I clear my throat. I don't want the conversation to

get heavy. Talking about loss — that will hurt too much. Right, I feel good. Like it's possible to be happy. I haven't felt that way since before Rosie died.

"Where are you from?" he asks.

Back to a light topic. Perfect. "Orange County."

"My uncle lived in Irvine for a while. It's not a terrible. A little—"

"Sterile? Void of personality? Full of people who care about the color of their neighbor's house more than anything else?" My jaw tenses. So much for breezy conversation.

I have nothing against Orange County in theory. It's gorgeous, safe, and filled with perfectly remodeled shopping centers. But it's also filled with people like my parents who prioritize keeping up appearances over everything else.

"You adore it," he teases. "Planning on buying one of those new condos by the Irvine Spectrum?"

I shake my head.

"Your parents still live there?"

I clear my throat. Talking about my parents is sure to drag this conversation into dark and heavy territory. I don't even talk about them with Kara. I'm not about to share this with Miles.

"I don't like to talk about my family," I say.

He nods with understanding. "Where are you going to medical school?"

"I don't want to talk about it." The decision is still weighing me down. Staying near home, in southern California, doesn't feel right. Going across the country doesn't feel right, either.

Miles leans closer. His eyes pierce mine. "I was inside you an hour ago, but your med school applications are too personal to discuss?"

I can't place his expression. His voice is light, like he's joking, but that doesn't feel quite right.

"Excuse me." He stands and makes his way to the bathroom.

My back is in knots. I don't know how I'm supposed to act with him. We're friends, but we're having sex. It's confusing.

I dig my phone out of my purse. Kara hasn't responded to my texts with any more pleas for information, and I'm not sure I'm ready to hand anything out. My emails aren't particularly interesting. Mostly stuff about class. One horrible, two-week-old email from my parents attempting to arrange Thanksgiving break.

I need to find a way to make that visit less horrible.

Anything will do.

I rack my brain for ideas as I put my phone on silent and return it to my purse.

The server stops at our table. I order a coffee for me and a water for Miles. I have no idea what he likes. Hell, I know almost nothing about him. He's arrogant. He's an amazing singer. And he went through something awful that tore his heart to shreds. He must have to write In Pieces.

But it's none of my business. We're having fun, no serious feelings involved. I take a deep breath and perfect my I'm having such effortless fun expression. It's terrible.

Miles returns from the bathroom as the server drops off my coffee. He orders his own coffee and settles back into his seat. His eyes pass over me like he's picking me apart.

My cheeks are warm. Hell, they're burning up. "I

shouldn't be so defensive, but I... I've never done anything like this before."

His eyes find mine. "It's simple really. We have fun."

I stir milk and sugar into my coffee. "Nothing is that simple."

"This is. We have amazing sex, we talk, we eat, we go to shows and make out backstage. When it stops being fun, we part ways."

"If you're adamantly anti-commitment, why do you want a fuck buddy?" I ask.

"Thought I'd try something new." His eyes connect with mine. "And I like you."

"It's that simple?"

He nods. "Why do you want a fuck buddy? Can't make it to twenty-one without fucking unless you're avoiding it."

"You're that hot," I tease. "So hot I lost my mind."

"Besides that."

"I need the distraction."

"You're going to wound me talking like that."

"I'm sure." I take a sip of my coffee. Sweet, sweet caffeine. It's enough to push away the mixed-up feelings brewing in my gut. I can focus on having fun. I can focus on today and not whenever it is that we part ways. "I'm applying to Harvard, Johns Hopkins, and Columbia."

"Those are all on the other side of the country."

"Exactly."

The server returns with Miles's coffee. We order our breakfasts.

He waits until we're alone. "I'm going to add another term to our arrangement. Anything we do together—I'm paying."

"I can pay for myself."

"I'm sure you can, but I insist." His expression is intense.

"Fine."

He smiles. It's different from the smug grin that is usually plastered on his face. It feels like he cares about me, like this is about more than a little fun.

I shift the focus to other areas of conversation. I explain the process of applying for medical school, starting with the MCATs and ending with pressing the "submit" button on my online application. If he finds it boring, he doesn't show it. He keeps his eyes on mine, wide, and rapt with attention.

He talks about Stanford, focusing on meeting Drew, starting Sinful Serenade, graduating just in time to start touring. The band is about three years old. They have two albums. According to Miles, the first is good but not great while the second is amazing. It was a crossover hit. Big on the alternative chart. Their last tour, which ended a few weeks ago, sold out in almost every date.

They're not Maroon Five, but they have the potential to be the next big thing. If they play their cards right.

He knows a lot about the music industry, about the pop machine and how true rock music struggles to make it up the charts. A lot of what he says goes right over my head, but I'm still drawn in by the passion in his voice.

He may act aloof or arrogant around his bandmates, but he's clearly committed to music and to Sinful Serenade.

After brunch, I expect a quick ride home on the accident waiting to happen, but Miles insists on walking over to Abbot Kinney. It's a cute neighborhood packed with boutiques, food trucks, and overpriced coffee shops.

We window-shop while sipping our iced green teas. There's this homemade Star Wars t-shirt in one of the boutiques. It must be infringing on all sorts of copyright laws.

Miles points to it. "Want me to buy you that?"

"I don't need any help looking like a nerd."

"You don't realize the effect you have on guys, do you?"

"I don't have any effect on guys."

He slides his hand around my hip. "You have this irresistible innocence. I'm surprised there aren't creeps trying to corrupt you twenty-four seven."

"I already have you."

"I can't be around twenty-four seven."

"Why not?" I step into a small shop and pretend to study the dresses. "What do you do when you're not torturing women with your sexy voice?"

He brushes my hair over one of my shoulders and runs his fingertips over my neck. "You think my voice is sexy?"

That blush spreads across my cheeks. I pick up a sweater and stare like I'm debating purchasing it. It's an ugly orange thing with red stripes. "You know it is."

He plucks the sweater from my hands and sets it back on the shelf. "I go to shows. Play video games with Drew or Pete. Try to tolerate Tom's bossiness."

"And when you're alone?"

He takes my hand and leads me back to the street. It's still warm and bright.

"I run. I think. I read," he says.

"You read?"

"You this rude to all your friends or only the ones who make you come?" He says it playfully.

"The latter." I make my way down the street. "What do you read?"

"Books."

"What books?"

"That's classified."

Okay... I let his weird non-answer go without rolling my eyes.

The conversation shifts into senseless teasing. We get ice cream from one of those artisanal food trucks. His tongue makes such beautiful motions in the frozen treat, lapping it up like it's his favorite thing in the world.

He catches me staring and shakes his head. "You don't have to picture me naked. I'm more than happy to get naked with you."

"I'm sure."

He points to an alley between two stores. "Right there works for me."

"I'm not sure I... not here."

His smile is so damn smug. He presses his hand into my lower back, turning me so that we're headed back to the motorcycle.

"I have to study," I say.

"That's a shame."

He teases me all the way back to the bike. It's a quick ride to my apartment. Then he's walking me to my door.

His hands go to my hips. He pulls my body into his and sinks his lips into mine.

He tastes so good. It feels so good, kissing him, having his body against mine.

I can feel the kiss in my bones. I can feel the affection in his clear blue eyes.

"Goodbye, Meg." He takes a step backwards.

"Goodbye." I wait until he's in the elevator to go inside.

He's gone, but his presence lingers in my mind.

I miss him. I want him in a way I don't quite understand.

CHAPTER ELEVEN

Miles and I text about nothing all week. Wednesday, I finish my shift and pull out my phone. A picture message greets me.

It's an STD test. From Miles. He's totally clean.

It's dated Monday. Two days ago. He got tested. For me. For us.

Miles: I don't want to assume you're on birth control. But I figured you'd like the option of skipping condoms.

Meg: I'm on the pill. It seemed like a good idea when I went to college.

Miles: I'll bring condoms. It's up to you.

Meg: Okay. I'll think about it.

Miles: I want to take you somewhere Friday. What time do you get off work?

Meg: Ten.

Miles: Send the address and I'm there.

After work Friday, I change in one of the handicapped bathrooms. This is the sexiest outfit I own—low cut chiffon blouse, tight black skirt, black wedges—but I don't feel like it fits. Eyeliner and red lipstick do little to help matters.

It's strange. I felt sexy when I was with him. I felt totally irresistible. But the outfit makes me feel awkward and stiff.

Oh, well. I'm not planning to spend much time in my clothes. Damn, I'd like to skip straight to me and Miles in bed together. It made sense. It felt good. I want to feel that good again.

I make my way through the ER.

A nurse winks at me. "About time you went out. You're too young to work so hard."

I nod a polite goodnight. The older nurses are always teasing me about wasting my youth. They don't understand that bars and parties aren't fun for me. They make me think about Rosie losing herself. I don't want to explain it to anyone.

But I do want to explain to Miles. I want him to understand. My heartbeat picks up. It's scary, how much I want him to understand.

The ER is quiet for a Friday night. The waiting room is sparse. The counter is empty except for a man with a bandage over his nose. He got into a fight.

He looks familiar.

He's shorter than I am. His hair is light. He's wearing one of those button-up shirts. The same that Rosie's boyfriend always wore.

No.

No, no, no.

That is Rosie's boyfriend. Jared.

What the hell is he doing here? He lives on the other side of town, closer to a dozen different hospitals.

He should be in jail by now. Or dead from an overdose. Not standing in the ER with a broken nose.

My breath picks up. My heart pounds against my chest. I turn so my back is to him. I can't risk him recognizing me. If he offers his condolences, I'll break another one of his bones.

He's hurt. Thank God. I shouldn't smirk—future doctors should never smirk over people's injuries— but it feels good to see him bruised. He deserves every bit of pain in the world. If it weren't for him, Rosie would still be alive.

"I've never seen that look before." It's Miles. He's three feet away, spread out on one of the ugly gray chairs.

"It's nothing."

"It's something." He stands and moves close enough to whisper. "You may as well tell me. You know I'll drag it out of you."

"Maybe I'm smirking because we're going to have sex."

"I know what that looks like, and it involves a lot more blushing and squeezing your knees together."

So I am that obvious. Doesn't matter. Someone broke Jared's nose. At least I know he deserved it.

Miles laughs. "Should I be jealous?"

"Of...?"

"You were staring at that guy." He motions to Jared. "Is he your ex-boyfriend or something?"

"Or something."

"What—he broke your heart, and you paid one of your friends to break his nose?"

"You really think it's broken?"

Miles nods. "Likely." His fingers brush against my wrist. "Did he cheat on you or something?"

"Or something."

He leans closer, lowering his voice to a whisper. "Want me to kick his ass?"

"Would you really?"

"For you, yeah."

"That's okay. Someone already did." I smile. It's the widest smile I've ever smiled. I should feel horrible about wishing this pain on Jared, but I don't.

Miles laughs and slides his hand around my waist. "Meg Smart. I never thought I'd see the day."

I clear my throat and adopt my most mature stance. "There is no day. Now, where are we going?"

"You're glad someone kicked that guy's ass."

"He deserves it."

Miles's eyes connect with mine. Joy spreads over his face. "Do you trust me?"

"That depends on what we're talking about."

"This guy hurt you. Right?"

"You could say that."

Miles pulls me towards the wall so we're out of the way. "I'm going to do something to hurt him back."

I should feel sick at the suggestion, but I don't. This asshole stole my sister's life from her.

He needs to hurt. He needs to bleed.

I nod. "Okay."

Jared is still filling out paperwork. I haven't seen him since before Rosie died. He didn't come to the funeral. At the time, it pissed me off, but now I'm glad. I would have killed him if I saw him that day.

I want to kill him now.

The two-faced asshole was so fucking polite to me. He acted like a gentleman, like he was a prince and he'd treat her like a princess. I guess his idea of royalty involves massive opiate indulgence.

He needs to pay for what he did.

He needs to hurt.

Miles grabs my arm hard. "Go wait outside. Now."

No. I need to tell Jared he's the scum of the earth.

"You're not getting in trouble on my watch," Miles says.

"I won't get in trouble," I say.

"The look on your face begs to differ." Miles lowers his voice. "You wouldn't be able to hurt him if you tried. You're not that kind of person."

My expression screws in irritation. What the hell does Miles know about what kind of person I am?

"Trust me." He leans closer. "Hitting him isn't going to make you feel better."

"I want to watch."

"Wait outside or it's not happening."

I grit my teeth. "Fine."

As long as Jared hurts. As long as he pays for what he did to my sister.

I go outside and plant on one of the benches in front of the building. Cool air sends goosebumps over my arms and legs. This outfit is not appropriate for the fall evening air.

Time slows. My excitement twists to panic. What if Miles really does hurt the guy? What if he's doing something illegal? What if he's going to get into real trouble?

I try to calm down, but deep breaths aren't working. I like Miles. We are friends. I don't want anything bad happening to him.

There are footsteps behind me. Miles. He sits on the bench next to me and drops something on my lap.

A wallet. Jared's wallet.

"What am I supposed to do with this?" I ask.

"Return it to the lost and found."

"But...what? Why?"

Miles smirks. "I have his address and credit card number now."

"And?"

"And he's going to send himself a few dozen custom t-shirts about what an awful asshole he is."

The stiffness in my neck relaxes. It's a prank. An illegal prank, but only a prank. It's not like Miles is going to wait outside the guy's house with a baseball bat.

Miles will be okay. He won't get hurt.

He leans close enough to whisper. "Unless you want to do something that will really hurt him."

My breath collects in my throat. "Like what?"

"The possibilities are endless. All sorts of accidents no one could ever trace back to us." Miles plays with the hem of my skirt. "It depends how much he hurt you."

"More than anyone else ever has."

"What happened?"

I want to tell him, but my tongue is sticky. It's better to keep this to myself. It's less dangerous. "I... I don't want to talk about it right now."

"As you wish." He slides the wallet into his pocket. "You must have loved him a lot to hate him so much."

Anger rises up inside of me. The thought sickens me. My hands curl into fists. "No."

Miles shakes his head. He doesn't believe me. He thinks I'm hung up on the asshole who destroyed my sister. Miles probably thinks that I'm in love with Jared, that he's the reason I don't want a relationship.

"I never loved him. I barely know him. He was my sister's boyfriend and he...he ruined her life."

"Call her. Let her decide what to do with him."

My heart sinks. Everything is heavy. I open my mouth to speak but no words come out. "I... I can't. She died a few months ago."

"Oh, fuck." He turns to me, his eyes wide with concern.

This isn't part of our deal. He's not supposed to be concerned, and I'm not supposed to let him take care of me.

"What happened?" His voice is so soft. It's the sweet Miles, the one who wrote all those songs.

I shake my head. I can't discuss this. I can't even say it out loud.

His voice gets softer. He runs his fingers through my hair. "What happened, Meg?"

"She..." It's hard to breathe. There. Inhale. Exhale. "She overdosed."

"An accident?"

"Yeah." I press my fingers together. This is too close, too personal. I need to get up, to get out of here, to be anywhere else. Jared doesn't matter. He's nothing. Just another loser who will dig his own grave.

"I'm sorry," he whispers.

His arms wrap around me. He pulls me into a tight hug. It's intimate. Too intimate. He's seeing inside me, seeing all the things I try to keep hidden.

I can't take it. But I can't move. I can't do anything but lean into Miles's touch.

He pulls me tighter. I slide my hands under his leather jacket and press them against his lower back, over the soft fabric of his t-shirt.

He's warm. He's here. But he's not mine. We'll never have that kind of relationship.

I take a deep breath. "I want to go home. Let's put the wallet in the lost and found."

"Okay. Where is that?"

"Give it to me. I'll do it."

Miles pulls the wallet from his pocket and hands it to me. I stare at the sky. There are big, gray clouds covering the moon. The stars are tiny and dull, like they can't bother to shine tonight.

"Meg." His voice is so soft.

"I'm fine." My throat is sore. My eyes sting with tears. I blink them away. I can't cry here.

"I'll take you home."

"No." I wipe my eyes with the back of my hand. "I'm going to say I found this out here. And then we're going out."

If I go home, I'll drown in how awful this feels. I have to convince him I'm okay enough to go out.

I march into the waiting room, drop off the wallet, and march back to Miles.

He's standing there, his eyes wide with affection. It's like he's desperate to do anything to make this hurt less.

His voice is a whisper. "Come here."

I stay put. This isn't what we're doing. I've already said too much. He's already seen too much, too deep inside me.

"Can we go?" I ask.

He shakes his head and wraps his arms around me. It's a tight hug. I want to push him off, to bang on his chest until he releases me.

But I can't. His body feels too good. I need the comfort too badly.

I take another ragged breath. I dig my fingers into the slick fabric of his leather jacket.

I can't cry in front of Miles. Not even if this is some other version of Miles, the one who hurts deep inside, who writes songs about the unspeakable agony of losing everything that matters.

"It's okay." His cheek brushes against mine. "I know how much it hurts."

I want to ask him how. I want to ask who he lost. I want to comfort him too. But I can't speak. I can't move.

I can't do anything but soak in the feeling of his arms against me.

This isn't what we're doing. We're casual. Not confidants.

After a few more breaths, I'm calm enough to release him. I pull back, slowly shaking him off. Cold hits me. It's brutal and sudden, like I'm shedding my favorite coat to step into a snowstorm.

His eyes stay glued to mine. "You look miserable."

I shake my head. "I'm fine."

His eyes turn to the street. "Don't make me call you on our 'no lies' clause."

"Can we please get out of here?"

He says nothing.

I need to turn the mood, to change him back to the other Miles. At least I know what that Miles wants. I make my voice light. "I'll go crazy if I have to make conversation with you for one more minute."

He smirks but he doesn't laugh. He's not quite back to snappy, sarcastic Miles. Not yet.

And I'm not back to acerbic Meg either. My defenses are down.

It's terrifying.

Miles wraps his hand around my wrist and leads me to his car. Or the car he borrowed from one of his band mates.

I settle into the passenger seat. My skirt rides up my thighs, but it does nothing to entice Miles to touch me.

He slides the key into the ignition. "You're not as good at pretending you're okay as you think you are."

"I don't want to talk about it."

"I'm not going to fuck you out of your misery." His lips curl into a smile. "I know. In my dreams, right?"

I nod.

"All this dreaming. I must be pretty fucking desperate." He brushes my knee. "Listen, Meg—"

"If the next words out of your mouth aren't something about how irresistible I am, you can save your breath."

"You're painfully irresistible." He trails his fingertips up my thigh. "I was thinking about fucking you the entire drive here." His eyes find mine. "Almost crashed this damn car."

Yes. Now. That makes sense. That feels good.

This hurts. It hurts so fucking badly.

Miles's voice gets low. Breathy. "I was planning on driving you to Malibu and fucking you in the backseat."

"The passenger seat isn't good enough?"

He smirks. "Only for round two." His hand slides over my thigh, back to my knee. "But I'm not going to be your human distraction. I don't have that kind of sex. No matter how badly I want to fuck someone."

I fight a sigh. Miles won't have sex with me, fine. I

have other ways of satisfying myself without his soft lips or his strong hands.

It won't be nearly as fun, but then it's not looking like this evening is going to be very fun.

He turns the key. "Don't sulk over it."

"You're the one who invited me out."

"We're out. If you want to spend the night pouting over not getting in my pants, I'll drive you home."

I pull the seatbelt over my chest. "What's the alternative?"

"I take you to Malibu. We have a conversation under the stars."

"I'm not really in the mood to talk."

He laughs. "You don't say."

I take a deep breath. I am irritable. I can't stand how mixed up I feel around Miles, how close I am to clinging to him and crying my heart out.

It's dangerous. Falling for him is the first step to falling apart. He's a drug. Different than the heroin that took hold of my sister's life but just as deadly.

I should go home. I should cry myself to sleep.

But I can't. I need someone.

I need him.

"I'm not cranky. I'm just hungry," I say. "Can we stop for something to eat?"

"Your wish is my command."

He turns the key and, mercifully, the radio fills the car with noise.

This is going to be a long night.

CHAPTER TWELVE

The only place open is a horribly expensive organic store. I try to buy my sashimi bowl and green tea but Miles insists. I guess I agreed to this term—anything we do, he pays. I'm too tired to object.

Just to screw with me, he buys strawberries and a bottle of chocolate syrup. I'm not that inexperienced. I know what people do with chocolate syrup. God, how I want him doing it to me, his tongue lapping the treat off my thighs and breasts.

In the car, I do my best to get comfortable. It's a long drive to Malibu, and there's almost no space between us.

I press my back into the leather seat and turn the radio to an earblasting volume. It's loud enough to drown my thoughts. I need a break from everything. I need to not hurt for a while.

Miles slides the knob until the music is low enough for a conversation. Thankfully, he doesn't attempt one. His attention stays on the road.

He drives just as fast as he does on his bike. The

city zips by. Then we're on Pacific Coast Highway and we're surrounded by ocean and sky.

I open the moonroof and watch the stars shine. There are patches of clouds in the dark sky, but we're far enough away from the city lights that the stars are bright.

There's something about being next to Miles. I feel so exposed and safe at once. It's like nothing outside this car, not even my memories of Rosie, can hurt me.

Him seeing me, knowing how close I am to breaking—that can hurt me.

"You know, when I mentioned conversation, I was assuming you'd also make an effort." His voice is light.

Okay. I can tease too. "Conversation isn't my strong suit."

"I can tell."

"Or yours."

He laughs. "We both know my strong suit. What's yours?"

I'm good at studying. At this point, it's probably my greatest skill. Not very useful outside of school, but I have another four years of that ahead of me.

Still, we're almost flirting. And flirting might convince Miles I want him as more than a distraction.

I do. I want him as more than a fuck buddy.

That can't happen. This is sex. Just sex.

"Spades," I say.

"How the hell do you come up with spades?"

I try to cobble together a joke, but the pieces don't fit "Well, it's obviously not hearts."

"And not comedy."

I flip him off playfully. My lips curl into a smile.

He laughs. "You're good at driving me out of my

mind."

"In what way?"

"You mean besides how fucking crazy I go thinking about touching you again?"

I take a deep breath. "Don't tease me if you're going to stick to that ridiculous no sex tonight declaration."

"Not that you care?"

"Go to hell."

He stops at a light. The first light in ages. It changes to green, and we turn off the main road into an empty beach parking lot. There's a sign with posted hours: six a.m. to ten p.m. It's past eleven, but that isn't about to stop Miles. He was ready to burn a guy's house down an hour ago.

"It's flattering," he says. "That it upsets you so much."

He parks the car and gets a blanket out of the trunk. Maybe that was his original plan for the night—sex on the beach under the stars.

Damn, that sounds romantic. It's better that we aren't feeding each other strawberries on the beach. I can't handle that.

I slip out of my shoes and dig my feet into the rough sand. The water is only a hundred feet away. The roar of crashing waves fills the salty air.

Miles lays the blanket next to a lifeguard stand and places our bounty of snacks on top of it. "I figured you'd rather not eat in the car."

"Thanks."

"You cold?"

"Only if you're about to offer me your shirt."

"Leather jacket's in the backseat."

The same backseat where he was going to fuck me.

Not that it matters. I shake my head, sit down, and focus on my dinner. I'm so hungry that even grocery store sashimi tastes good. Actually, it tastes amazing. Soft tuna, chewy rice, spicy wasabi.

Miles is deep in thought, but I have no clue what he's thinking. I have no idea how to broach the topic.

Once I'm finished eating, I move on to my other need. I undo the top button of my blouse and push my chest forward.

His eyes go to my chest. His tongue slides over his lips. But he doesn't touch me.

He does break the silence. "We are friends. You can talk to me."

"I'm not interested."

"Pretty sure I should take offense to that."

"Then take offense. But it's not something I want to talk about. And certainly not with you. You made it clear that you don't want that kind of closeness. That we're not confidants."

His voice gets low. "You're drowning in something. You don't have to tell me what it is, but I'm not going to watch without throwing a life vest."

Great. Sensitive Miles is out and he's speaking in metaphors. I have to convince him I'm fine even if I don't believe it myself.

I stare into his beautiful blue eyes. "Thank you for the sentiment. But I'm fine. My sister died three months ago. I still miss her sometimes, but it's nothing out of the ordinary."

"She was a drug addict, wasn't she?"

I scowl. I hate thinking of Rosie like that, but she was a drug addict at that point. "That's not any of your business."

"If it affects our relationship, it is."

"What relationship is that? We've had sex and breakfast." I finish my food and drop my fork in the bowl.

There's a tightness in my chest. I don't want to discuss this with Miles. Hell, I don't want to discuss this with anyone. I thought we were on the same page.

I take a deep breath. I can convince him it's nothing. "My sister, Rosie, starting doing drugs behind my back. It went on for about a year. She lied the whole time, and I looked the other way, because I didn't want to believe it was possible. I was studying for the MCAT, and I didn't have any spare energy to worry about her."

"Why are you trying to convince me you're over it?"

"I'm not trying to convince you of anything."

"You'll never be over it. Not really."

"How do you know what I'll be over?"

"I know how it feels to lose the person who matters more to you than anyone." His eyes go to the sand.

My heart is in civil war. I want to tell him he's wrong and offer him comfort. "Are you going to share those details with me?"

"That's not my point."

"It's mine. If you won't even tell me who you lost, why should I tell you anything about how I feel?" I grit my teeth. "Whoever you are, can you bring back the Miles I met last month?"

"Even that guy would notice how upset you are."

"Fine. I'm upset. You did your friend duty and asked what was wrong. I did my friend duty and gave you the details. Can we close the book on this conversation?"

"No."

"Then take me home."

He stares at me.

"Is there a reason why you're cross-examining me?"

He scoots closer. "It's the decent thing to do."

"You never struck me as a decent guy."

He shrugs. "You're lucky I don't offend easily."

"I can try harder to offend."

He rests his hand on mine. There's something in his eyes. He's uncertain. It's the first time I've seen Miles anything but confident.

"It's not something I talk about," I say. "It's not personal."

He shifts onto his back, his eyes on the stars. "Fine. But I'm still not having sex with you tonight."

Even without Miles's questions, I feel a pull to reveal myself, to share my pain with him. I want to feel the way I do when I listen to his songs, like he understands me and I understand him.

Why is that intimacy so elusive when we speak?

I close my eyes and sink into the sand. The gentle breeze sends a chill down my spine. I rub my arms with my palms but it only helps so much.

Miles wraps his arms around me and pulls my body into his. It's like slipping into my favorite hoodie—warm and comforting.

Everything that happened with Rosie hurts. Every time I see someone with a drink and a smile, every time I hear her name, every time I find one of her things—it hurts somewhere so deep I can't breathe.

Minutes pass. Maybe hours. I'm aware of nothing except the waves, the breeze, and Miles's breath. He pulls me closer, wrapping his arm around me and stroking my hair. This isn't the Miles I saw fucking some girl at a party. It's not the guy who teased me about being a virgin. It's the guy who wrote In Pieces, the one who knows what it feels like to lose everything that matters.

So why can't I talk to him? My lips refuse to move. I think up a million ways to start the conversation. Who did you write In Pieces about? How long ago was it? Does it hurt less? I used to live with Rosie, in a two bedroom. She died finals week. I was so depressed I missed two finals. I had to beg my teachers to let me make them up. My GPA took a hit. It's still not what it needs to be. What did you lose? How far did you fall?

I want to tell him, to tell someone. I don't talk to anyone about it. Not even Kara.

Still, my lips refuse to move.

I try to focus on the stars, something to center me and keep my mind from drifting to places it shouldn't go. It doesn't work. Vivid mental images form. Miles as my doting boyfriend, walking me to class, sharing my sashimi, whispering sweet nothings under the stars.

I don't want a boyfriend. He doesn't do boyfriend. It should be a perfect arrangement. Only he keeps acting sweet, like he's going to sew the pieces of my broken heart back together.

I sink into Miles. This time, I soak up every ounce of comfort. Minutes pass. Hours even.

He taps me on the shoulder and whispers, "are you asleep?"

"Yes," I murmur.

He chuckles. "Dreaming about anything good?"

"You could say that."

He lifts me, taking me into his arms and carrying me over the sand. My ear is against his chest, and I can hear his steady heartbeat. Whatever this is, I need it tonight.

He lays me on the passenger seat and presses his lips against my cheek. He looks at me like he knows I'm awake. "I was considering fucking you in that lifeguard stand."

"You should know that I hate you."

"I know." He slides into the driver's seat. "My uncle's place is nearby, but he's not around. I'm going to take you there."

I close my eyes and listen to the air rushing through the moonroof. I feel nothing except the soft vibrations of the car. Then Miles's arms are around me. His hands are pressed into my thigh. My head is against his shoulders. My body fits into his perfectly, even more perfectly than when we have sex.

We're in a strange house, up the stairs, in a bedroom. It feels like a guest room. It's clean and untouched. The bed is even made.

Miles lays me down and undresses me. He does it slowly. His fingertips linger on my skin.

Even though his touch is more sweet than sexual, I burn up with need. My blouse is gone. Then my skirt. I'm still in my bra and panties. That won't do. This feeling, this pain won't do. I need him with me, comforting me, erasing everything else.

I unhook my bra and slide it off my shoulders. His eyes pass over my body, but he doesn't touch me.

"Please," I say. "It can be quick."

He shakes his head. "It won't make you feel better. Trust me. I've tried."

He's wrong. I push my panties to my ankles and kick them off. Miles's eyes are glued to me. He's under my thumb but only enough to watch. Not enough to give me what I want.

I spread my legs and sprawl over the bed in an obvious invitation.

He climbs in next to me, placing his body behind mine. "I'm not fucking you." He slides his arm around my waist. "If you ask again, I'm leaving."

"Why?"

"Because if you ask two more times, I'll say yes, and that isn't happening." He runs his fingers through my hair. "Go to sleep. You'll feel better in the morning."

He's wrong again. I'll feel worse in the morning. Rosie will still be gone. And I'll still be heavy from the loss.

"If I feel worse, will you fuck me in the morning?" I ask.

He nods. "Sounds fair."

I melt around him. He pulls me closer.

I'm not going to cry on his shoulder. He's not going to fall in love with me.

But he's in bed with me, holding me.

It feels so fucking good, him holding me.

Like we're confidants. Like we're lovers. Like we're going to share every ugly thing in our hearts.

CHAPTER THIRTEEN

I wake up alone.

He's gone. The other side of the bed is cold. He's been gone for hours.

I'm in a stranger's house, in a strange, lifeless room.

At least the view is amazing—a long stretch of the deep blue Pacific Ocean and the backyard just below the window. It's straight off a postcard. Aqua pool. Lush garden. Bright yellow sun.

And there's Miles, lying on a lounge chair in his boxers, paperback book in his hands. He's not so much reading as staring off into space with a tortured expression.

I know almost nothing about the Miles behind the sharp wit. He was trying to pry me apart last night. Maybe it wasn't on purpose, but he wanted more from me. He wanted to hear about Rosie and all the other things that still hurt.

But why? Either this is casual or it's more. I need to know which it is. I need to know if it's safe to let him in.

I want to pry him apart, look at all the places he hurts, and put him back together.

Maybe we can have that intimacy. Maybe this can be more.

I find the bathroom. There's a box of disposable toothbrushes under the counter. I try to think up an explanation besides a harem of equally disposable women, but I fail.

The rest of the house is just as beautiful as its surroundings. Everything is clean, bright, and beige. The rooms are huge, the ceilings are high, the furniture is understated. It's like the mansion version of an Apple store. There's something untouchable about this place, like no one lives here. And there's Miles, in the backyard, looking just as untouchable as the clean glass table.

He stirs as I pull the sliding door open. His eyes find mine.

There's a weight in my chest. I shouldn't want so badly to ask how he feels, to know how he hurts and what I can do to take it away.

He pushes off the seat and stretches his arms over his head. His boxers slide down his stomach ever so slightly. They're an inch above his...

"Good morning." He takes three steps towards me. "You must've slept well. It's almost noon."

"You should've woken me."

He slides his hand around my waist. "I did. You had some choice words about it."

"Like asking what the hell you're doing inviting me for sex then taking me to some strange house to sleep?"

"Similar, but with a lot more insults and

profanity." His lips curl into a smile. "You're cute when you swear."

How is it possible I don't remember any of this? I must've been half asleep. I only hope I gave Miles the lecture he really deserves. I take a deep breath. "Thank you."

His eyes find mine. His expression shifts. Not playful or sarcastic but serious. Like he really is worried about me. "Are you okay?"

Cool, calm, composed. That's what he does, so that's what I'll do. "You wrote that song. You know what it's like to lose everything that matters to you."

He nods.

"Are you okay?"

"Fair point."

That's it. No admission of feelings. No hurt on his face. There's no sign anyone or anything has ever hurt Miles. He's so utterly unflappable.

He asked me to talk. I can ask him the same thing.

I stare into his clear blue eyes. "Do you want to talk about it?"

He shifts his weight between his legs. "I don't talk about that with anyone."

The statement is a lead wall. There's no getting past it or around it. This must be how he felt last night—locked out of my head and my heart. It stings in a way it shouldn't. Not given how casual this is supposed to be.

I take a step towards the kitchen. "Do you have anything with caffeine?"

He nods to the coffeemaker sitting on the counter inside. "It's a few hours old."

So he's been up for a few hours. This image flashes through my mind—Miles lying on that lounge chair, his gaze fixed on the horizon, his thoughts drifting away.

I follow him to the kitchen and fix a cup of coffee.

The beverage does nothing to chase away the uneasy feeling in my gut. I want to know Miles's thoughts but that's not part of our arrangement.

He nudges me with his shoulder. "You're more obvious than you think you are, Meg."

He brushes his hand over my lower back. Damn, I want that hand on me.

I try to play it cool. Focus on my coffee. Sit at the perfect kitchen table. Ignore the fact that Miles is wearing boxers. He could be doing it to seduce me or to drive me mad.

I smile and sip my drink. I am the epitome of cool. I could not be more cool.

He opens the fridge and pulls out a carton of eggs. "Scrambled okay?"

"That's fine."

He takes a perfect white bowl from a cabinet, cracks half a dozen perfect white eggs, and stirs with a perfect white whisk.

His back is to me. His muscles are ever so slightly flexed. Those are strong shoulders and lats. He must do a lot more to work out than run.

My mind flashes with another set of images. These are more appealing. Miles in all sorts of compromising positions with me, his muscles flexed, his breath strained.

Miles turns off the stove and scoops the eggs onto two perfect white plates and sets them on the table. They're good—fluffy and cooked just right. Better than anything I can cook.

We eat in silence. Tension hangs over the table.

Does he expect me to explain what happened last night? I want to, but only if he'll let me in too. Only if we'll be more than fuck buddies.

I finish my last bite and set my fork next to my plate. "Thanks for breakfast."

"Are you still hungry?"

"I have food at home."

Miles makes a show of pushing out of his seat slowly. The sunlight falls over his body just so. His torso looks even more defined. His back looks stronger.

Somehow, he looks even more attractive.

Miles pulls a carton of strawberries from the fridge, rinses them in a perfect white colander, and pours them onto an equally perfect white plate. "I can't let you go home until I'm done with you."

I lick my lips. He watches me, grinning.

Ahem. "Done how?"

"Last time I went for four, but I do like to break records."

That heat is back. This time, I do nothing to fight it. My skin tingles, desperate for his touch.

His eyes pass over my body. There's nothing I can do to hide my reaction now. I want him and badly.

I take one of the strawberries and press it to my lips. The flesh is soft and sweet. There's some way I'm supposed to react here, but I don't know what it is.

Miles laughs. "You're nervous again. It's cute."

I eat the damn strawberry. So much for matching his advanced-level seduction. "That's one opinion on the matter."

He slides his tongue over the tip of a berry and sucks on it like it's some part of me.

He wants to break a record. That means five

orgasms. He must mean today. Five orgasms in one screw would kill me.

He moves closer, undoes my top button, presses his lips against my neck. "You were begging me last night."

"Not begging."

He undoes another button, and the blouse flops open. He slides his fingers over the edges of my bra. "You were desperate."

I dig my nails into my thighs. "Not entirely."

"It took everything I had to turn you down." He sinks his teeth into my neck and slides his hand inside my bra.

"Why did you?"

"I don't want you thinking about anything else when I touch you." He slides his fingertips over my nipple.

"I won't. I couldn't. I'm not even sure what day it is."

His breath gets heavy. He undoes the rest of the buttons and pushes the blouse off my shoulders. "I need to hear you come again."

"Okay."

He laughs, his voice sincere. "You really are adorable."

"No."

"Would you prefer sexy as all hell?" He does away with my bra.

I gasp as he cups my breasts.

"Yes." I press my eyelids together. We're talking about something, but it seems irrelevant. I don't care what he calls me as long as he keeps touching me.

"This will be easier on the couch."

"Right." I toss my clothes aside and follow him.

His eyes pass over my body. "Definitely sexy as all hell."

I kick off my skirt.

Miles's hands slide over my hips, under the sides of my panties. He digs his fingertips into my skin and presses his body against mine one part at a time--his hips, his stomach, his chest, his mouth.

He tastes like strawberries.

I can feel his erection through his boxers. I want so badly to wrap my hands around it, to prove I really am sexy as all hell.

I dig my hands into his hair like I'm holding on for dear life. His kiss is intense. It engulfs me.

He grabs my hips and scoops me onto the couch. I'm flat on my back, one leg hanging over the side of the couch, the other pressed against the cushion. Miles stands above me, light falling over every perfect inch of his body.

He's stares at me, into me, through me. It doesn't feel casual, but then again, what could possibly be casual about him being inside me?

He moves onto the couch, planting his body on top of mine. I wrap my legs around him and pull him closer. Damn, that feels good.

His fingertips skim my sides, my stomach, my chest. His hands feel good on my skin. He should never be allowed to do anything with his hands except touch me.

I arch my back, straining to feel his cock against my sex. Underwear is in the way, but I can feel him through the thin cotton fabric. God, he feels good.

His lips find mine. His kiss is softer. He's slowing down.

Like hell. I slide my tongue into his mouth and

swirl it around his. His body shifts. I rock my hips, grinding my crotch against his. The friction sends waves of pleasure through me.

He groans. His lips go to my neck. My collarbone. Then they're on my nipple, sucking on it like it's his plaything. I'm his plaything. He can do whatever he wants to me as long as he doesn't stop.

His fingers brush against my thigh, closer, and closer, and closer. He runs them against my clit, over my panties. "I'm going to eat you out. Have you done that before?"

"No," I breathe. "But I don't want you to go easy on me."

"Couldn't even if I wanted to."

He presses his lips into my stomach. My belly button. My inner thigh.

He tugs my panties all the way to my feet.

Then his mouth is on me. It's different than his hands. Softer. Wetter.

I lean my head back and surrender to the sensation. His tongue hits every nerve ending I have. Pleasure surges through my body, collecting in my sex. I'm close already.

"Miles," I groan. I dig my hands into his hair.

He licks me again, and again. I rock my hips in an attempt to contain the sensation. It's intense, way more intense than sex.

I'm light. I'm free. I'm flying. Damn, I'm flying.

Almost.

One more lick, and I go over the edge. It's fucking amazing. Every bit of tension in my body releases. A wave of ecstasy washes over me.

I groan his name again and again.

"Mhmm." He pins me to the couch, his hands firm

against my hips.

He's still going. His tongue slides from my sex to my clit. Around my outer lips. He moves with long, slow strokes. With fast, hard ones. Front to back, side to side, zig zag.

Pleasure builds. It's more intense. Almost too intense.

I throw my head back and dig my nails into his shoulders. Still, it's intense.

With the next flick of his tongue, an orgasm crashes over me. I scream his name as I come.

The world is beautiful. It's hard to believe that anything has ever hurt before.

I collapse on the couch, soaking in every drop of pleasure.

Miles presses himself up. He runs his fingertips over my thighs, an invitation to continue.

I nod a yes.

He pulls me off the couch. I'm not sure where we're going, only that I want to be there, with him, making him feel as good as I do.

We go up the stairs, to the door at the end of the hallway. It's a massive bathroom with a huge shower.

It's as gorgeous as everything else in this house—glass walls, aluminum fixtures, nonslip mat rolled over the floor.

Miles turns on the water and moves me under it. I tilt my head back to rinse my hair.

A tiny groan escapes his lips. He's staring like he wants to consume me, like he's desperate to touch me. Right now, I have him where I want him.

The power is thrilling. I'm going to revel in it.

He moves under the shower head, tilting his head back the way I did. His body is close to mine. Water is streaming over his chest and stomach.

He returns to a normal position and points to a rack in the corner. "Shampoo."

"Of course." The rack is filled to the brim with organic soaps and shampoos. I pick the only brand I recognize, squeeze it into my hands, run it through my hair and return it to the rack.

He smirks. "You're going to pay for that insolence."

"I'd like to see you try."

I go to run a hand through my hair, but Miles stops me. He digs his fingers into my scalp. I groan, shifting my body towards his reflexively.

Patience is out of the question. I need him groaning in my ear.

I need him. Period.

He runs his hands through my hair, brings me back to the shower head, and helps me rinse.

"This doesn't feel like punishment," I say.

"Mhmm." He presses his lips into my neck. "It will."

My breath catches in my throat. "When?"

"When you leave this shower without fucking me."

I am utterly unable to contain a gasp. "That will punish you more than it punishes me."

He murmurs another "Mhmm." He presses his lips into mine. His hands find my chest, and he rubs my nipples.

The water is streaming over us. Everything is slick and wet. Every motion of his fingertips is enough to drive me mad.

He releases the kiss. "That was just for starters."

"I like starters."

He smiles. "You're so damn cute you might ruin

my plan entirely."

I move back to the rack, squeeze shampoo in my hands, and return to him. "We discussed this." I run my hands through his thick hair.

I guide him under the water so he can rinse.

I'm not going to remind him, not with words anyway.

We do the same with conditioner, kissing in between the application and the rinse. Then it's soap. He squeezes bodywash into his hands and rubs every inch of my skin. It takes everything I have not to scream, not to beg him to fuck me right here and now.

He helps me rinse off, and it's my turn to torture him. I still have the control and I want to keep it. I rub bodywash over every inch of him. Once my hands are nothing but water, I rub his cock for good measure. He's hard.

I like the feeling of him in my hands, the way he groans when I stroke him.

He's my plaything now, and I know exactly what I want to do to him.

I wrap my hands around his cock and stroke him. He kisses me, hard, groaning into my mouth. He's shaking. Because of me.

Right now, he's all mine.

I pull my lips from his. I kiss his shoulders and chest, grabbing on to his hips for support.

"Meg..."

"Yes?" I slide to my knees and press my lips against his perfect stomach.

He digs his hands into my hair. "You're sexy as hell."

It occurs to me that I've never done this before.

With Miles in front of me, I'm not hesitant or shy. I know everything I need to know. I'm going to do whatever it takes to make him feel as good as I felt on the couch.

I slide my tongue around the head of his cock. He shudders, so I do it again. Again. Again. I suck on his tip. He's hard, but his skin is soft. And it tastes like Miles.

I take as much of him as I can. His deep groan echoes around the glass shower. It pushes me forward. I need that sound in my ears. I need to make him come.

I press my tongue against his base, sucking harder.

His groans get louder. "Sexy by every definition of the word."

Harder.

His thighs shake. He tugs at my hair. Perfect. My body courses with pleasure. I need to take him there. I need to feel him come.

I take him deeper. Flick my tongue against his head. He groans, pinching my nipples hard enough to send pangs of pleasure to my core.

"Sexiest girl I ever met," he breathes.

I run my tongue around his head until he's shaking. Until his groans are low and deep. His heavy breath fills the space.

He squeezes my nipple. "Mhmm."

He's almost there. Almost mine. I press my hands into his ass, pushing him deeper.

His grip tightens. His thighs clench.

He comes, filling my mouth. It's sweet and salty and a little strange, but I like feeling his orgasm, tasting it. When he's finished, I swallow hard.

Satisfaction spreads through me. Different than an

orgasm, but just as good. I made him come. I made him desperate.

He pulls me to my feet and wraps his arms around me. Then his lips are on mine and I feel a different kind of need.

The whole world rearranges. I have no idea where I stand, what this means, what it is we're doing here.

CHAPTER FOURTEEN

My clothes aren't in the spare room. They're still on the floor downstairs. I hug my towel to my chest and move to the living room.

Miles is sitting on the couch. Next to my neatly arranged clothing.

Okay then.

I take my time sliding into my bra. Miles is still under my thumb. Still watching me with rapt attention.

Damn, I like having his attention.

I shimmy into my skirt and slide my blouse over my shoulders. I do only the middle three buttons.

But my underwear is nowhere to be seen.

There's a devilish grin on Miles's face. I'm sure he has something to do with this, but I'm not going to admit it's an issue. So I don't have underwear, so what?

"Let's get sushi for lunch." He pulls a condom from the front pocket of his jeans and pulls me onto his lap. "You can have your panties when I'm done with you."

He presses his lips to mine and slides his hand under my skirt.

It would be silly to object.

The fusion Japanese restaurant is right on the water. Ocean and blue sky are the backdrop to the shady patio.

We're the only people out here. It's midafternoon, that time between lunch and dinner. A breeze blows over my shoulders. I shiver and hug my arms to my chest. Miles slides his leather jacket off his arms and drapes it over my shoulders.

A perfect gentleman.

My heartbeat picks up. I'm sure I'm getting the wrong idea again. I'm just another girl in a long list of Miles's playthings.

I push my concerns aside. It's not every day I'm wined and dined—well, dined, at least—by a hot rock star. And it's certainly not every day he makes me come more times than I can count.

Miles watches me open the menu. He laughs, a deep I'm obviously making fun of Meg kind of laugh. I'm sure my jaw is hanging, but the prices here are insane.

"You really are adorable," he says.

I fold the menu together and cross my legs. I'll show him adorable. "Those weren't your words in the shower."

He bites his lip, and his eyes light up. It's sexy as all hell, but it is not a look of defeat.

"Order whatever you want," he says. "It's on me."

"I know."

He's smirking again. I entertain him. No, it's worse. I amuse him.

Okay, fine. There's only one way to put an end to this. I need to convince Miles I'm on his level. That I'm not intimidated by his money, or his body, or his gorgeous voice.

When our server arrives, I pick the most expensive sashimi on the menu, and I order two of everything. Well, four of everything since sashimi comes two pieces to an order. I request salt instead of soy sauce. I snap the menu closed and hand it to the server.

"And to drink?" he asks.

Damn. I order a green tea and offer my best smile. The whole unflappable thing does come off a little cold, and I'm not going to be one of those people who's an asshole to waitstaff.

Miles is still staring at me like I'm a puppy. Apparently, he's not impressed by my display. He requests his usual.

The server leaves. I take a long sip of my water. I stare at the ocean—it's only thirty feet away—to avoid the look in his eyes.

"You really like sashimi," he says.

"Yes."

He laughs. "You okay, Meg? You seem a little out of sorts."

I bring my gaze back to him. "I'm fine." It's a lie. I'm not fine. I'm crumbling. His eyes are beautiful and they're filled with affection.

"I'm not cute," I say.

"We'll have to agree to disagree there."

"Fine. But I'd rather you not keep bringing it up." I cross and uncross my legs. This seat suddenly feels uncomfortable. I don't want to amuse him. I want to affect him. I want to matter to him.

He lowers his voice. "What's so bad about being cute?"

"It's what you say about your little sister. Or about someone who is clueless and totally uncool."

"No," he says. "It's the girl who blushes when you compliment her, who tries to prove she's a badass by ordering enough sashimi for three people."

"I'm going to eat all of it."

He smiles. "And that—you get defensive about everything."

"I'm not defensive." That isn't helping me prove my point. I give up. "Fine. You're right. I'm adorable and clueless and awkward and you're sexy and suave and in control. Should I keep going?"

He lowers his voice. "It's not a competition. I like you the way you are."

"But..." I bite my lip. I'm not helping my case. "Okay."

"We're friends." His eyes find mine. "I want you to enjoy this as much as I do, Meg. If calling you adorable really makes you that miserable, I'll stop. But I'd rather not. I love watching you blush."

I swallow hard. "Okay."

"You sure?"

I nod. There's something about his voice when he calls me adorable. I hate feeling cute, but I love the sound of his voice when he says it. I'm affecting him. Maybe I'm not driving him mad with lust. Maybe I don't have him under my spell. But I am affecting him.

"I don't think you're amusing," he says. "I think you're funny. Charming in a unique way."

My cheeks flush.

"You have a beautiful smile. It's rare. Makes me feel like I've won a prize when I can get you to smile."

His expression is sincere. Does he really think that much of me? His words aren't at all casual. They're the words of someone with deep affection. They're the words of a lover, not a fuck buddy.

I clear my throat. "You really think we're friends and not just two people hooking up?"

He nods.

"So you'd tell me if there was anything I needed to know about you? Anything you usually keep secret."

He raises an eyebrow. "You getting at something?"

"Just… you've been pushing a lot about Rosie. I thought that maybe you'd been through something like that."

"My uncle died last year."

"So that house—"

"It's mine."

"He's the one you inherited from?"

Miles nods.

"Oh, I'm sorry that you lost him."

"Thank you." His eyes go to the ocean. "Took me six months to smile after he died. It's still a struggle some days. So I know it still hurts you, that your sister lied to you. I can only imagine." His expression fills with vulnerability. "I'm not going to lie to you like that."

For the first time ever, Miles isn't confident. There's uncertainty all over his face. His brow is knotted, his eyes turned down.

"There's nothing you need to know," he says. "I promise."

The words don't feel quite right, but I can't bring myself to ask him to promise.

Back at his uncle's place—his place, I guess—I change into a pair of extra boxers and a t-shirt. His extra clothes. Not some random thing he keeps around for the disposable women he brings here.

We settle onto the couch.

Miles slides his arm around my shoulder. I rest my head on his chest. It's comfortable, being here with him. It's normal.

He turns on the TV and his PS4 and scrolls through a streaming service.

He runs a hand through my hair. "This is what you want to watch, right?"

He navigates to The Lost World. He's mocking me.

"Clever," I say.

"It's 'clever girl,' and that's in the first movie."

"Clever boy."

"I'd love to watch dinosaurs destroy San Diego, but if you'd rather watch something else, go for it." He hands me the remote.

"You're going to mock me whatever I pick."

His breath is warm on my ear. He runs his hand along the neckline of my t-shirt, his t-shirt. "Likely."

I arch my back, pressing my chest into his hands. "Convince me to pick something."

"Convince you how?" His fingertips skim my skin.

"Like that," I breathe.

"I like the confidence."

"You're stalling."

He slides his hand into my shirt, his fingertips brushing my nipple. "Why would I do that?"

"It's smart, really. You're pressed against me on

141

the couch. You get to mock me and have your way with me at the same time."

He smiles. "Some part of this you don't like?"

"No." I lean into his touch. "Keep going."

"After you pick a movie."

I'm not doing anything with him touching me. I close my eyes, squeezing the remote to contain myself. He runs his fingers over my chest, holding my body against his.

"We can watch whatever," I say.

"Mhmm." He sucks on my earlobe. "You pick."

"You're going to make fun of me."

"You're not going to pay attention to the movie, anyway. You pick."

His teeth scrape against my earlobe as he squeezes my nipples. I can't contain it anymore. I groan and press my body into his.

"Miles..."

"I'm not familiar with a movie by that name."

He's trying to kill me. There's no other reasonable explanation.

He brings his lips to my neck and pulls me onto his lap. Then his hands are on my boxers, well, his boxers. He pulls them to my knees.

"Miles… you can't… don't tease me…"

"Me, tease? Never." He sinks his teeth into my neck and pulls the boxers off my hips.

"I don't care about a movie."

"I know."

He strokes my inner thighs with a light touch. He gets closer, closer, closer. I throw my head back and relax my body into his. Movies are stupid. Movies are so much less amazing than this.

I lift my arms and Miles pulls my t-shirt, his t-shirt,

over my head. I'm on his lap, naked, in the middle of the living room, the stupid TV still waiting for my movie selection.

No way in hell I'm selecting a movie now.

He grabs my wrist and plants my hands on the couch, right outside his thighs. His lips find my neck again. He sucks on my skin. Desire spreads to my limbs.

He can tease me all he wants if it's going to end like this.

I press my palms into the couch. I'm his plaything, and I'm not about to object to this performance.

He strokes my thighs with a light touch, getting closer, and closer, and closer. He's an inch away from my sex.

He draws zigzags over my thigh with his fingertips. My body hums with desire. Miles's touch is everything I need. The only thing I need.

"I've never cared less about a movie," I say.

"I know."

His breath is warm on my neck, my ear. He sucks on my lobe again. The pressure is intense, and every motion of his tongue sends another shockwave of pleasure through me.

Miles can't give me anything more than sex, but, my God, can he give me sex.

"Touch me," I breathe.

"Good things come to those who wait."

"I hate waiting."

"I know." He sinks his teeth into my neck again just enough to feel amazing. His fingers skim my sex. "Fuck, Meg, how do you get so wet?"

"You."

He groans and sinks his teeth into my neck again.

Finally, his fingertips skim my clit. Oh. Hell. Yes. His touch sends sparks through my body. It takes everything I have not to pant.

I arch my back, rocking my hips to press myself against his hand. He strokes me with slow, steady attention. His touch is light and delicate, and every part of me is desperate for him. I can't contain my breath. I can't do anything but surrender to the sensation.

He sinks his teeth into my neck. It's harder now, and every bite amplifies the pleasure building inside me. His touch gets harder, faster, rougher. He rubs my clit with long strokes, his fingers skimming my sex.

He slides a finger inside me. I gasp. It's exactly what I need. Then it's two fingers.

I arch my back to push him deeper. He presses his free hand against my chest, holding my body against his, by back against his chest.

The pressure builds. Almost. It's intense. I didn't think my body had anything left, but I'm almost there again. I take a sharp breath, soaking in the sound of his groans, the feel of his cotton t-shirt against my back.

I'm naked on his lap. I'm about to come. He has all the cards, and I don't give a damn. As long as he keeps touching me, keeps making me feel this good.

My body fills with pleasure. It starts inside me and radiates through my core—to my stomach, hips, chest, thighs, lips. The fire inside me is so intense nothing could ever put it out.

I groan. Almost. Almost. I squeeze the couch as an orgasm rocks through me. Pleasure spreads all the way to my fingers and toes.

He holds me close for a while. Until my breath returns to normal. Until I almost believe I could walk.

His lips press against my neck. "Did that help you decide on a movie?"

"Shut up."

"That's no way to thank the man who made you scream so loudly you almost broke the glass."

"Don't be cocky," I murmur.

"If you promise to stay that loud. I like it." He helps me off the couch and takes my hand. "Come on. I have something to show you."

I follow him upstairs. He opens a bedroom door flips on the lights.

It occurs to me that, once again, I'm naked and he's fully dressed. Somehow, I'm not bothered. I love the way he looks at me like he wants to consume me. It makes me feel powerful and desirable.

He points to a bookshelf. "Notice anything?"

Holy shit. There are three or four dozen Star Wars novels here.

"You're a nerd," I say.

"Our secret." He slides his arm around my waist. "I have a reputation to maintain."

I nod. Miles told me a secret. We have a secret. Besides the whole friends-with-benefits thing. It's not a big secret, but it feels personal.

My lips curl into a smile. "You care what other people think of you."

"Everyone does."

"But you act like you don't. You act like nothing could ever hurt you."

"You know that isn't true."

I slide my hand around his waist and look into his eyes. "Tell me another secret."

"Damn, it's hard to turn down a naked woman."

"You did last night."

"You know why I did." He runs his fingers through my hair. "How secret?"

"Very secret."

He chuckles. "I went as Harry Potter for Halloween all throughout middle school."

"You did not."

He nods. "I was shorter, smaller. My mom loved making my costume. She loved that kind of thing, the magic, the justice." His eyes go to the floor. "I was twelve or thirteen. Older kid took my fake glasses, threw them on the ground, and stepped on them."

"What did you do?"

"I flipped. Tried to hit him but I couldn't. He was bigger, stronger. The rest of the year, I never heard the end of it. Taught me the value of not reacting to things. Then I got bigger, learned how to hit. That was that."

"You stopped showing your emotions and started beating people up because a bully picked on your Harry Potter costume?"

"No. What is it you always call me?"

"Aloof."

"I'm aloof because I don't want anyone to know my weaknesses. I don't want anyone to know what hurts me." His expression gets intense.

"But your songs. You're confessing to the whole world."

"Yeah."

"What's the difference?"

"I'm in control. I'm the one on stage, commanding attention, making girls scream." His eyes meet mine. He runs his fingertips up and down my back. "Most people don't listen closely to the words. They don't see what's right in front of their faces."

I lean into his touch. It's difficult to concentrate what with his hands being on my naked body. But I can tell this is important. This really is a secret.

I stare back. "I did. I listened to that song a thousand times. That guy who was singing. He was my closest friend. He was the only person who knew where I hurt."

"I still know where you hurt."

"But I don't… it's not equal."

"You do." He takes a step backwards. "You know more than anybody else does."

He sits on the bed, his eyes filling with a look I can't place. It's sad but there's more to it than that. Nostalgia, maybe.

This was his uncle's place. It must mean a lot to him.

"This house seems untouched," I say.

"Don't come here by myself. It feels empty without Damon. Feels quiet without his laugh."

I scan the bookshelf. It's up to date. It has three Star Wars books that came out over the summer. So he is here sometimes. Once at least.

"Do you have a favorite?" I nod to the books.

"No."

"Do you like other sci-fi or just Star Wars?"

"Mostly Star Wars. And Futurama."

My eyes find his. "Did you ever play Podracer or Rogue Squadron?"

Now, he's looking at me like I'm the nerd. "Never had the chance."

"You know what this means?"

He smiles. "What?"

"We're watching Star Wars."

"Which one?"

"All of them."

"You'll be here until four a.m."

"Do you have something better to do?"

He laughs. "You really are cute."

"Okay, fine. I'm cute. But you have nothing better to do than watch twelve hours of Star Wars films."

"Can't think of anything I'd rather do."

I don't even care that he calls me cute. I haven't been this excited in months. I'm practically bouncing.

Miles looks just as excited.

It feels good, being with him and doing little things. Doing nothing.

"If you only want to watch one or two movies, I get that. I don't want to impose," I say.

"No, I like you here." He pulls me into the bed. "I like your company."

"Is that what the kids are calling it?"

"I love fucking you. But I like talking to you too." He slides his hands under my ass and guides me onto my back. "I like you here. House doesn't feel empty." He pulls his t-shirt over his head. "The guys in the band, you may not have noticed, but they watch me for signs I'm gonna break again."

"When did you break the first time?"

He says nothing.

I run my hands through his hair. "Does it still hurt?"

"Not as much. It's been a year almost." He presses his lips to my neck. "I like talking to you, Meg, but you're going to need to put some clothes on if you want to keep talking." He drags his fingertips over my chest. "You want to talk or you want to do this?"

I answer by unbuttoning his jeans.

CHAPTER FIFTEEN

We watch every Star Wars film. Miles knows every line, and he delights in reciting them with me. Well, he delights in mocking me, too—in mocking my very obvious crush on Han Solo. What can I say? Maybe I do have a thing for scoundrels.

It's almost dawn when we go to bed, but this time Miles doesn't put me in the spare room. We sleep together on his bed, in his bedroom. It's not the biggest bed, but it feels so good to be pressed against him. His body fits perfectly with mine. I fall asleep almost instantly, and I wake up in his arms.

Miles stirs when I get out of bed. He drags me to the bathroom, and we take another shower together. It's as amazing as before. We kiss, touch, and help each other with soap and shampoo.

After, he makes me breakfast and coffee. It's like we're playing house, like we're playing pretend at being grownups in a grown-up relationship. I know I'm twenty-one, and he must not be more than a few years older, but I've never really felt like an adult.

This, though, being in this house alone with him—it feels real.

Miles snickers when we leave for Kara's. "You've been wearing that outfit for almost three days."

"So?"

"Something tells me you don't normally wear low-cut tops and short skirts to hang out with your best friend. Not that I object."

He's right. I never dress up to see Kara. At best, I wear a t-shirt and jeans. I need clean clothes, especially clean underwear. There's no way I'm going commando to hang out with my best friend.

"So drop me at my place. I'll change."

He shakes his head. "No, I'll take you to a boutique I know."

"I'm not a doll."

"And you won't be on display to anyone but me." He leads me to the front door. "But I'll feel awful about ripping off your panties if I didn't buy them."

"No you won't."

He smirks. "Okay, I won't. But I'm still buying you something to wear today."

"That's not necessary."

"You're not going to win this one, Meg. You should give up resisting if you don't want to be late to meet with your friend."

"I don't need an outfit. And I don't need you to buy me any kind of lingerie."

He presses his lips into my cheek. "All this time you're spending resisting. We could be spending it in the dressing room together."

"Oh." Oh.

I get in the car without any further objections.

The boutique is better than I could possibly imagine. Not the clothes—I couldn't possibly care less about clothes. Miles drags me into the dressing room. One hand under my skirt, one hand over my mouth, he rubs me until I can barely muffle my screams, then rubs me some more. I come three times despite my fear that the sales girl will throw us out.

I pick out a pair of jeans, a tank top, and a lacy black lingerie set. Everything here is outrageously expensive—more than I make in a month—but he insists.

We—well, I—am right on time to Kara's place. She opens the door and takes in my clothes with curiosity.

"I've never seen that outfit before."

"It's new."

She shakes her head, not buying my version of the story. "Those are expensive jeans."

I nod.

"Is there some reason why you're keeping this a secret?"

"I don't want you to freak out."

"Name one time when I ever freaked out." She throws me serious side eye. "English Breakfast okay?"

"Sure."

She moves to the kitchen and turns on her electric kettle.

I turn over my options as she fixes tea. I trust Kara more than I trust anyone. I should want to tell her about everything with Miles.

She returns to the main room with two mugs of tea. She sets one down on the end table and hands the other to me. There's infinite patience in her eyes, like she could wait eight million years for an explanation.

I sip my tea to buy another ten seconds.

"I was with Miles," I say.

She gasps then clears her throat as if to cover her surprise. "And what were you doing with Miles?"

"We slept together."

"Holy shit, Megara Smart. How the fuck did you not tell me this?"

"It's no big deal."

"Bullshit. Don't act like you don't give a damn. You lost your virginity to Miles. That's huge. Is he huge?"

My cheeks burn.

"He is!" She squeals. "Let's put the issue of your secrecy aside for a moment." Kara leans in close, her eyes wide. "What was it like fucking him?"

"Good."

She stares at me. "Good? You call that a detail? I want a better fucking detail!"

"Is great a better detail?"

"Technically, great is better than good."

"You sound like an English teacher."

"Thank you." She taps her fingers against her jeans. "So…"

"Very, really good. He's good at everything, and he's more tender than you'd expect. But it's just sex. It's really not a big deal."

"Not buying it, sweetie." She shifts to the other side of the couch. "Was it only once or have you been seeing him?"

"A few times. We're… friends with benefits."

"And what, he picked you up last night and dropped you off here with a change of clothes?" She studies me like she's looking for cracks.

"This is why I didn't want to say anything."

"What is?"

"Stop looking at me like I'm fragile. I'm not going to break because of a little casual sex."

"Fine. As long as it feels casual to you. Does it?"

Damn, is she a mind reader? It doesn't exactly feel casual. But he's been clear about not wanting more. And I don't want more. "I don't want feelings for anyone. What if a medical school in New York is my best option? I don't want anything affecting my decision. Certainly not feelings for a guy."

"But you have feelings for him?"

"We're friends." I think. I hope.

"Hmmm." She nods. "Okay. You're a big girl. I'll drop it if you give me every detail!"

"Every detail?"

"Not a blow by blow." She laughs. "Just tell me what's going on. You know, like we're best friends or something."

"That would be something."

"Wouldn't it?"

"Okay." I take a deep breath, and I start at the beginning. I'm vague about the sex and about how mixed up he makes me feel, but I include all the other important details.

When I'm finished, she throws together a plan. There's a Sinful Serenade show Saturday and the two of us simply must make an impression. She has just the outfit I can borrow. Our height and cup-size differences are not an issue.

"You know how we're best friends and we tell each other things?" I ask.

"I don't like where this is going."

"Why are you trying to make an impression if

you're set on staying just friends with Drew? You do like him."

"It's not about whether or not I'll like him. He'll never want me that way. And it's not worth the risk of things changing. When he got back in touch last winter, it felt like I'd found my favorite dress. I didn't realize how much I'd missed him until I heard his voice again. How good it felt just sitting next to him at dinner or during a movie." Her eyes get dreamy. "He's such a good friend. Overprotective, yeah, but he's sweet. And he makes me laugh. I can't lose that. Nothing would be worse than losing that."

"What if he started dating someone else?"

She frowns. "It's going to happen eventually. He's handsome and famous. Girls are always stopping him to ask for his autograph. They're always touching him. Their stupid hands on his arm like they deserve to touch him." She shakes her head. "Is it so wrong that I want him to look at me like he's desperate to rip off my clothes?"

"Depends what you'd do if he offered to rip your clothes off."

"He won't."

"But if he did?"

She lets out a sigh of pleasure. "I have to read five hundred pages tonight. I can't think about Drew ripping off my clothes or I won't make it through the first sentence." She pulls her knees into her chest. "What would you do if Miles developed feelings for you?"

"He won't."

"But if he did?"

"I have no idea."

I'm in a daze the rest of brunch. Mostly, we talk about school. Midterms. Her plans to go home, to San Francisco, for Thanksgiving break. My attempts to avoid going home to see my parents for even a single weekend. The house still hurts too much.

At home, there's something waiting by my apartment door—a wrapped box, complete with an aqua-blue bow. The card is simple.

Good luck studying tonight.

- Miles

I set inside, throw myself onto the bed, and unwrap the box. It's a Nintendo 64 and two faded, gray cartridge games—Star Wars Episode I: Racer and Star Wars: Rogue Squadron.

How the hell did he track down two twenty-year-old games? I haven't seen either of these, or a Nintendo 64, in ages.

I connect the wires to the TV the same way I did when I was a kid—red to red, white to white, yellow to yellow.

I text Miles.

Meg: Thank you. I love it.

Miles: Always happy to bring you pleasure.

Meg: You're very distracting. My grades are going to suffer.

Miles: I can take it back if you don't trust yourself.

Meg: No! You can't! It's the sweetest gift anyone has ever given me.

Miles: You're a nerd.

Meg: You are too.

Miles: That's our secret.

We have a secret. We have other secrets. We have a level of intimacy I don't quite understand.

Does Miles have feelings for me? It's possible. Guys don't buy hard-to-find video games for girls they're apathetic about.

My phone buzzes.

Miles: Kara tell you about our show Saturday?

Meg: She did. I even managed to make plans to go with her. I'm not sure how. I'm not very quick today. Someone kept me up all night then used up all my energy this morning.

Miles: You didn't like coming in the dressing room?

Meg: I'm not complaining.

Miles: It's Saturday. We go on around nine. We're working out some of our new material. Our manager's idea. I'll put you on the list.

Meg: Okay.

Miles: I'll pick you up. Give Kara the chance to take Drew home.

Meg: I don't think that's happening.

Miles: Not yet. But it could. Your friend is hot and Drew isn't fucking anybody. Everybody in the band knows he's not fucking anybody. He's pissy nonstop. Guy needs to get laid bad.

Meg: You think Kara is hot?

Miles: Not as hot as you, but yeah, she's attractive. And she's a sweet girl. I don't have any interest. Don't have any interest in touching anyone but you.

Meg: This is really strange sweet talk.

Miles: You can tell me you think Drew is hot if it makes you feel better.

Meg: It kinda does. He is hot.

Miles: How could you say that? You're destroying my confidence, Meg. I can't believe you even look at other men.

Meg: I don't. Not really.

Miles: Good.

Meg: You really think he's pissy nonstop? That's not a nice thing to say about your friend.

Miles: I'd say it to his face. Guy knows he's not all rainbows and sunshine.

Meg: Yeah?

Miles: Yeah. He has a vision. Only Tom has a different vision. Shit gets heated in the studio.

Meg: He punched you in the face once?

Miles: Yeah. I was being an ass.

Meg: You, an ass? That's shocking.

Miles: I know. I'm usually so polite.

Meg: And not at all full of yourself.

Miles: Not at all.

Meg: Do you have a vision too?

Miles: Yeah, but I approach songs differently than they do. Tom wants to be popular. Drew wants to make this killer rock music. He thinks he's a guitar legend. And he's right. He's good. But it's not necessarily what will get the most radio play. Then Pete, our bassist, he stays out of the fray so nobody will notice he gets to do whatever he wants with the bassline.

Meg: And you?

Miles: I own the vocals, the lyrics, the emotional arc of the song. Band knows better than to fuck that.

Meg: It's probably because you're so beautiful. They do whatever they can to appease you so you'll stick around.

Miles: Undoubtedly. You must be tired. You're not usually this honest.

Meg: I am tired.

Miles: Tell your friend that Drew hasn't fucked

anyone else in a while.

Meg: I'm not sure she wants to know. She insists they need to stay friends.

Miles: Trust me. That's not how these things work.

Meg: It's terrifying, but I think I do trust you.

Miles: Enough to go bareback next time?

Meg: Yes.

Miles: Fuck. Saturday still six days away?

Meg: Last I checked.

Miles: I can come over right now.

Meg: I have to study. Is it that much better without a condom?

Miles: Fuck. Barely remember. Last time I went bareback was in highschool. Tried a monogamous relationship for an entire month.

Meg: You did not.

Miles: I did. It failed. Horribly. Sure you're that busy? You can kick me out of bed when we're done.

Meg: But I can't.

Miles: Yeah, you'd probably beg me to go again. Okay. Go study. I'll be counting the minutes to Saturday.

Meg: Me too.

CHAPTER SIXTEEN

The club is lit in shades of neon purple. The first floor is already packed. Most of the crowd is casual— jeans, t-shirts, sneakers. A handful of women are dressed to impress.

Kara and I fit into the latter group. Somehow, I don't care that I'm treading the line between classy and trashy. Between the tight, low cut top and the short skirt, I know I'm going to make Miles want me as badly as I want him.

Kara squeezes my hand and drags me up the stairs. She pushes past another set of musician guys all the way to Drew. She finds him like he has a homing beacon.

He does a double take when he sees her outfit. Mission accomplished.

"Who lets you out of the house dressed like that?" He raises a brow.

She shrugs like she wears this everywhere. They hug hello. I step aside to give them room. I'm not sure where Kara gets her insecurity. Drew is absolutely looking at her like he wants to fuck her. He's not as obvious about it as Miles is, but he's obvious enough.

He catches me watching him and redirects his stare towards the opposite wall.

I scan the room for Miles. There. He's leaning against the wall talking to a busty woman with long blond hair. Well then.

His eyes find mine, and he immediately excuses himself. Hell, he practically throws the buxom blond out of his way. I nod, but I stay put.

Today, he's coming to me.

A dozen steps and he's next to me. He slides his arm around my waist and leans in to whisper in my ear.

"Let's go out back. Won't be able to think until I'm inside you." He drags his fingertips over the waist of my skirt. "You look fucking amazing."

"I know."

"Damn, I like when you're confident." He nods to the stairs.

"Is there time?" It's eight-thirty. He's due on stage in half an hour.

Miles nods. His eyes are heavy. It's like he wants me so badly he can't articulate a single word.

"Hey, Megan." A familiar voice interrupts.

It's the blond drummer. Tom.

"It's Meg," I say.

Miles throws his friend an incredulous look. "Can't this wait?"

"No, it can't." Tom offers me an apologetic smile then he's back to Miles. "Now."

Miles frowns. He's upset. As upset as he was on the beach. More even.

He shakes off his expression, but it's still there in his eyes and his posture. He's unsure of something.

I want to know what it is.

I watch Tom pull Miles aside. There's not a lot of room up here. They're almost within earshot. I take a seat on the couch and scoot closer. Until they are within earshot.

"You're fucking her?" Tom asks.

"You take issue with casual sex all of a sudden?"

"Does she know?"

"No."

"Fuck, Miles. You trying to give me a headache?" Tom shakes his head. "Are you going to tell her?"

"How the fuck is that your business?" Miles asks.

"If you don't tell her, I will," Tom says.

Miles's voice is low, angry. "Fuck off."

There's a weight shifting on the couch. Someone sits next to me. It's an older man in a bright orange suit. He's balding but he still keeps his hair in a ponytail.

"Meg, right?" He offers his hand. "I'm Aiden. I'm the Sinful Serenade manager."

Okay... I don't see what I could possibly have to say to this guy, but I can be polite. "Yeah, Meg. Nice to meet you."

He looks to Tom and Miles, still in a heated debate. "There's no polite way to say this, Meg, but I need you to go away."

"Excuse me?"

"Miles can't have a girlfriend. He's never written a love song. Girls like that. They like that he's broken, that he's unconquered territory. But now he's writing this song. It's not quite a love song. But it's too close." There's no self-awareness in Aiden's beady eyes. He delivers his suggestion like he's reciting the weather report. "He's going to be the next Adam Levine. Do you want to stand in his way?"

"We're..." Not friends but we're not together. "We're not boyfriend and girlfriend. But that's really none of your business."

"Everyone has a price, sweetheart. Don't make me work to find yours."

There's a hand around my arm. It pulls me off the couch and presses me against a hard body. Miles.

"You okay?" he whispers.

I nod.

Miles glares at Aiden. "Don't talk to my friends."

Tom and Miles share a look of understanding. Then Tom is the one on the couch, having harsh words with the manager.

Fame is fucked up.

Miles wraps his arms around me. His voice is soft, sweet. "Did he touch you?"

"No."

"Good... he has a reputation. It's a long story, but stay away from him."

I nod. Miles sounds worried. He's worried about me. He cares about me.

But what was Tom talking about? They have a secret. Miles wrote a new song, a love song? My mind is racing. I can't keep up.

"What did your friend want to talk about?" I ask.

"Band stuff."

"Sure it wasn't about me?"

"What did Aiden say to you?" Miles asks.

"He doesn't want you to have a girlfriend. For your image. Girls need to think you're a slut, I guess."

Miles laughs. "Yeah, he would say that. But you're

not my girlfriend. So we're good."

"Yeah. Should I worry about being on a gossip page? My parents will flip over me dating a rock star."

"Want to bet?"

"Maybe."

His eyes find mine. "Your parents will love me."

"You're cocky." But it's possible he's right. He's a Stanford graduate. He's charming. He's handsome. Except for the tattoos, he looks like a perfectly nice boy.

Miles laughs. "You know they will."

"But how do you know?"

"Cause I know you." He runs his fingertips over my tank top. "And I know Orange County parents. Where do yours live?"

"Newport Beach."

"Spoiled rich girl." He shakes his head in mock outrage.

"Yeah, and your Malibu mansion is just a place to hang your hat?"

He nods. "When's the last time you saw them?"

"You're trying to make me forget you and Tom were whispering secrets."

"It was nothing. When's the last time you saw your parents?"

It wasn't nothing. There's tension in Miles's face. His brow is furrowed. His shoulders are tight.

He's upset. This is a big secret. Do I trust him enough to let it go?

I'm not sure.

I stare back into his gorgeous blue eyes. "Haven't seen them since the day I left for school."

"They miss you? Beg you to visit?"

"All the time."

"Offer to come up for lunch or dinner?"

"They come up all the time. I make excuses."

"Tell me next time. I'll come with you. As your boyfriend."

"You want to meet my parents?"

He traces the neckline of my top. "I'll keep them off your back."

His voice is heavy with need, but I'm not sure if he's desperate for me or for the end of this conversation.

I need to think.

I press my lips to his. Damn, his lips are soft. I can feel the kiss all the way to my toes. It isn't helping me think.

"Excuse me." I take a step backwards. "Bathroom."

He nods.

There's something in his eyes, something I can't place. I turn and make my way down the stairs.

Everything in this room is red and shiny, and the lights above our heads are a particularly fluorescent purple.

And Kara is here. She's standing at the sink touching up her lipstick. She makes eye contact through the mirror. "You okay?"

I nod.

"You look upset."

"It's nothing." I think it's nothing. I go to the mirror and check my makeup. It's fine but I need some excuse for why I'm here.

More lipstick can't hurt. It can't help either. Miles already wants to fuck me. What I need is something to convince him I'm worth his trust.

Do they make a shade called girl you tell your secrets to? Mine is some play on cherry red.

"Whatever is happening with Miles, it shouldn't leave you with that expression on your face." She plays with her tube of lipstick. "Like you just got hit by a truck."

I clear my throat. "It's nothing. I'm just not in the mood to be at a party anymore."

"Want to talk about it?"

I shake my head. "No. I… I'm just glad I can trust you. You're the only person in my life I can really trust."

"I'm not so sure we have the same definition of the word trust," she says. "Look at me and swear on your love of, um, what's that character called again? The hard-drinking robot?"

"Bender."

"Swear on your love of Bender that you're okay."

Do I really look that miserable? I do feel unsettled. Why is Miles suddenly pulling back? We're supposed to have terms. No lies. No secrets.

I can't do this if he's going to whisper secrets with his bandmate.

Maybe he'll tell me. I'll ask again, give him another chance to tell me.

Kara slides onto the counter.

"I don't love Bender that much." I slide onto the counter next to her. "Something up with Drew?"

"You're not going to distract me unless you swear."

"I swear that I'll be okay." Eventually. "You know, Miles told me that Drew hasn't slept with anyone in a while."

"Really. That's interesting." She clears her throat, fighting her blush. "He invited me to dinner after the set. But I got the feeling everyone's invited."

"I doubt anyone is going to jump on that train. Including me. I'll say no and hang out here."

"You sure?"

"Yeah. Well, I might take a cab. But I'll be fine."

"You know, Miles wrote a song about you. Heard through the grapevine that he's playing it tonight."

"Oh."

Kara is my best friend, and I trust her with almost anything. Just not how I feel about Miles. I can't even say it out loud. It would be admitting to giving in to the temptation that destroyed my sister.

I clear my throat. "So we're both totally inept with men."

"That appears to be the case, yes."

Kara fixes her makeup and mine and drags me back to the upstairs VIP section. The band is no longer here. The manager, Aiden, assures us that Sinful Serenade is getting ready to go on stage.

I get comfortable on one of the black cubes posing as a normal seat. Kara sits next to me. It's too loud for meaningful conversation, so we trade gossip about Professor Rivers, our poetry professor.

The stage lights go dark. Almost show time. The crowd starts screaming. This is a small space. After all, the band is working on their new material. Miles is singing a song about me. They can't show that off to a large audience. Not when it isn't finished.

How can he be writing a song about me?

The lights go on. The song starts.

It's In Pieces.

I can't bring myself to look at the stage. Certainly

not to look at Miles. I press my eyelids together.

His voice seeps into my veins.

Three weeks now.
Can't sleep.
Two weeks now.
Gaping hole in my chest shows no signs of recovery.

That word, a joke, you laugh.
"Running away again, kid?"
A minute here
and then you're gone.

His pain swirls around me, mixing with mine. It's a roller coaster. The only thing I can do is hold on and try to survive the ride.

I pry my eyelids apart. I can't place the expression on his face. But I know what the song means. I know it means he hurts. And I hurt. But together, we hurt a little less.

Or do I have that all wrong?

His voice cuts clear across the room. "Would you like to hear something off the new album?"

The crowd cheers. Every girl in this club is screaming with glee, including Kara, who's at an ear-bursting volume. I'm sure twenty pairs of panties drop, but who am I to judge?

"It's called No Way in Hell. About someone very special." His eyes are on me.

Drew strums his guitar. The song starts. It's something fast and hard, and there's a desperation to the music.

Miles's voice fills the room.

Three a.m. and I can't sleep.
A common refrain, I know.
As a sentiment, it's cheap.
Someone to call, to hold,
to love. No way that word—
She smiles and I drift away—

Oh hell no.
This can't be.
No way I, no way she.
Anyone else, maybe,
but not me.
I don't do this kind of thing.

There's no doubt about it. He's singing about me. It's not like before. This song is about me. And he's singing it to me. I close my eyes, willing my ears to shut, willing my lungs to breathe, willing my heart to steady.

Morning now and I can't think
of anything but her laugh, her cries
the sound she makes when I sink
my teeth. Oh wow, those details
are mine to keep, but she's not
And suddenly I want-

Oh hell no.
This can't be.
No way I, no way she.
Anyone else, maybe,
but not me.
I don't do this kind of thing.

My body refuses to behave. It refuses to do anything but soak in Miles's song. All the emotion in his voice is crashing all over me. He hurts. Somewhere deep inside him, he hurts, and God help me, I want to be the one to take that pain away.

CHAPTER SEVENTEEN

After the set, the band reappears in the VIP area. Drew and Kara practically disappear. One second here, then they're not quite holding hands on their way out the back door.

And now I'm sitting on my stupid black cube, with the other guys from the band around me. Tom has a pretty redhead on his lap. She giggles, staring at him like he's a prize.

The dark-haired bassist introduces himself. "Meg, right?"

I nod. "Meg Smart."

"Pete Steele." He shakes his head and turns to Tom. "You do have a room."

Tom shrugs. He sips his drink, casually wrapping his arm around the redhead like she's a fancy trophy.

She looks happy. I guess it's not my place to judge.

Miles plops next to me. He spreads his knees wide like he's going to entice me to drop to my knees and blow him in front of his friends.

Not that I'm thinking about taking him back to my

place and ripping his clothes off.

I can't do that. I can't touch him until I give him a chance to explain.

"Damn, you're tacky." Pete addresses Tom. "Almost as bad as Drew running off without a goodbye. Must be desperate."

Tom motions to me. "That's her best friend."

Miles smirks, trailing his fingers over my outer thigh.

I bite my tongue to keep from reacting to his touch. "I have a name and it's Meg."

"You know what's up with them, Meg?" Pete asks.

"They're only friends," I say.

Pete nods. "Yeah, I bet. With all due respect to your friend, no way I'd do anything other than drag her to the backseat if I were Drew."

"You mean, if you weren't too busy sexting Cindy?" Tom asks.

"Jealous 'cause your longest relationship was three minutes?" Pete asks.

"It was three hours," Tom says.

"You assholes are awful gossips," Miles says.

"Should hear what he says about you." Pete taps something into his phone.

"You should try not getting into trouble," Tom says. "Then I wouldn't have to gossip."

Miles narrows his eyes. "Or how about this, Tom? You keep your mouth shut. Then I won't have to use my fist to shut you up."

Tom rolls his eyes.

Pete shakes his head.

Clearly, this is a conversation with history. I'm not part of the history. I'm not in the circle of friends.

Maybe there is something to the concept of asking

nicely. I make eye contact with Tom. "What kind of trouble does Miles get into?"

Tom and Miles share a look of understanding. So much for Tom's claim to tell me if Miles doesn't. It's clear the guys have some kind of code.

It doesn't help my confidence.

Miles pulls me onto his lap. His cock is right under my sex. I'm wearing the lace underwear he bought me at the boutique. It's practically transparent.

I squeeze my knees together. There's no sense in flashing the other guys in the band.

Miles presses his lips against my neck, holding me the way Tom is holding the pretty redhead——like I'm a trophy.

He addresses the other guys. "Don't mention this to the Guitar Prince, okay?"

"You call Drew the Guitar Prince?" I ask.

Pete nods. "Should hear what we call Tom behind his back."

"Fuck you." The drummer pouts.

Pete points to the redhead in Tom's lap. "I'm not one to wait in line." He throws his hand over the side of his mouth, like he's going to whisper. "It's Sticks for Brains. Not the most creative, but it gets the point across."

"Guitar Prince and Miles can coast on talent. What the hell are you offering?" Tom asks.

"Sex appeal." Pete smiles.

"Can it, Sticks," Miles says. "We all know you're not going to fire your brother."

I look from Pete to Tom. Tom has green eyes and dirty blond hair, a mix of young Brad Pitt and Kurt Cobain. Pete has dark eyes and black hair. They're both handsome and well-built, but they look nothing alike.

"Don't worry about me, Meg," Pete says. "I don't share any bloodlines with Sticks. We're foster brothers."

"Adopted," Tom corrects.

I bite my tongue, silently praying for any other conversation topic. Anything besides family.

Tom kisses his pretty lap girl on the cheek and sends her away. Once she's out of earshot, he leans in close and makes eye contact with Miles. "I'm not sure what you two are doing, but Drew will kill you if you fuck things up with that slutty girl, and then I'll be out a guitarist and a singer."

My hands curl into fists. "Hey, asshole, that's my best friend, and she's not slutty. She just has big boobs. And even if she was, she wouldn't appreciate you talking about her like that. So why don't you shut the fuck up?"

"Or you'll ask Miles to shut me up," Tom offers.

Miles presses his lips into my neck. "Please ask. I'd love an excuse."

I shake my head. "I don't want to hear another word about my friend or about Drew. Got it?"

Tom nods. There's annoyance all over his face, but he nods.

Pete laughs. "Damn, you're not even getting pussy and you're whipped. Banging those drum sticks must be frying your brain."

"You play bass in an emo band, asshole. Do you actually do anything?" Tom asks.

"You still doubt that I'm the sexiest member of Sinful Serenade?" Pete asks. "Meg, back me up. I'm way hotter than your boy toy, right?"

Tom butts in before I can even fathom a response.

"'Cause that whole 'girl you know I've got steady rhythm' thing is so hot."

Pete winks at me. "Meg knows what I'm talking about."

I blush and squeeze my legs together again. Miles laughs, and he tilts me so my knees are facing away from the guys, so I'm only at risk of flashing the wall.

"Cindy knows what he's talking about," Miles says. "And we've heard what he's talking about in lurid detail."

Pete blushes, but there's a wealth of confidence in his eyes. "You have to admit—I last a long time."

"And he's quite creative, too," Miles says.

I'm lost. I turn to Miles. "You're going to have to explain this to me."

Miles runs his fingertips along my thighs, right under the hem of my skirt. "Pete is a phone sex devotee."

Pete shrugs, playing sheepish but clearly proud as hell. "You'd both understand if you ever tried taking a relationship on the road." He chuckles. "Or if you ever tried a relationship. Period."

I turn ever so slightly, so I'm looking into Miles's eyes. I still can't place his expression.

Feelings well up in my stomach. Is this what relationships feel like? I have affection for him, I do. I'm just not sure where the line stops. We are friends. We do have sex. But is there more to it than that?

"Jesus, now Miles has to prove he has the skilled hands," Tom says.

Pete shakes his head. "Miles convinces girls he's tortured inside, that he needs them to wipe his pain away."

"Right," Tom says.

Pete chuckles. "He has a mouth and he knows how to use it."

"Is that right, Meg?" Tom asks.

I turn back to them. "My lips are sealed."

Miles whispers in my ear, "Want to get out of here?"

A rush of heat passes through me. I do want to get out of here. I do want Miles to take me home and to drag me to bed. But not like this, not with him guarding all his secrets.

I turn to him the best I can. "Only if you're going to explain what Tom was talking about. Or should I ask him right now?"

Miles grabs my hips and slides me off his lap. We're almost facing each other, and his expression is almost serious. The closest thing to serious I've seen in quite a while.

He nods.

I nod.

And suddenly, this chat with the band is the most boring conversation I've ever been a part of.

We take a cab to my place, touching instead of talking.

He trails his fingers over my thighs, all the way under my skirt and so, so close, but not quite where they need to be.

My body is at war with my heart. His hands feel so good. His breath feels so good. Hell, his words feel so good, so perfect, so easy.

He wants me. Maybe this is the only way he'll ever want me. Maybe this is as good as it's ever going to get.

But I made our terms for a reason. No secrets, no lies. He's keeping a secret from me.

I can't have that. Not after everything with Rosie.

No matter how badly my body is screaming, begging my brain to take a hike for the rest of the evening, I can't give in.

He slides his hand under the fabric of my top. All that heat rushes through me. I can't bring myself to ask him to stop. I can't even admit I might need him to stop.

Instead I close my eyes and surrender to the sensation he stirs inside me. His hands belong on my body. His lips belong on my skin. It feels so good, the two of us together.

I don't want to give it up.

But I might have to. He gets one chance to tell me the truth. That's it.

The car stops. Dammit. We're parked outside my apartment. No more of this. We have to step back into the ugly world, and I have to demand an explanation.

Miles pays the cabbie and escorts me to my apartment. The elevator feels tiny. The hallway feels tinier. The key is slippery in my hands, and my legs have never felt more wobbly.

We step inside my apartment. Miles presses the door closed behind me. He takes my hands, pulls them over my head, and pins me to the door.

His body is heavy against mine. His kiss is hot, needy. Like this is more than sex to him.

Like he needs more than my body.

Miles tugs my skirt down to my knees. He drags his hand to my thighs.

No teasing this time. He strokes me over my

panties.

"I need you." He tugs at my top and pulls it off my arms.

I'm pressed against the door, almost naked, and he's still wearing all his clothes.

He still has all the cards.

I break his grasp, plant on the bed, and wrap a sheet around my chest.

Miles stares into my eyes. "Megan."

"It's Megara. Not Megan. It's right on my driver's license. And, no, it's not from the Disney movie. It's a mythology thing."

"You have a driver's license?"

"Yeah."

"You never drive."

"Not really the point."

"Tom was just running his mouth off. It was nothing."

"If it was nothing, tell me." I take a deep breath. I have to be strong here. I have to resist how much I want him. "I only left with you because you said you'd talk to me."

He runs a hand through his hair. His brow knots with frustration.

"Miles. We agreed. No secrets. No lies. I heard you two talking. He asked if you'd told me something. He threatened to tell me if you didn't."

"It's nothing." Miles sits next to me. His eyes turn to the ground. His voice softens. "Tom is nosy. That's it."

"If it's nothing, tell me."

"I can't talk about that." He leans closer. "That's how it is. We agreed that this is casual."

"We agreed not to keep secrets."

His eyes darken. "I'm not talking about that. Take it or leave it." His voice drops to something. It's needy. "This isn't supposed to be complicated."

"You're the one making it complicated." I push myself off the bed and press my back against the wall. It only puts three feet between me and Miles. That's about as good as I can do in this apartment. "Why won't you tell me if it's nothing?"

"Meg. Don't do this. We have a good thing here."

"You're the one doing it." I pull the sheet tighter around my chest. "You asked me if I trust you. I do. I want to keep trusting you. Please. Just tell me."

He swallows hard. "I can't."

"Then you need to leave."

Miles pushes himself to his feet. His eyes meet mine. "Wouldn't you rather I leave after?"

"I'm not in the mood anymore." No matter how much my body objects.

"This is supposed to be fun."

"Yeah, well it's not fun for me anymore." I press my palm flat against his chest. "If you're not going to tell me then fucking leave."

"Meg..."

"Now."

He holds my gaze for a moment. There's something in his eyes—that same hurt I saw earlier—but he blinks and it's gone.

I press my eyelids together.

The door slams shut.

That's it. He's gone.

I'm affecting him.

But somehow it's not any consolation.

CHAPTER EIGHTEEN

Routine washes away any hint of Miles. I go to class. I go to work. I go to Kara's on Sunday and try to avoid any topic related to men or music—especially men who make music.

The goal proves impossible. She turns twenty-one at the end of October, and she's throwing a birthday-slash-Halloween-slash-week-before-midterms party at the Sinful Mansion in Hollywood. I consider calling Drew and begging him to take over my duties as best friend.

The next two weeks are miserable. Sinful Serenade launches their new single No Way in Hell—the song about me.

It's an overnight success. It hits number one on the alternative chart, number four on the pop chart. The music video hits ten million downloads by the end of its first week. The thing is gorgeous and stark. It's in black and white. Half is the band playing on the beach, waves crashing around them. The other half is Miles in an empty bedroom, his eyes filled with hurt.

I understood In Pieces like the words were written in my soul. Why can't I figure this song out? I'm sure it's about me. But I'm not sure what it means.

How can he write a song about me in one breath then tell me I don't deserve to look into his heart in the next?

The song follows me everywhere. It's on every Spotify playlist and Google Play Music station. The damn thing plays every hour on KROQ. I can't go into a store or a restaurant or a coffee shop without hearing it.

The words mock me.

Three a.m. and I can't sleep.
A common refrain, I know.
As a sentiment, it's cheap.
Someone to call, to hold,
to love. No way that word—
She smiles and I drift away—

Oh hell no.
This can't be.
No way I, no way she.
Anyone else, maybe,
but not me.
I don't do this kind of thing.

Love. He's using the word love in reference to me. He can share his feelings with the world, but he can't share them with me.

He's not talking to me. Not texting me. He doesn't apologize. He doesn't even ask to cash in on our benefits.

I mean nothing to him.

CHAPTER NINETEEN

The Friday before Halloween is particularly busy. I barely have the energy to make it through my shift. Kara's party is tomorrow night. I have no idea how I'm supposed to survive the war my heart and my body are going to wage being in the same room as Miles.

A teenage girl is rushed into the ER. She's unconscious, barely breathing. Her lips are blue. She's thin enough the breeze could break her, and her arms are covered in track marks.

One is fresh.

A few hours old max.

Her mother is at her side. She's clueless. She's lost. Confused. She had no idea her daughter was on drugs.

How could she have no idea? There's no way this girl is any older than sixteen. She's covered in track marks. How the hell did Mom miss that?

The girl is dying.

Dr. Anderson, the doctor I scribe for, pushes me out of the way. "Take five, Meg."

I can't move. I can't pry my eyes away from the girl.

One of the nurses pushes me out of the way. They're rushing to her. But it's too late. It's not going to work.

I know how this goes. The paramedics should've given her Naloxone. It's supposed to counter the opiates in heroin. It's supposed to restart her heart and her breathing.

The sounds around me swirl together until they're this awful mix of air conditioning, squeaking rubber soles, the erratic beep of the heart rate monitor as the girl's pulse fades away. Nothing they're doing is working. This girl is too far gone. There's nothing anyone can do.

Just like Rosie.

I hide out in one of the single-stall bathrooms, trying and failing to will myself to go home. I can't sit in my bed alone. All I'll feel is her absence. We used to live together in a two-bedroom place in the same building. The landlord was understanding when she died—helped me move all my stuff into a studio and offered a discounted rent.

I miss my big sister so much. She was funny and bright and full of life. She understood things that flew right over my head. I thought she had it all figured out, that she knew the secret to balancing school and having a life.

That she really was that effortlessly happy.

I wish she was here. I wish I could tell her how much I miss her, how much worse our parents got after she died. They've always pretended but now they're shells of themselves. They're broken.

She'd know what to do to fix them. She'd know

how to cheer me up. She'd definitely know what to do about Miles. She'd take me out, get me drunk, and send me home with the perfect guy to wipe my memory clean. Then, she'd take me to brunch, stuff me with pancakes, and squeal over me finally growing up.

She had me fooled. She seemed okay for so long. She'd look me in the eyes and smile, and I'd feel it in my gut—everything had to be okay if my sister could smile like that. Even though I knew better, I believed it was okay. She'd never lied to me before, not like that.

I call Kara. I've kept all my grief to myself for so long. I can't do it anymore. I need to be with someone who understands so I can cry my heart out. It's stupid I didn't do it sooner. Kara's dad died when she was in high school. She knows how this feels, knows enough to drag me out for my own good, knows enough not to press for details.

Damn. Voicemail. I call again. Voicemail again. One more try.

"Hey, Kara, just wanted to say hey… text me tomorrow." I end the call and wrap my fingers around the smooth plastic of my phone.

I need to feel something else, something beyond how much I miss my sister. There's no one else to call. None of my other friends would understand. My parents certainly don't understand. There's no one who knows what this feels like.

No one except Miles.

I dial before my senses can catch up with me.

Damn. Voicemail.

"Hey, Miles. I thought I wanted to talk to you, but now I'm not sure. I'll see you tomorrow I guess. I…"

I hang up before I can tell him I miss him.

It's a half-hour walk to the top of the hill where Rosie and I used to hang out. We called our outings hikes but we spent most of the time talking about school and friends and especially about our parents.

There are houses here, expensive ones. We used to make fun of their blandness. Everything is beige. Everyone drives a black sedan or luxury car. Everyone looks perfect on the outside. Like our parents do.

Like she did.

I find an empty patch of grass and take in the view of the city. I can see the entire UCLA campus. To the left is Century City. To the right is the ocean. It's cloudy tonight. I can't see downtown. I can't see the stars.

I can't see the path to being okay without her.

My phone buzzes. It's Miles. Calling me back.

I stare at the screen. My fingers refuse to move. I'm not sure I can handle hearing his voice. It's already in my head, singing that song over and over.

Again, my phone buzzes. This time, it's a text.

Miles: Are you okay?

Meg: No.

Miles: Where are you? I'll pick you up.

Meg: Is that a good idea?

Miles: I'll take you home. If you want me to leave after that, I will.

I send him the address of the nearest house. It's pure impulse. I want him here. I want his arms around me.

Miles: What happened?

Meg: There was this girl in the ER… I'm not sure I should discuss this with you.

Miles: Let me help you. I want to.

Meg: Would you let me help you?

I stare at the phone for minutes, but there's no response. That's as good as a no.

The world is heavy. I pull my knees to my chest and bring my gaze to the sky. Still no stars but the half-moon is a beautiful shade of silver.

The neighborhood is quiet. No sounds except the wind Then there's a car. It parks. The door opens. Footsteps come closer.

Someone kneels next to me.

"Hey." Miles slides his arms around me. "Come on. You'll be okay."

I shake my head. But I soak in all the comfort of his arms anyway.

CHAPTER TWENTY

He won't share himself with me but he's here, in my apartment, taking care of me, singing songs about me.

How the hell am I supposed to make sense of that?

I tug at the zipper of my hoodie and shrug it off my shoulders. "You want something to drink?"

"Whatever you're having."

"Do you drink?"

"Drink what?" He sets my bag on the counter.

"Alcohol."

"There's never been any alcohol in your fridge."

"There was none at your place in Malibu?"

His brow furrows. "You checked?"

"No, but am I wrong?"

"You're right. There's no alcohol there."

I look at the available beverages. It's green tea, water, or grapefruit juice. I pour two glasses of juice and hand one to Miles.

"Thanks." He takes a sip and sets the glass on the counter. It's a delicate movement. Careful.

"Do you drink?" I ask.

"No," he says. "You don't either."

"Why not?"

"I don't like the person it makes me." He moves into the kitchen. His eyes find mine. "I want to help you, Meg. I know what it's like to lose someone."

"I don't want to talk." I hold strong. This time, I'm the one who wants sex and he's the one who wants conversation. But it's not like he's offering to tear his heart out for me. It's still him withholding what I want. "I want to fuck you."

"I'm not your shiny distraction."

"You won't be my distraction. You won't share your secrets. What will you do?"

"Listen to you."

"Listen to me pour my heart out while you stay closed off?"

He says nothing. There's all this vulnerability in his eyes, but still, he says nothing.

I down my juice in one long gulp and place my cup in the sink. "I'm going to shower first."

"What makes you sure there will be a second?"

"If you're going to leave, lock the door behind you. Okay?"

I keep my eyes on his as I slip out of my shirt and pants. Miles watches with rapt attention. But he stays put. Even as I slide my bra off my shoulders and push my panties to my knees.

He grunts with approval but he doesn't move.

It's been a long week. The warm water soothes my tense muscles. But the heat isn't enough release. I need his body against mine. I need him in here with me.

I take my time with soap, shampoo, and

conditioner. The shower is safe and warm. I'm alone. No one can see me crumble.

Cold air surrounds me as I step out of my safety bubble. I walk into the main room. Miles is still standing there, but now he has a towel in his hands. He keeps his eyes on mine as he wraps the towel around me and cinches it tightly.

Why did he have to withhold that secret? I want to keep things fun. I want to feel the way I did when I got to the show—like I was in for a hell of a night.

Like the world was beautiful.

This is supposed to be a pleasant distraction.

But it's not. He sees through me. He sees everything I hide from everyone else.

His voice is low. "You've turned my cock against me."

"Have I?"

He nods. "It's agony doing anything besides tearing that towel off your body."

I drop the towel. His tongue slides over his lips. His fingers dig into his jeans.

Still, he stays put.

"You're killing me here," he groans.

I take a seat on my bed. "You're killing yourself."

"I'm not doing this. Not with you so miserable."

"Then don't. But you're the one turning your cock against you. He and I have the same idea for how this should go."

He nods and slides onto the bed next to me. He takes his time pulling off his t-shirt, kicking off his shoes. Then it's his socks. His jeans.

There's a casual intimacy to it, like he's undressing before bed, like we're old lovers.

I lay on my side. He lies behind me, nuzzling his

head into the crook of my neck. His breath sends shivers down my spine.

I bite my tongue to keep from begging.

"Lay with me." He runs his fingertips over my shoulders.

I melt into his touch. Whatever he wants, I want him doing it to me.

His chest is pressed against my back, his crotch against my ass. "My uncle. He had cancer. In his pancreas. I didn't take it well. I ran off. Got into fights. Drank too much. Fucked a bunch of women without exchanging first names." He pulls the comforter over us. "I spun out of control. Worse than I ever had before."

"What do you mean?"

"I mean I fucked up, and I wasn't there for him. The guy was dying and I was stewing in self-pity over it. Same problems I'd refused to deal with for years."

He pulls me closer, his palm flat against my stomach. His heartbeat pounds against my back, his breath warms my neck.

There's something missing from his words. Something he isn't saying.

He presses his lips against my cheek. "I know it hurts. I know you miss her. I know it feels like it will never stop hurting. But you need to realize it's not your fault."

"How do you know?"

"'Cause I know." His voice waivers. "Trust me."

"How? Tell me how. I want to trust you, Miles. I really do. Tell me what it is you're hiding and I will."

"I can't."

His lips brush my neck. He drags his fingertips over my hips like he's doodling lyrics on a piece of paper.

My racing heart slows. One by one, my muscles relax. I'm a puddle again, melting into him.

The world disappears. It's nothing but us in this bed, our bodies perfectly tangled.

"You sure you don't want to talk about it?" His voice is soft and sweet. It's like he cares, like he's the sensitive Miles who sings all those songs.

I shake my head.

"You might as well," he says. "Since you're not going to get laid."

I let out a growl.

He laughs. "You'll feel better."

"I'll feel better with your cock inside me."

He groans.

Maybe I can convince him. "That's how I need your help. I don't care how you do it, but I need to stop thinking."

"You need to get this off your chest."

My chest does feel heavy. Maybe he's right. "If I do and I still feel like shit, will you admit I'm right?"

"Yeah. But I'm still not gonna be your shiny distraction." His voice wavers like he's considering being my shiny distraction.

I take a deep breath. I can convince him. "There was this patient today. She was young, a teenager. Her mom was with her, screaming, but completely clueless. She had no idea her daughter was a drug addict. There were track marks all over the girl's arms and legs, but Mom had no idea."

"I'm sorry."

"Rosie was the most important person in my life. She was my best friend, and we never lied to each other. That's what our parents did to us. They would lie right to our faces. When my cousin ran off and joined the army, they pretended it wasn't because of a fight with his parents. When my mom lost her job at the hospital, they told me she decided to quit. She was miserable every day she was unemployed, but she said it was fine. Every time anything went wrong, they pretended like it was nothing, like everything was fine. Rosie was older. She'd dealt with it longer, and she saw through it before I did. So she made me swear that we'd never bullshit each other like that."

"Yeah?"

"Yeah. And it worked. We got into so many fights over our honesty, but we always made up. When she graduated, everything started going wrong. She said she wanted to take a gap year. It was a lie. An obvious lie I should've called her on. She bombed her MCAT. She spent the next six months studying, but she still bombed it the second time. The third time. She stopped talking about retaking the test. It was like she gave up on being a doctor. It was the first time she failed at anything, and she was miserable about it. Miserable with this big, happy, everything is okay expression. I'm sure she thought she was helping me—my life has been class, work, and studying for the MCAT since sophomore year—but it didn't help. It was just the first lie to drive us apart."

"It's not your fault, Meg. That's what drugs do to people. They get them wrapped up in all this bullshit. Drug addicts are great liars. There's nothing you could have done."

"But that's the thing. It wasn't drugs at first. It was a test. Then it was her future. She gave up."

Miles takes a sharp breath.

"It broke my heart when she died."

"I know." He runs his fingertips over my arm. "I'm sorry."

I swallow hard. "That's why I can't do this with you. Not if you're going to hide something from me."

His breath is low, desperate. "If you knew the whole story, you'd kick me out again."

"That's not true. Do you really trust me that little?"

"No. I trust you more than I trust anyone."

"Then why won't you tell me?"

"I can't talk about it yet." He drags his fingertips over my shoulders. "I've never been disappointed over a relationship ending before."

"This is a relationship?"

"Us, being friends with benefits. I won't tell you my secret. I'm breaking the terms." He pulls me closer. "It's up to you. I don't want to leave. Don't want to stop."

"I don't want to stop. I want to be able to trust you."

"But if you can't have that?"

"I want to stop thinking." I lean into his touch. "I want to feel good."

"As far as I'm concerned, we're still together. Still monogamous."

"It's been weeks."

"Only want you." He slides his hand to my hip. "You still want to go bareback?"

I nod and turn to face him. There's all this pain in his clear blue eyes. Is this really the end? I don't want it to be over.

He drags his fingertips over my chest.

There must be a way I can keep him mine for a while longer.

"Talk to me, Meg." He teases my nipple with his

thumb. "I've been going crazy thinking about you."

"You think about me?"

"All the time." He presses his lips to my neck. "I miss the way you taste."

"You've been thinking about fucking me."

He shakes his head. "About you. I miss your moans. I miss your laugh. I miss the way your body fits into mine."

It's like he can give me anything but himself. But I can live with that. If I get this I can live with that.

I look back into his eyes. "This is on my terms, Miles. It's just sex. You do what I want. You come when I call."

His lips curl into a smile. "I like the sound of that."

I laugh despite myself. "I mean come over."

His fingers trace the outline of my smile. "I love your laugh."

"No. You don't say things like that. This is sex. That's it. You don't get to say you miss me, that you love me laugh, that you want to tape my heart back together. Not if you're going to keep everything to yourself."

He nods and grabs my hips. He turns me over, so I'm flat on my back. Then he's straddling me, his crotch grinding against mine.

I missed him too.

I dig my hands into his hair and bring my lips to his. The kiss is hot, electric.

This is exactly what I need. Right now, he's giving me exactly what I need.

Miles runs his fingers over my nipples. I moan into his mouth, bucking my hips, scraping my nails against his skin.

"You feel so good," he groans.

He sucks hard on my nipples, first one, then the other.

My body screams with want. This is all we have, but this is perfect.

He kisses his way down my stomach. Over my inner thigh. "I've been dreaming about this."

He moves closer. Almost.

Palms flat against the inside of my knees, he pushes my legs onto the bed so I'm splayed open for him. His plaything again, but God, do I love the way he plays.

He runs his tongue over my sex. Pleasure screams through me as my body remembers how good this feels, how much it misses him.

He sucks on my outer lips. Then it's the gentle scrape of his teeth. He works his way to my clit, his fingers trailing over my inner thighs.

"Miles," I groan. I dig my hands into his hair.

His tongue slides over my clit.

Anything teasing or gentle is gone. His mouth is on me, and he's licking me in every place that craves his tongue. My body reacts quickly. The knot inside me is intense, and he's the only thing that can undo it.

He's the only thing that can make me feel good.

He licks me, dragging his fingertips over my thighs. I groan. All the ugly parts of the day fade away. Right now, I feel good. Right now, there's pleasure in the world.

Hell, the world is fucking beautiful.

His tongue, his mouth, his lips—they're perfect. He explores my sex until I'm shaking then he focuses right on that spot.

His mouth is soft, warm, so perfectly wet. That knot of pleasure inside me grows and grows, until it's so tight, so intense I scream.

The neighbors will pound on the walls. I don't care. I scream until I'm sure I'm breaking glass.

He licks me again, and it sends me over the edge. That knot unravels and pleasure washes through my body. My muscles relax, my legs flopping against the bed.

He drags his lips over my stomach, stopping at my breasts to draw circles around my nipples. "You're sexier than I remembered." He sucks on my nipple until I squeak.

He bites my nipple. Lust shoots through me again, washing away whatever thought was forming in my brain. Conversation… we have no use for that. The only appropriate sound is a throaty groan.

He moves to my other nipple and sucks gently. I moan, rocking my hips against him, scraping my nails against his back.

"I missed you," he says.

"You missed this."

"No." He flicks his tongue against my nipple. "I missed you." His hands plant around my shoulders, and he meets my gaze. "Do you believe me?"

He's staring at me, staring through me. But there's something in his gorgeous eyes—I do believe him.

"Fuck me," I breathe.

"Fuck, yes."

Miles cups my ass, bringing my body towards his. And there it is. The tip of his cock strains against my sex.

No condom. There's nothing between us. Nothing but our bodies joining.

He sighs as he enters me. Any hint of tension or doubt flees my body. This is exactly where I need to be. Hell, this is everything I need.

I arch my back and bring my legs to his chest, my ankles over his shoulders. It's tighter and deeper than it was before.

Miles kisses me. It's still needy, still desperate. He moans against my lips, his tongue swirling around mine, exploring every inch of my mouth.

He tastes like me.

He thrusts into me. I bring my hands back to his hair, holding him close.

Miles makes a move to pull his mouth off me, to groan or sigh or maybe scream my name, but I hold him close.

Right now, he's mine.

Right now, the world is beautiful.

I arch my back and rock my hips, pushing him deeper. He follows my lead. Faster. Harder. Deeper. So he's mine, and I'm his, and he's so deep inside me I might scream.

But I don't. I groan into his mouth, and I tug at his hair, and I kiss him like I'll never get another chance to kiss him again.

That knot returns. He feels so good inside me, and the more he shakes, the more he moans, the more his fingers dig into my skin…

The pressure inside me builds. It's so tight, so intense.

Miles pulls his mouth off mine. He groans into my neck, sending vibrations across my shoulders and back.

His eyes find mine. It's like I can see inside him, see all those things that make him hurt. It's too much. I press my eyes closed and kiss him.

He thrusts into me again, and again, moaning into

my mouth, tugging at my hair. Everything inside me winds up until it's so, so tight. And then he's shaking, and he's screaming, and he's sinking his teeth into my skin.

Everything inside me releases in a wave of ecstasy. I hold him tightly, riding it as long as I can. He's there, too. His cock pulses inside me as he rocks me through another orgasm.

He groans.

His teeth sink into my neck, one last time, and he comes, filling me.

Miles collapses next to me. He pulls me close, holding me the way he did last night.

"Better than I remembered," he groans.

"You have a terrible memory."

"Or it's like that song—I love fucking you more today than yesterday, but not as much as tomorrow."

I murmur something that's supposed to sound like shut up but it comes out more hell yes, please test this hypothesis with me tomorrow.

I wake up alone. The bed is empty. The apartment is empty. He's not here.

There's no note, no text, no contact from him at all.

Is he honoring my request to keep things strictly sexual or is he running off before I can start picking the lock that guards his heart?

I'm not sure. But the ache in my gut convinces me of one thing—I want him here.

I'm going to have him here.

I'm going to make it impossible for him to resist me.

CHAPTER TWENTY-ONE

I catch a ride with Kara and hang out on the couch while she sets up for her party. Tom tries to make conversation. Then Pete. I send them both away, claiming a pressing desire to read, and hide out on the upstairs terrace.

Really, I'm trying to build up the confidence to change into my costume. It's in my bag, in Kara's car. I know it will affect Miles. I know exactly the reaction it will cause—his jaw will drop and his teeth will sink into his lower lip—but I'm concerned about the reaction it inspires in others.

It's not as if reminding Miles he wants me will help matters. He knows he wants me. The problem is that he won't offer himself to me. I need to accept that. It's just sex. Just pleasure. Just feeling good. Him locking me out of his heart—that doesn't feel good. That stings worse than anything has since Rosie died.

My heart needs to get over how much it wants his. That's not happening.

The sunset casts an orange glow over the hills. The

view here is gorgeous—the Hollywood sign, the downtown L.A. skyline, the gridlocked streets all the way to the coast.

Rock stars get all the breaks.

"How come every time I see you, you look like you're waiting to be mounted?" Miles positions his body next to mine.

Instantly, my senses are overwhelmed. I remind myself that emotional intimacy is off the table, but my damn heart refuses to comprehend.

I stare into his gorgeous blue eyes. He's still defensive. I can't take it.

I push myself to my feet. "Excuse me."

"Talk to me."

"You were gone this morning. No note, no goodbye, nothing."

"I had to take care of something."

"What?"

"Band shit. It's not interesting." He rubs my shoulder. "I don't get to say I miss you. I don't get to say I love your laugh. Sounds like you shouldn't expect me to leave you notes telling you where I'm going to be."

He's making a compelling point. I hate that he's making a compelling point. I hate how reasonable he is. The acid churning in my stomach feels entirely unreasonable.

I am the one who demanded we dial back the feelings. Why can't my heart get on board with that?

I clear my throat. "You're right. As usual. Does it ever get tiring being right?" It's half teasing, half aggressive.

"Sometimes."

"Why did you come over last night?" I ask. "Why

did you hold me and ask about my sister?"

"You called me." Miles looks up at me. "I'm respecting your terms, Meg."

"Is that what you want—for this to be all benefits, no friendship included?"

"It's what we agreed to." His expression shifts, back to cool and unflappable.

My heartbeat picks up. I still can't cause the reaction I want. But I can take my power back. I can be in the one in control of this.

"Excuse me. I need to change for the party." I nod goodbye. "I'll see you later."

His eyes stay on me, but, still, he says nothing.

Downstairs, the party is filling up. I plow through two dozen people to find Kara. She's already tipsy. Verging on drunk, even.

She slurs her words. "Sweetie, where have you been? Do you want a drink? You should have a drink."

Okay. Past verging and all the way into drunk. It's her birthday. Not the time for a lecture.

"Maybe later. Right now, I need my costume," I say.

"Right!" She bounces to her purse, digs through it, and hands me her car keys. "Knock 'em dead."

I change in the backseat of her car, stuff my clothes into a backpack, and dump it on the patio furniture. No matter how many times I adjust the costume, I feel uncomfortable. This thing is tiny. Gold bikini Princess Leia seemed like a good idea this morning. At the moment, I'm stuck on how many inches of skin I'm exposing.

I take a deep breath and check my reflection in the window. I look good. Nerdy but sexy.

I'm in control. I'm going to affect Miles.

After three more deep breaths, I make my way inside. The party isn't quite as crowded as the last one was. It's more college students than beautiful people. Nice of the band to let Kara invite all her friends to their place.

I fight my desire to hide from the action. Big smile, shoulders back, I'm confident. I may not love parties but I love having Miles under my thumb.

Tonight, I'm the casual, cool, effortless one.

Drew spots me and waves. I wave back, my best nice to see you, but please God leave me here on this couch alone wave.

It doesn't work. He strolls over and plops down next to me. He's dressed as a police officer. It suits him.

His tone is serious. "Can I ask you something personal?"

My heart thuds against my chest. Please don't let it involve Miles. "Sure."

"You miserable because you hate parties or because of Miles?"

Dammit. No luck today. "I'm not miserable."

"I barely know you and I still know that's bullshit."

"I'm not. I'm not happy but I'm… It's hard to explain."

He raises a brow. "Don't think you have to explain your intentions in that outfit."

I shrug like I wear this every Halloween.

He scans the crowd. I can't make out the expression on his face. Drew is unreadable.

"I meant what I said about Miles—I'll kick his ass

if he hurts you."

"That seems extreme."

"I've been around extreme too long to notice."

"Can I ask you something?"

He nods. "Fair is fair."

"Do you want to be with Kara? As her boyfriend?"

He holds a poker face. "Kara's amazing. She smart, funny, sweet. I'd have to be blind not to realize she's fucking gorgeous. But I'm not about to throw away what I have with Kara for a relationship that's doomed to fail."

"What if it's not doomed to fail?"

"Not worth the risk."

A month ago, I'd have nodded in agreement. Relationships suck. They always fail. Look at Rosie and Jared.

But right now I'm not sure I agree. Miles and I share something special, an understanding, an intimacy. I've never felt that way with anyone before.

It's tearing me up inside, how much I want him. But it feels good when I have him. Being with him feels better than anything else ever has.

Okay. My heart refuses to accept that this is casual. At least I'm aware of its failings.

Something catches Drew's eye. It's Kara. She's dressed as a mermaid. Her teal figure-hugging dress has a scale pattern. Sequins adorn the sweetheart neckline, emphasizing her large breasts. The dress flares at the knee, creating a proper mermaid tail. With her long, dark hair hanging over her shoulders, she has the whole mermaid sex goddess thing on lock.

Drew pants like a dog. It takes him a full minute to catch his breath.

He nods a goodbye, all cool like he isn't thinking

about throwing Kara on his bed and using the handcuffs attached to his belt to keep her there.

"Let me know if you need a ride." He lowers his voice. "There are condoms in all the bathrooms. Just don't fuck in my room."

"I'm not going to—"

He raises a brow, incredulous. "I'll keep this conversation between us."

"Thank you."

"None of my business." He makes his way to Kara.

Who does the guy think he's kidding? His reaction is exactly the one I'm trying to inspire in Miles. There's no way Drew and Kara are going to be able to resist each other for long. Not with the way they keep teasing each other.

I hang out by the beverage table, nursing a tall glass of grapefruit juice.

Tom interrupts my peace. "All the couples in like costumes have to dance together."

"What are you talking about?"

Tom isn't wearing a costume. Unless his costume is guy who doesn't keep secrets. Maybe Miles took that one.

Tom drags me to the suddenly empty dance floor. Everyone has made room for the poor suckers in couples' costumes, apparently. There are two superheroes, a Buttercup and a Dread Pirate Roberts, and there's Miles, dressed as Han freaking Solo.

His pupils dilate. His tongue slides over his lips. He wants me. Badly. I'm affecting him.

I have him under my thumb.

His lips curl into a smile. He offers his hand. "Princess."

I can't help but smile. There's no doubt in my mind—he's wearing that costume for me. He's letting other people see the nerdiness he usually keeps secret for me.

I take his hand. My smile spreads ear to ear. "Scoundrel."

He slides his arms around my waist and pulls me close. A few people cheer. Tom scurries around, forcing more people together. I'm sure he's doing this at Kara's request, but I still don't like being this close to the spotlight.

The music is fast—a pop song I don't recognize. I can't keep up. But I don't have to.

Miles moves slow. I wrap my arms around his neck and bring my body closer to his. Whatever the circumstance, his arms feel nice. Better than nice. His arms make me feel better than anything ever has.

I'm fucked. There's no resisting the pull he has over my heart.

We dance for the entire song. Then it's over, and his arms are at his side. I mumble an excuse me and disappear into the crowd. Everyone around me is dancing or screaming or chanting shots! It's worse in the kitchen. A dozen people are crowded around a table, playing Kings Cup. I know some of them from school. But worse, they know me as that buzzkill girl who never drinks and never has any fun.

One of my classmates—I think her name is Sally—waves me over. "Hey, Meg, wanna play?"

"No thanks. I have uh…" I try to think up an excuse that won't end with someone asking why I'm not drinking.

"There you are." Miles slides his arms around my waist. He nods to my fellow students. "Sorry to drag

Meg away from you, but I need her desperately."

Sally's face lights up with joy. Hell, the girl looks like she's about to wet herself. I nod, yes, obviously, I can't play your drinking game because I'm needed desperately by the hot rock star. See, I'm fun. I'm cool. I'm not a buzzkill.

Miles leads me outside. It's dark and cool, and he looks damn beautiful under the light of the moon.

He brushes my hair from my eyes.

I can see his breath, that bit of heat escaping his body. Hell, I can see right into his eyes. It doesn't tell me enough. I don't know what he's thinking.

"You're sober, aren't you?" I ask.

He nods.

"I think we're the only two sober people at this party."

"You looking for a ride home?" he asks.

"No." I move to the patio furniture. My backpack is still on the table. I sit next to it. "I don't know. Were you looking to get out of here?"

He sits next to me. "Soon. What about your friend?"

"She's fine. Drew cleared his room for her."

"His room or his bed?"

"You can't tell by his mood?"

Miles laughs. "I can, actually. He's not fucking her."

"Is he that obvious?"

Miles nods. "Is she?"

"Sort of. We haven't talked about guys in a while. I've been trying hard not to think about anything but midterms and medical school."

"Have you made any decisions about where you're applying?"

"Not yet." I pull my gaze back to Miles's eyes. There's so much in them, so much I'm never going to figure out. "But I don't want to think about it tonight."

"Princess, I think you might be taking advantage of me."

My lips curl into a smile.

"Just because you're royalty, that doesn't mean you can use me for my body. Even if I am a scoundrel."

"No?" I take his hand and place it over the curve of my hip, so his fingers graze my bare skin. "You're not desperate for me to take this off?"

He shakes his head.

"So you're desperate for me to leave it on?" I press my body against his. "You have a fantasy of screwing the princess?"

"You sure this is what you want?"

I nod.

"Then let's go."

"Where?"

"My place in Malibu."

"Now?"

He stands and offers his hand. "Hey, Princess, I've got the fastest ship in the galaxy. I can get you wherever you want to go in the blink of an eye."

"You mean the death bike, don't you?"

He smirks. "You'll hurt her feelings."

CHAPTER TWENTY-TWO

I change back into my clothes for the ride to his place. It's still freezing and terrifying on the motorcycle. But that's nothing compared to all the feelings stirring inside me.

We spend the night on the couch, watching science fiction movies. Truth be told, there isn't that much watching going on. Mostly kissing, touching, fucking. It feels amazing, being this close to him. It's like we're in our own little world. Our own bubble.

Like nothing can bring us down.

We spend the night together in his bed. Spend the morning on the couch, sipping coffee and kissing and not really watching The Matrix movies.

The house is beautiful and bright but this time, it's touchable. It's intimate. It's mine. He's mine. I know he's not, that we agreed to keep this all benefits, no friendship but it feels like he's mine.

I press my lips into his. He tastes good. His legs feel good between mine. His chest feels good against mine.

But there's this sound. This annoying melody. It's familiar. It's loud. Dammit.

That's the ringtone I assigned for my parents. And I've been dodging their texts for weeks. There's no more dodging. Once they escalate to phone call, they call and call and call.

"Sorry, I have to take this." I push off the couch and grab my phone. Deep breath. "Hey, Mom. How are you?"

"I've been worried. Did you get my message about Thanksgiving?"

"Yes."

Miles runs his fingers over my shoulder. He whispers, "Tell them you've been busy because you're seeing someone."

"Excuse me." I put my phone over the speaker and turn to Miles. "Are you crazy?"

"Trust me. Tell her you have a boyfriend. It will give you something to talk about besides medical school and your sister."

He's making a compelling argument.

"I'll still come with you," he says. "For Thanksgiving. Hell, invite them to meet us at Nobu tonight. I'll impress them by paying."

"That would impress them."

"I know." He brushes my hair from my eyes. "You have to admit I'm charming. For a scoundrel."

"I don't have to admit that, no."

"But you know it's true."

"Megara." Mom's voice flows through the speaker. "Are you there?"

"Tell her," Miles mouths.

He's right. I should tell her. It's a perfect distraction. The visit will be a million times easier if I have Miles by my side. Being in that house alone, or with just Mom and Dad… It still hurts.

"I'm sorry Mom. That's just… that's Miles. My boyfriend." I take a deep breath. "We've been dating a few months now. And it's kept me busy."

"You're seeing someone?" Her voice is neutral.

"Yeah. He's great. Really, really great. Smart." Damn, what does she want to hear? I've never had to worry about my mom approving of a guy.

"Tell her I went to Stanford," Miles whispers.

That's good. "He's a little older. Graduated from Stanford a few years ago."

"Oh, that's great, sweetie. Miles, was it?" she asks.

"Yes. Miles. You'd like him." Why would she like him? Dammit, how does this parents meeting the boyfriend thing work?

"What's your mom like to do for fun?" Miles whispers.

"Give me a second, Mom." I cover the receiver with my hand and whisper to Miles. "She doesn't have time for fun. She's a surgeon." I rack my brain. Nobody in my family has had fun in a while. "She likes mythology. And foreign films."

"Skip that part. Invite me over for Thanksgiving," he says. "Trust me. She'll be excited that you want to introduce me."

That doesn't sound like Mom, but I'll try. I turn back to my cell. "Sorry, Mom. He's a little distracting. He really wants to meet you guys. Do you think he could come with me for Thanksgiving?"

"You're coming home?" Her voice perks up. "Of course, honey. We were hoping you'd come home. You don't have work?"

"No. My supervisor gave me the entire week off."

I bite my tongue. There's no getting out of this now. "Miles, he doesn't have a lot of family around here. I know he'll appreciate this."

"Yes. It will be nice having company since we don't…" Her voice breaks. "You two can stay the weekend. Or just Thursday. Your father is working Friday but it's the early shift. Then the weekend—well, you know the drill."

Ah, the virtues of having a surgeon and an ER doctor for parents. They're always working. If I'd been the type to get in trouble, I could have taken advantage of their busy schedules during high school.

Actually, it's remarkable that they both have Thanksgiving off. Usually, we have dinner at an off time to accommodate their schedules.

"Have you thought about schools?" Mom asks. "UCI's program is improving. You could stay here. It would save you the trouble of finding a place."

"I'm thinking an East Coast school." This isn't where I want this conversation going. I look to Miles for direction.

He shakes his head. "Ask her how she's doing. About work or a hobby."

Yes, of course. It sounds so obvious when he says it. I turn my attention to my phone. "How is work?"

"Busy, of course. Dr. Lee is opening a private practice. She invited me to join, but I'm not sure I can leave the hospital." Mom's voice lifts. This is something she can talk about. "Is Miles at your place, honey? Or are you at his?"

"His."

"And you're being safe?"

Oh God. I'm going to die of embarrassment. But this is nothing. Mom is a surgeon who specializes in gynecology. I'm shocked she isn't using more explicit words.

"Yes, we are," I say.

Miles chuckles.

I put my hand over the phone's mic. "This is not funny."

"You're smiling," he says.

Damn, I am smiling. Okay, it's a little funny.

He motions for the phone.

It's not a bad idea, him talking to her. "Mom, Miles wants to talk to you. To say hi. He's really excited to meet you. Is that okay?"

"He sounds like a polite young man."

Now that is funny. I laugh. It's a belly laugh, one of the best laughs I've had in a while. My mom thinks my rock star fuck buddy is a polite young man.

It's absurd.

I hand the phone to Miles.

Miles laughs. He covers the receiver with his hands. "You are so fucking bad at this."

I flip him off playfully.

"Hey, Dr. Smart. This is Miles. Meg has told me so much about you." His eyes stay on mine. He's smiling ear to ear.

He sweet-talks my mom. I can tell she's charmed from over here. He's welcome to stay as long as he wants. He's thrilled to finally meet my parents he's supposedly heard so much about.

He even says goodbye and ends the call without passing it back to me.

After lunch, Miles takes me home. It's midterms week. No time for anything but school. I kiss him goodbye, warn him I'll be unavailable, and devote the entirety of my night to studying.

I don't stop until I'm about to fall asleep at my desk.

I brush my teeth and throw myself onto my bed. My phone is still blinking. There's a text from Miles.

Miles: You ready for midterms?

Meg: Not yet. I need to study. I'm not sure I'll ever be done studying. No time for distracting rock stars with very distracting mouths.

Miles: And hands.

Meg: Yes, and we could add cocks while we're at it.

Miles: Only have the one. That not enough for you?

Meg: You know what I mean!

Miles: I'll get a sex toy.

Meg: Don't start. I have to go to bed. First midterm is at nine a.m.

Miles: Studying all night tomorrow?

Meg: All night every night.

Miles: Been thinking. Sure would be a nice benefit if you could take a relaxing study break at home.

Meg: Yeah?

Miles: Without ever leaving your bed.

Meg: I'm listening. Well, reading.

Miles: Text me tomorrow when you're done studying. For your reward.

Meg: I'm not a puppy.

Miles: You'll like it.

Meg: I'll consider it. Goodnight.

Miles: Dream about me.

I dream about finals. That same awful dream where I wake up late and arrive just as class is getting out. It doesn't happen. I'm early to every exam. I come home. I collapse, drink tea, study my ass off, and fall asleep at my desk. When I wake, my phone is buzzing with a text from Miles.

Miles: Guess that's failure. Don't worry. You can collect your reward tomorrow.

Miles: I dreamt about you.

Miles: Tell you about it later.

Cryptic, as usual. I try to put his flirting out of mind. I have an early test. I need sleep.

It doesn't work. I toss and turn. My body refuses to relax when it comes to the subject of Miles Webb.

It wants him. Whatever it is he's offering, it wants that.

I reply.

Meg: I'm awake and I'm all studied up.

Miles: You are a good girl.

Meg: And you're a very bad boy.

Miles: That's such a stereotype, Megara. I expected better.

I cringe at the sight of my full name. It hasn't come up since that night. My thoughts go straight back to that awful fight. I was right here, desperate for one single fucking card to play and coming up empty.

There's the sound of a guitar intro. My phone is ringing with a tone I never set. According to the display, Miles is calling me.

It hits me. It's playing that song No Way In Hell. He programmed it into my phone as his personal ringtone.

I answer, playing dumb. "Who is this?"

"Just a young man who is very good with his mouth."

My lips curl into a smile. My concerns fade away.

He's making me feel good. That's what matters.

"Is that right?" I tease back.

He laughs. "Mhmm. You swear you're done studying."

"On my love of Jurassic Park."

"And you're awake?"

There's something different about hearing him on the phone. He's closer and farther away all at once. It's like his breath and his voice are right in my ear. Or maybe it's his tone. He almost sounds nervous.

"Wide awake," I say.

"Put your phone on speaker."

I do.

"What are you wearing?"

"Shorts and a tank top."

"Mhmm." His voice gets heavy. "Take off the shorts."

I wait for some sign that he's joking, but there isn't one.

"Do you want to hear me come or do you want to go to bed alone?"

CHAPTER TWENTY-THREE

I'm hot everywhere. Not just my cheeks but my chest, stomach, and back too. I open the window. The cool air does nothing to lessen the heat building in my body.

Miles wants to listen to me come? The guy makes sexy sounds for a living, and he wants to hear mine over the phone.

I'm back at the night of our not exactly a breakup again, only this time, I'm at the club, listening to Miles and Tom mock Pete for his constant phone sex. The night flies by, and I'm here, half naked and about to cry because Miles can't bring himself to explain.

My body skips over the heartbreak part. The heat racing through me pools between my legs. The damn thing can't be helped. It has an addiction to Miles. There's no other explanation.

My head is failing to pull back, failing to protect me. I guess the studying really tired it out.

Miles's exhale flows through the speakers. He's waiting, and he's not doing it patiently. Technically speaking, the ball is in my court. I can say yes or say no.

Technically speaking, this arrangement is entirely on my terms.

My eyes flutter closed. The breeze sends a shiver up my legs and thighs. No underwear tonight. No bra. Just this tiny tank top and shorts, like when I was on the couch with Miles.

No, I can't go there. If I'm going to do this, I need to be in this moment. And damn I want to enjoy this moment.

"You swear you're not fucking with me?" I ask.

"I'll prove it."

He's quiet for a minute. Then my phone buzzes with a picture message. It's Miles, in his bed, alone. His hand is tugging at the waistband of his boxers.

God, he's so freaking yummy it's ridiculous.

"You want more?" he asks.

A blush spreads across my cheeks. It's not like I'm used to guys offering to send me nude pictures.

Okay. He sent me a picture in his underwear. It's only fair I do the same. Even if I'm not wearing any underwear. I pull my tank top to my bellybutton so my breasts are on display.

I've never taken a sexy picture of myself before. I know all the ways it's a bad idea, all the ways it could hurt me, but I don't care.

This feels too good for me to care.

I snap a picture of my chest and neck and send it to Miles.

He lets out a groan. "Fuck, Meg, you're killing me."

Yes. Perfect. I'm going to be the one in control here. "How so?"

"I miss your tits."

"You saw them last week."

"I want to see them every day. To see that look on your face when I suck on your nipples."

So much for control. I'm melting. Heat rushes through my body. Whatever it is we're doing, I can't stop until I get what he promised me, until he's groaning in my ear.

"What else?" I ask.

"Take off your shorts," he says.

I do. "Take off your boxers."

There's a low groan and then silence. A moment later, my phone buzzes. He took off his boxers and sent me a picture. That must be…

I look at my new picture message. It's Miles. All of him. He's naked and hard, his hand wrapped around his cock. I always thought it was strange when women wanted these pictures, but now I understand. That's Miles, hard and desperate and out of his mind because of me.

"I've never done this before," I say.

"Me either."

"Really?"

"Really."

I pull my tank top over my head and toss it aside. I'm naked on my bed. If I close my eyes, I almost feel like he's here, like he's watching me. I run my fingertips over my chest. "I don't know what to say."

"I don't care what you say. I just want to hear you come."

Dammit, I'm on fire. This is perfect.

I don't want to hear anything except his breath and his moans. Maybe my name rolling off his tongue like he's so desperate he can't find another word to explain his pleasure.

I set the phone on the bed next to me, between my mouth and my ears. My hand trails over my chest, teasing my nipples the way Miles does.

It's good already. Not as good as him, but close. I play with my nipples until his breath is as heavy and strained as mine is. Then I trail my hand down my stomach, below my belly button, between my legs.

My breath hitches in my throat. "You have to do it, too."

His voice is heavy. "After. I want to hear you first."

My eyes flutter closed. It's not as if I've never touched myself before. I made it to twenty-one without ever having sex. I touched myself plenty. But never with an audience.

My breath goes all the way to my core. He's never done this before either. No reason to be self-conscious.

I slide my hand between my legs with a soft touch. It's a tease, at first, the kind of thing Miles would do. I work my way to my clit then back off again. Slowly. Until I can't take it anymore.

Through the speakers, his breath is heavy. Desperate. It stirs something in me. Makes me just as desperate.

No more waiting. No more gentleness. I rub myself hard.

It's not as good as when Miles touches me. It's lacking a certain patience, a certain heat. But it's still damn good.

The pressure inside me builds at record speed. I lose control of my breath. Of the sounds escaping my lips. I let out a soft moan. Then a louder one. My hand moves faster, drawing circles over my clit. I make the circles smaller and tighter until they're in just the right spot.

"Oh." My voice picks up. I'm almost screaming.

No room for shyness now. His voice is louder, heavier, more desperate. I'm affecting him, and that feels so damn good.

I rub myself until I'm at the brink. Deep down, I know this won't be enough to satisfy my craving. I need more than Miles's breath in my ear. I need his hands and his mouth and his cock.

The ache between my legs is so intense. Almost more than I can take. The pleasure in my arms and legs and chest spins inward, pooling in my core until it's a deep, desperate pressure.

A groan flows through the speakers. It sends me right over the edge. That pleasure drives a little deeper, squeezing me until I can't breathe. One more brush of my fingers and I come. My orgasm is pulses of ecstasy. The pressure releases bit by bit, spilling into the purest, deepest bliss.

Miles lets out a low moan. "Don't know how I can follow that."

My cheeks flush. "You moan more than that on one Sinful Serenade track."

"Depends on the track." He growls. "You sound so fucking sexy. Can't remember the last time I was this hard."

"I want to hear you, too." No awkwardness. I have to say it. "I want to hear you come."

No snappy retort. There's some shifting, sheets moving, a body planting on the bed. He must be getting into position.

His breath gets heavier and heavier. He must not

have control of it any longer. It's strained and desperate. I relax into my bed, letting the sounds of his pleasure wash over me. He moans, low and deep and purely animal. The moans get louder and lower. It's so much better than anything on any song—and I've paid very close attention.

"Mhmm."

He's not wasting time either. Everything that flows through my speakers is desperate and needy, like he wants this as much as I did. His groans run together. Louder. Higher. Like he can't control them at all.

There. He's coming. I'm not sure how I can tell, but I can. His voice strains. His breath gets choppy. He lets out one last moan, louder than I've ever heard before. Then, he's sighing in pleasure. His breath steadies. Still strained, but not completely out of control.

"Relaxed?" he asks.

"More like keyed up and wishing you were here."

"Happy to listen to you go again."

"I should get to bed."

"When's your last midterm?"

"Friday night. Why?"

"No reason." He exhales slowly. "Goodnight, Meg. And good luck."

"Goodnight."

I hang up the phone, pull the sheets over my head, and try desperately to fill the craving I have for Miles.

I fail.

The week is a blur of textbooks and tests. By Friday afternoon, the only thing I want is the sweet embrace of my sheets. I need a million hours of sleep.

The elevator is all the way on the top floor, so I take the stairs to my apartment. Every step is pure agony.

And there he is, the only thing better than those million hours of sleep. Miles is leaning against my door, his hands in the pockets of his leather jacket, his lips pursed like there's something right on the tip of his tongue.

"You survived." He smiles.

I nod.

"I bet you'd like to celebrate that."

"Okay."

"If that's not a problem for you."

"I can clear my schedule." I fish my keys out of my backpack, open the apartment, and pull Miles inside with me.

The room is a verifiable mess. Paper everywhere, clothes strewn over the floor, dishes piled in the sink.

Miles shakes his head. "I like what you've done with the place."

"Thank you. I'm trying something new with the dishes. And the laundry. And the shower."

"Dirty girl."

My lips curl into a smile. "Not quite yet." I toss my backpack on the ground. "How long were you waiting?"

"Not long." He runs his fingertips over my chin, tilting my head so he's peering right into my eyes. "But it would've been worth waiting longer."

"And what is it you're waiting for?"

He presses his lips into mine. His hands slide into my hair as his tongue swirls around mine. The kiss breaks and he pulls back. "That."

My heart thumps against my chest. I've ignored

my body for days. It's time to give it a little attention.

His fingers skim my wrists. "I've been thinking about you all week."

Okay, it's time to have some fun. I tease him. "I'm been thinking about midterms all week."

He pulls his shirt over his head. "What are you thinking about now?"

"There was this angular velocity question."

"Are you only in science classes?"

I trace the lines of his chest. "Who's thinking about midterms now?"

He pulls me onto the bed. The gesture is messy. I slip and land on my side. He shakes his head like he's going to punish me.

"You think you're clever?" he asks.

"Absolutely."

He unzips my hoodie. Then his hands are on my stomach. My skin burns at his touch. Midterms seem so irrelevant now, but I'm not done teasing him yet. It's too much fun.

"And molecular biology," I say. "That was impossible."

He tugs at my t-shirt. I lift my arms to help him get it off.

His eyes pass over me slowly. Then it's his fingers skimming my sides. "You should have said hard."

My cheeks flush. "I, um..."

He unhooks my bra and pulls it off my arms. "Um…?"

I plant my hands on his chest and press my crotch into his. Hard. Yes, he is absolutely hard.

Deep breath. I want him desperately, but I want his smile as much as I want his cock. "And my Roman Poetry elective."

He unzips my jeans and pulls them off my ass. "That's a shit choice for an elective."

He runs his fingertips over the waist of my panties. A gasp escapes my lips. Midterms. Electives. They're so quaint, so far away, so much less important than this.

I rub my crotch against his. "It's better than you'd expect."

He shakes his head. "You're making this hard."

"I can tell."

He smirks. "But I'm going to beat midterms."

"You really can't." I press my lips to his. Damn, he tastes good. And I feel good. Light. Like I can float.

"That so?"

I nod. "It's all biology."

He laughs.

Then he makes me forget what year it is.

CHAPTER TWENTY-FOUR

The next three weeks are a blur. Miles seeps further and further into my life. He texts me during the day. I text back between classes, while I eat lunch, on the walk home from the hospital. It's little things—jokes about Star Wars or promises to make me come until I'm screaming his name or details about our day—but I smile every time I see a new text from him.

This feels good. Better than it should.

For once, I allow myself to soak up the joy. He picks me up from work every Friday night and drops me off at Kara's every Sunday morning. The time between, at his place in Malibu, is ours and ours alone. It's like the rest of the world doesn't exist. Like nothing can ever hurt us.

Time goes so fast. All of a sudden, it's the day before Thanksgiving, and Miles is at school. A surprise. He takes me out for sushi and a special showing of The Matrix. Then he drives me home and makes me come more times than I can count.

When I wake, Miles is already dressed and ready to go. I speed through my morning routine, packing and dressing as carefully as I can manage.

There. Done. Now to spend two days at my parents' house. I can handle that.

Miles's eyes pass over me. "You look nice."

Nice is hardly the compliment I expect from Miles, but it's exactly right. I'm in my most parent-pleasing outfit—a polka-dot cardigan, skinny jeans, ankle boots.

"Thank you."

He focuses on the v-neckline of my sweater. "Are you wearing anything under that?"

"Yes. My parents will not be cool with us making out in front of them."

"I'm not sure. Your mom was asking if you're having safe sex."

"I will leave! I swear I will."

He laughs. "And go where?"

"Anyplace I don't have to die of embarrassment."

He pulls me into a hug and presses his lips to mine. "You won't die. I promise."

"I don't know if I can do this," I whisper.

"You can. Come on." He takes my hand and leads me to his car downstairs.

I let him take the lead, putting our things in the trunk, opening the door for me. Then we're in the car, the engine is on, we're heading towards Newport Beach.

"You hungry?" he asks.

I shake my head. I'm not sure I can eat right now.

"Want coffee?"

"Later."

The car moves fast, but it's not crazy fast like that first night we met. It's reasonable.

I turn on the radio. It's tuned to KROQ and what do you know, No Way in Hell pours out of the speakers.

Three a.m. and I can't sleep.
A common refrain, I know.
As a sentiment, it's cheap.
Someone to call, to hold,
to love, no way, that word—
She smiles and I drift away—

My cheeks flush. I stammer something incomprehensible and change the station.

"You know, most girls feel flattered when someone writes a song about them," he says.

I press my back against the seat. "You've never said that it's about me."

His fingers curl around the wheel. "It is."

"Oh."

"You're cute when you're nervous."

I turn my attention to the window, but there's nothing to see. Only overpasses, exit signs, rows of condos. "Why did you write a song about me?"

"Something came over me, an itch, and the song was the only way to scratch it."

I take a deep breath. "That isn't an answer."

"Yes, it is." He turns to me for a moment then his eyes are back on the road. "It's just not the answer you want."

I want him to look at me and tell me his feelings, to explain what it means—the itch he can't scratch.

The song sounds like it's about falling in love.

Is he falling in love with me?

The radio station goes to commercial. It's for some fast-food restaurant, some supposedly cheap and delicious breakfast item. The hum of the road, the wind leaking through the not-quite-airtight windows, fills the car.

Miles is supposed to be my secret weapon in getting through this awful weekend. If he's going to be defensive and make up bullshit about why he wrote a song about me... I can't deal with that.

I guess it's up to me to turn the mood.

"Is this your car?" I ask.

"Yeah."

"Then why do you always ride the death bike?"

"I like having something powerful between my legs."

"Besides your cock?"

He chuckles. "You're not supposed to spell out the joke."

"Yeah, but I like thinking about your cock." I take a deep breath. It doesn't help sooth me. What is he doing writing songs about falling in love with me then insisting I'm ruining our relationship by making it serious?

I tap my fingers against the windowsill. It's frustrating, the way he's so unclear about his intentions.

"I can't explain it. If I could, I wouldn't have to write the song." His voice gets low. "I felt something. I wrote the song. The end."

"Thanks. You really cleared things up."

"You're cranky today."

"Fuck off."

"Let's stop for breakfast."

"I'm not hungry."

I close my eyes and pretend to nap. Despite my insistence Miles takes the next exit.

He parks at a Starbucks. "Come on. I'll buy you coffee, green tea, whatever your heart desires."

My stomach rumbles. I am hungry. But that isn't why I'm cranky.

He must realize that I'm cranky over his non-answer. He felt an itch, the song scratched it. What a load of bullshit.

I follow Miles into the coffee shop. He slides his arm around my waist, pulling me closer. It's like we're a normal couple. Like we're actually happy we're seeing my family for the holiday.

The girl behind the counter recognizes Miles instantly. Her eyes light up. Her tongue slides over her lips. "Welcome!"

Miles smirks. "You want to grab a seat?"

"So you can flirt with the employee?"

He trails his fingers over the edge of my cardigan than over my skin. "I only flirt with you." His hand slides to my lower back. "I just don't want to subject anyone else to your hunger-induced mood."

"Maybe my mood is bullshit induced."

"Only one way to find out." He steps up to the register. Plants his palms flat and leans in towards the employee like he's about to share a secret. "Black coffee for me. Large. And for my friend—" He motions to me.

"Large latte. Extra shot."

"And," Miles says.

"One of the egg sandwiches. The one with spinach."

The girl nods. She stares adoringly at Miles. "I love

Sinful Serenade."

He winks at her. "Thanks, honey."

"Would you sign something?" Her eyes go wide. She reaches under the counter and hands him a marker.

He nods, signs a napkin, and hands it back to her.

I flop on one of the cushy armchairs and check my phone. Nothing but a text from my mom to drive safely. Everyone else is far, far away. Kara is in San Francisco. I text her Happy Thanksgiving.

Miles slides into the cushy chair next to mine. He hands me my drink and my egg sandwich.

His expression is attentive. What the hell do I do with that?

I get up for sugar and a wooden stir stick. I can feel his eyes on me as I fix my drink. It's good. Sweet and creamy and incredibly full of caffeine.

Deep breath. I return to my seat with grace. I'm calm. I'm going to make the most of things.

My eyes meet his. "Why did you really invite yourself home with me?"

"The answer to that question is self-evident."

"Jesus, I forgot you were going to be a lawyer." I take another sip. More sweet, sweet caffeine. How did people live before caffeine? It must've been hell.

"I want to help you. With your parents."

"Wouldn't you rather see your family?" I ask.

"Sinful Serenade is my family." His voice gets low. "I don't usually talk about my family."

"I'm not going to push you." It's clear that pushing him to talk to me fails. And it's not at all pushing someone who would rather stay closed off.

His eyes turn to the ground. "Here's the thing, Meg. I'm only telling you this so you understand why

I'll never fall in love with you."

My breath catches in my throat. "I know. We're friends."

Miles stares through me. "And you're sure you're okay with that?"

"Absolutely." I press my hand into my jeans. "This relationship is just sex."

He nods. "My dad left when I was in middle school. Bored of the whole suburban thing. I was angry. I did nothing but play my guitar and get into trouble. But my mom… she fell apart. She couldn't get out of bed, couldn't even bother to get herself to the shower. It broke her heart. That's what love does, it breaks your heart."

Miles's eyes fill up with this mix of hatred and frustration. His dad leaving must have hurt so much. And then his mom… he's never talked about her before.

"But she… now…" I can't bring myself to ask the question. I already know it leads down some dark and stormy path. He has no family that matters. His mom must not be…

His gaze drifts to the window. He focuses on something far off in the distance, like he's lost in thought. It must be a whole minute before he looks back to me.

"She killed herself," he says.

My stomach drops with a thud. My fingers slip. Oh no. My cup hits the ground. Then there's coffee everywhere. "Oh, God. I better get that."

I jump out of my seat. Napkins. I need napkins. They're by the counter, by the perky employee who doesn't know that Miles doesn't do boyfriend, that he believes love can only break you.

I grab a stack.

The perky employee spots the puddle of coffee. "I can get that."

"No, it's okay." She's not hearing it. She slides out from the counter with a white washcloth, rushes to Miles, drops to her knees, and mops up the coffee.

His eyes find mine, but he says nothing. I try to turn myself into stone. I try to give nothing away, but everything around me feels heavy.

He's gone through so much. He hurts so much. And he mentions it casually in the middle of a coffee shop. By the way, my mom killed herself and that's why I have all these intimacy issues. Want to fuck in the bathroom?

Deep breath.

The employee finishes mopping. She smiles at Miles. At me. Totally oblivious to the change in atmosphere.

"I'll make you another. Latte, extra shot, right?" she asks.

I nod and return to my seat. "Sorry."

"That's about what I expected." He picks up the remaining half of my sandwich and hands it to me. "You're clumsy when you're hungry."

"I'm sorry you went through all that."

There's vulnerability in his expression. "I survived."

My heart thuds against my chest. "You're alone."

His expression hardens. "I've been alone a long time. It's easier that way."

"Oh."

Miles is silent. Of course he's silent. He's been alone a long time. It's easier that way.

Alone.

Without anyone.
Without me.
It's easier that way.
It's better that way.
He's happier that way.
He's happier without me.

CHAPTER TWENTY-FIVE

We park in the driveway of my parents' Newport Beach house. Miles grabs our suitcases from the trunk. I try to help but he pulls the suitcases out of reach. Okay. I guess my mom will appreciate him acting like a gentleman.

The oak door is locked. I knock instead of fishing for my keys. Mom will also appreciate the chance to make an entrance.

Nerves rise up in my stomach. The last time I was here, I felt like I was suffocating. Everything was off and wrong, and Rosie's absence was haunting me.

Miles sets the suitcases on the concrete.

Then his arm is around my waist and I'm sure it's going to be okay.

Mom answers the door. "Honey, I missed you." She takes a long look at Miles and nods a hello. "I'm Susan Smart."

"Miles Webb. Nice to finally meet you." He shakes her hand. "I can see where Meg gets her looks."

Mom blushes. "Thank you. Come in." She pushes

the door open. "How was the drive?"

"Good. Not too much traffic." I step inside and scan the living room. It's as gorgeous and pristine as I remember. But something is missing. There used to be trophies on the mantle—Rosie's volleyball trophies. They're gone. One more piece of her is gone.

"Can I get you anything? Coffee? Tea? A snack, maybe?"

I bite my tongue. "How about we put away our bags first?"

She nods and leads us up the stairs. There used to be half a dozen framed pictures on this wall—family photos, the cheesy ones sent as Christmas cards—but they're all gone.

Mom smiles. "Did you kids want to stay in Meg's room or would you like to stay in the spare room, Miles?"

My jaw drops. We don't have a spare room. We have Rosie's room.

I know we have to move on eventually. I know people grieve in different ways. And maybe it hurts Mom too much to have Rosie's stuff here...

But how can she call that the spare room?

How can she take down all those pictures and hide all those trophies?

Miles steps in. It's like he can tell I'm about to snap.

"Thank you so much, Dr. Smart." Miles looks to me. "What do you think, honey? Want me to stay with you?"

I nod.

He turns to Mom. "You sure it's all right?"

She nods. "Yes, it's good for you, sleeping next to

someone you love. The touch produces oxytocin. That's the love hormone. It's what makes you feel all warm and fuzzy." She offers a half-smile. "Dopamine too."

"I know dopamine. The pleasure hormone." Miles offers her a very full smile.

"Yes." Mom turns to me. "I'm glad you found someone smart."

"He did go to Stanford, the show-off." I try my best I'm having such effortless fun joking about my boyfriend smile. It's horrible.

He places our suitcases in my room then slides his arm around me. He leans in to whisper, "Should I tell her I have a motorcycle?"

I laugh. I'm tempted to tell her myself. I have no idea how Mom will act towards the bad-boy version of Miles. Ever since Rosie died, she's been unpredictable.

Mom leads us downstairs. "How did you two meet? Meg doesn't talk about guys very often."

"She's studious." Miles plays with my hair. "She's quite the nerd, really."

Mom smiles. "She went as Princess Leia for Halloween five years in a row."

"This year too," he says. "I'm a friend of Kara's. Well, a friend of a friend."

She nods. "What do you do, Miles? Meg didn't mention it."

"I work in the entertainment industry." He winks at me. "Not that interesting."

"Do you need any help with dinner?" I ask.

"No, it's all prepared except the turkey, and that's in the oven." She motions to the table, directing us to sit. "Coffee or tea, you two?"

"Green tea." Miles smiles. "If it's not too much trouble."

I'm not sure if he's teasing me or taking care of me. Both maybe. Whatever it is, I like it.

I lean in to whisper, "Thank you. This is already less awful."

"You want me to tell her about Sinful Serenade?"

"Up to you."

"Most parents don't react well to the knowledge their daughter is having a torrid love affair with a rock star."

"Because you've met so many girls' parents?"

"Seen it happen."

"To who?"

He shrugs.

Mom steps into the room. She sets out a teapot and three mugs. "I haven't used this thing in forever." She looks at Miles. "Meg is very busy. Can't get home much."

"I'm sure that's partly my fault." He smiles wide, charm turned to a thousand.

"You look familiar, Miles. Are you from around here?"

"I lived in Irvine for a while. But that's probably not it. I'm in this band. Sinful Serenade. We have this song that plays a hundred times a day on KROQ."

Mom smiles. "I haven't listened to KROQ since high school."

"It's about the same. Foo Fighters, Red Hot Chili Peppers, and Nirvana around the clock."

Mom blushes, totally charmed. "You're sweet, but those bands came long after I finished high school."

"I can't believe that."

She turns to us, friendly but maternal, too. "Do

you do well?"

He nods. "Well enough." Under the table, he slides his hand over my thigh. "I write songs on the side. It's go big or go home, but I've had a few hits."

Mom's eyes light up. "Really?"

Miles names a few songs that put the popular in pop. Mom's demeanor changes. It's not that she's horribly superficial. Just, around here, money talks. It takes a lot to impress a family of doctors. Apparently, "millionaire songwriter with gorgeous blue eyes" is enough to do it.

I zone out as Mom grills Miles. He's perfect and charming—the picture of a sweet, supportive boyfriend. He leans his head against my shoulder and praises my wit, my beauty, my excellent work ethic. He speculates wildly about some future we'll never see—where he tours based on my school schedule and settles down in the city where I do my residency.

For a guy who doesn't do boyfriend, he sure is good at playing one.

We have a late dinner. The table in the dining room is covered with the good linens, the good china, the good silverware. It's the kind of meal royalty eats.

Dad sits next to Mom, scooping potatoes absentmindedly. He's not really all here, doesn't seem to have much to say. He hasn't had much to say since Rosie died, and he's on the same "let's just never discuss it again" wavelength as my mom.

He pays careful attention to Miles, but there's no sign that Dad objects to my so-called boyfriend. Dad isn't even bothered by the tattoos that peek out from

Miles's t-shirt.

This is what I wanted, the attention on Miles instead of me. But it feels wrong for them to so easily accept him. Shouldn't they be prying about his intentions? Shouldn't they be worried about their little girl?

Miles is too charming, too good at convincing them he adores me.

Mom clears her throat. "You know, I'm so thankful to have my daughter and her friend here. And she's healthy, and she's going to medical school next year." She holds up her glass of wine like she's toasting me. "You're going to do great anywhere."

"Thank you." I hold my water to my chest, avoiding anything close to a toast. "It'll be nice to finally get out of southern California. Spread my wings and see the world." And get away from this house and the way it tears open a hole in my gut.

"If that's what you want." Mom sips her wine slowly. She sets the glass down, folds her hands, and looks directly at me. "Megara, honey, what are you thankful for?"

I bite my lip, fighting my temptation to call out the bullshit. This is supposed to be a nice family dinner. I'm not going to ruin it by pointing out how much we're pretending that Rosie isn't here.

"For honesty," I say.

Mom frowns, not sure what to make of that. "It is important." She pats Dad's hand. "Especially in a relationship."

The mood shifts and her desperate attempt to pretend like my sister never existed disappears. Her expression is misery. The memory must be hitting her like a ton of bricks.

I know that feeling. It's a horrible feeling. Half of me wants to rush to comfort her. But the other half can't forgive her for erasing Rosie from the house.

I know it isn't fair. She's coping the only way she knows how.

But it's still wrong that there's no sign Rosie ever existed.

Mom shakes her head and that hurt is gone. Back to an everything is okay smile. "I miss Rosie, too. I wish she was here. But she's not. She's gone, and keeping her stuff around isn't going to bring her back."

I offer my best smile. This conversation won't go anywhere unless we're honest, and I can tell she's not ready to admit how much it hurts. I'm not sure I'm ready either.

Miles cuts in. "I'm thankful for your hospitality." He smiles, all charm.

"My pleasure," Mom says. She turns to me. "You've really found a nice young man."

I make eye contact with Miles. "He's the perfect boyfriend."

He raises an eyebrow.

"He bought me an N64," I say. "You remember how Rosie and I used to play with ours? The one cousin Jimmy gave us. For a while, she loved racing games."

Mom frowns. "Yes, I remember. I remember a lot about your sister. More than I want to remember." A tear forms in her eye.

I pull together some kind of an apology, some way to connect over how much this hurts.

Nothing comes together. I have no idea what I should say here.

Mom pushes out from the table. "Excuse me, Megara, Miles. I'm developing a headache. I'm going to lie down."

Dad looks at her with concern. She waves like it's fine and makes her way up the stairs. Her steps are calm and even, but I'm pretty sure her hands are shaking.

Miles makes effortless conversation with my father, never missing a beat. It's sports, movies, requests for embarrassing stories about me. After dinner, they take to the TV. Dad flips around channels, eventually settling on a rerun of some kind.

I creep upstairs. If my mom really wants to talk about Rosie, I want to be there with her.

The door to her room is open a sliver. She's sitting on the bed, in the dark, her hands wrapped around a silver frame.

That frame used to be on the wall. One of the family pictures. An old one, when we were kids, before everything went wrong.

There are tears running down her cheeks. They're silent, like she doesn't want anyone to know it hurts.

I grab onto the doorknob, but I can't bring myself to push the door open.

What would I say?

I don't have the answers. I don't have a clue how to handle this.

My grip on the knob releases. Better to go to my room, alone. Better to cry, alone, where I won't hurt anyone else.

A few hours pass. I pull my comforter over my head and read one of my Star Wars books. The words don't make an impact. Everything about this house is suffocating.

My dad goes to sleep. The lights go out. Miles joins me on the bed and wraps his arms around me. He goes right for the gold. His hands slide under my cardigan, tracing the outline of my bra.

"We can get this off now," he says.

The heat rushing through my body is the first pleasant thing I've felt all day, but my parents are three doors down. "Not here."

His lips skim my neck. "You're right." He sinks his teeth into my skin. "No way you can stay quiet."

"I can. But you like it when I'm loud."

"Fuck yes." He runs his fingers over my inner thighs. "There's someplace I want to take you."

"Yeah?"

"You'll like it." He pulls me off the bed. "Of course, you'll be coming so hard you'll barely be aware of your surroundings."

I like it already.

CHAPTER TWENTY-SIX

We take Pacific Coast Highway south to a long, empty street that cuts through the hills. Everything is dark except for the stars and the moon.

I rest my eyes. It's late, and this day stretched on forever. Miles has my head spinning. I don't know which way is up or down. That's enough to drive me mad, but the house, my parents... it's like my sister never existed.

The car slows to a stop. We're at a red light. Miles has that same determined expression. He knows where we're going. He knows what he's doing. He knows exactly what he's getting out of this relationship.

He turns onto a steep, winding road. There's some kind of lab at the top of the hill. We stop just short of it to pull onto a large patch of dirt. It's a makeshift vista point.

Miles turns off the car. "Take a look."

We make our way to the edge of the hill. The quiet suburbs go on forever, this mass of twinkling lights.

The black sky is dotted with stars I've never seen before.

"This was the closest thing we had to a make-out spot in high school," he says.

Miles lived in Irvine for a while. It's only twenty minutes from here. Hell, UCI is barely fifteen minutes from my parents' house.

It would make sense to go to school there. It would save me time, money, effort.

But it would hurt too.

I clear my throat. "Did you... come here a lot?"

"Yeah. But I was always alone."

My tense muscles relax. "Always?"

"Unless someone changed the definition of always so that it means sometimes."

I don't bother with a comeback. There's too much to take in. This place is beautiful, and I'm the first girl Miles has ever brought here. I try not to let it mean anything. My heart thuds against my chest.

I pull my arms over it to keep all the warmth in my body.

Miles slides his arm around my shoulders. "Cold?"

"Yeah."

"Come here." He slides into the backseat, pulling me with him.

His body is close to mine. Inches away. There's just enough light to make out the expression on his face. He looks sad. But I don't know what that means.

He's warm, and he smells good. I need that, need him comforting me.

His fingers skim my chin. He guides me into a kiss. It's soft and sweet, the kind of kiss that should mean I love you. But this one can't.

That's not possible.

I tug at his leather jacket. I need him closer. I need it to mean I love you.

When the kiss breaks, Miles stares into my eyes. "Are you okay?"

I shake my head. He shouldn't ask things like that. He shouldn't act so damn sweet.

"What is it?"

My lungs fail me. My vocal chords fail me. My mouth is sticky and confused. There's no easy way to explain this, but I want to try. "My parents... they erased my sister's existence from the house. It's not right."

"They're trying to cope."

"I know. But that doesn't make it easier."

He runs his hand through my hair. "They care about you. Let them."

I close my eyes. His touch is delicate. His voice is soft. But he's never going to love me and he's better off alone.

I pull back. "Who the hell do you think you are to tell me to let someone care about me?"

He doesn't falter. "Fair enough."

It doesn't bother him. I hate that it doesn't bother him.

His lips skim my neck. Heat surges through me. All I need to do is close my eyes and surrender to his body against mine. It doesn't matter if he'll break my heart later. It doesn't matter that my parents are erasing my sister's existence.

This moment is the only thing that matters.

I lean into his lips. He moves faster, scraping his teeth against my skin, tugging at my cardigan.

"This is all I can offer you," he says.

Every place he touches is on fire, desperate for

more of him, whatever he can offer. "I know."

He pulls my sweater over my head. "You've hurt so much. I can't bring myself to add to that."

His eyes find mine. They're dead serious, and there's such a sweetness to his gaze. He does care about me, even if it's only enough not to completely discard me.

I turn away, staring at the perfect view outside. "Then stop saying things like that. If you care about me, don't act like you're going to fall in love with me."

His voice is even. "Fair enough."

"And that. Stop with that. You have all the cards in this relationship. Stop bragging about how fucking collected you are."

He runs his hands over my shoulders, pulling my bra straps down. "I'm not collected." He unclasps my bra and rubs my nipples. "It's just that all my attention is already focused somewhere else." He takes my hand and slides it over the bulge in his jeans.

My breath catches in my throat. "That's not the same thing."

He pinches my nipples, sending pangs of desire all the way to my toes. My body screams with want. It won't forgive me if I do anything besides touch him.

"I do care about you." He pulls my jeans and panties to my feet in one fell swoop. "But this is the only way I can show you."

"I know."

His fingertips skim my thighs. "Are sure you're okay with that?"

I let my eyes flutter closed. "I have to take it or leave it."

Miles runs his hand over my calf, the inside of my knee, my thigh. "You can leave it."

"I'd believe you if you weren't about to fuck me."

He grabs my knees and arranges me so I'm on top of him. "I can stop. I'd rather not, but I can."

"Don't. I want you to show me how you care about me." I squeeze my eyelids together.

If this really is all Miles can offer, then it has to be enough. I need him to show me how he cares, even if it's with his cock inside me.

He rubs my shoulders, bringing my body onto his. The backseat is too small for two tall people. One of my legs is squeezed between his knee and the seat. The other is skimming the floor.

Miles is three inches from me. He brushes a hair behind my ear. His fingers slide over the curve of my chin. It's soft and sweet, like he loves me.

"You okay?" he asks.

"Show me."

He presses his palm flat against my back. "Look at me."

I pry my eyes open. He's staring at me, staring through me. It's like he can see inside me, see how close I am to crumbling.

"You don't look okay." His voice is just as soft and sweet as his touch.

"Don't pretend it matters to you."

"It does." He wraps his arms around me and holds me close. "You look like you're about to cry."

I press myself up, so we're eye to eye. "Show me, whatever that means, or drive me home."

He holds my gaze. It feels like forever passes, but it can't be more than a minute. Then, his eyes flutter closed, and his lips find mine.

It's the same kiss as before. One that would mean I love you in a normal relationship. His hands slide to my ass, his touch soft and delicate.

We're inches apart. His cock is just under my sex.

He takes my hips and guides me onto him. It's slow and gentle, and then he's all the way inside me.

I plant my hands on his shoulders and bring my body closer. We're face to face. Staring into each other's eyes. He keeps his grip on my hips, guiding my movements to drive his cock deeper inside me.

He stares at me like he loves me.

I close my eyes and press my lips into his. Soft. Sweet. Perfect. Or, it would be, if this whole situation weren't so hopelessly fucked.

He holds me close, shifting into me with a steady rhythm. His lips stay on mine. His tongue explores my mouth. It's gentle and delicate, like he wants more of me.

I kiss him back. I swirl my tongue around his. I rub my body against his. The pleasure builds in that same soft, slow way, until it's too much to take.

Miles breaks the kiss. He stares into my eyes, runs his hand through my hair. His pupils dilate. His fingers dig into my skin.

"Meg…" It's a soft groan, but it's filled with desire.

He keeps things slow. My sex clenches. More. More. More. It feels like it's going on forever, like it's never going to stop.

I press my lips into his, kissing him harder. But, still, he stays slow. He rocks into me. He holds close.

The pressure inside me builds. More. More. More. It's so much. It's too much. An orgasm wells up in me. I moan into his mouth. More. I still need more. I kiss him harder, hold him closer.

Pleasure rocks through me, all the way to my

fingers and toes. But I'm greedy, and I still want more.

I dig my hands into his hair. I squeeze my thighs against his. I rock my hips to meet him.

Miles groans into my mouth. His fingers dig into my skin. He thrusts ever so slightly harder. Pleasure wells up in me again. It's faster this time, more intense.

He breaks the kiss. Stares into my eyes. Nervous energy passes through me. He's inside me. I'm about to come. But the way he's staring at me... I've got no clue what it means.

I stare back. I dig my nails into his shoulders.

Pleasure floods my body. I can't fight it anymore. I cry out as an orgasm spills through me, mixing up all the feelings inside me, so I'm half in ecstasy, half in hell.

He holds me tightly, thrusting into me with that same perfect rhythm. I hold his gaze, groaning as another orgasm builds.

He moans, still holding me tightly, still thrusting into me. A shudder runs through his body. Almost. His teeth sink into his lip.

Still, he moves with that same rhythm, slow and steady. He shakes, harder, harder.

His eyes stay glued to mine. I watch his face contorting. His breath gets heavier. His groans get lower, louder. He squeezes my hips. There. His eyes roll back as he comes.

He rocks into me one last time, and he fills me.

It sends me over the edge again. For a few moments, everything else fades away. I only feel the pleasure coursing through my fingers and toes. I only feel good.

My resolve fades. I collapse my body onto his, trying hard to hold onto everything that feels good.

Miles relaxes into the seat. He squeezes me tighter, holds my body against his.

His heart is pounding against his chest, against my chest. His breath is in my hair. This means something, I'm sure of it. But I've got no clue what that something is.

CHAPTER TWENTY-SEVEN

I wake up alone. No one is home. Dad is at work. No telling where Mom is. Probably, she's as uncomfortable in this house as I am.

There isn't a peep on my phone. No telling where Miles is either.

I eat breakfast with the TV. Even with two hundred channels, there's nothing that can tear my attention away from him. Wherever he is. Whatever he's doing.

I fix a cup of coffee. A second. A third. My mouth goes dry. My fingers shake. It's a lot of caffeine, but it's a nice enough buzz—probably the most pleasant thing I'll feel all day.

I still remember last Thanksgiving. Shit was already bad with Rosie. She was already pretending, already on drugs. But the four-day weekend was a perfect respite. It was the four of us, but really the two of us. We watched movies all night, plowing through the pumpkin pie, the pecan pie, the chocolate pie. There was a lot of pie. We spent the entire day shopping, emptying our checking accounts. And, for the first time since she started dating that awful Jared, it felt like she was my sister and not my enemy. It felt like we were being honest.

She was probably high the whole time.

I push off the couch and inspect the mantel. There are tiny dents in the plaster in all the spots that used to house Rosie's trophies. I was so jealous of those trophies. Rosie had everything—perfect grades, perfect friends, perfect boyfriend. She was athletic, smart, fun.

But with the drugs, she was nothing anymore. All those parts of her disappeared.

The back door slides open.

"Can I skip breakfast and have you instead?" Miles shuts the door. He stands in front of the sleek glass windows, shirtless and dripping with sweat. His eyes meet mine. "You okay?"

"No. I hate it here. I hate everything about this house."

"It will get better."

"How? You don't stay at your uncle's place in Malibu alone. Tell me how it gets better."

"I stay there with you." He moves closer. "You want to join me in the shower?"

I shake my head. I can't handle that right now.

"Talk to me, Meg. I'm here because I want to help you."

"Which is it—do you want to help me or do you want to be alone? Do you care about me or is this strictly sexual?"

His brow furrows. "Suit yourself."

He storms up the stairs and slams the door behind

him.

I want so badly to join him. I want so badly to have my body pressed against his, nothing between us but the running water.

I want to be his plaything. But I need to be his everything.

It's Black Friday. Might as well go shopping. I text Mom, suggesting we meet for dinner at the nearest mall, Fashion Island. We nail down a restaurant and a time. The organic place, seven o'clock.

Leaves most of the day for me and Miles.

He's sitting on the couch, scribbling something in a tiny notebook. Lyrics, probably. Does he have another itch he needs to scratch?

I sit next to him. "We're meeting my parents for dinner at seven at Fashion Island."

"Mhmm."

His eyes stay on the paper. His body is turned away from mine, locking me out.

Deep breath. "You want to go now? We can walk around. Watch the koi swim."

"Sure." He closes his notebook and slides it into his pocket. His eyes turn to me, studying me, picking me apart. "You eat breakfast?"

"Yeah."

"So you won't be cranky?"

"Shut up." I grab my purse and make my way to the door. "You coming or what?"

"Such threats from someone who doesn't have the keys to the car."

"I know how to drive. I choose not to."

"Why not?" He meets me at the door.

There's this tightness in my chest. "I shared a car with Rosie. She used it more, so, when she died, I brought it back here. I can get to work and school fine on foot."

"And it makes you think about her?"

"Yeah."

"That's why your parents put her stuff away." His eyes bore into mine. "It hurt them having it around."

"I know that." I hug my arms to my chest. "But that doesn't make me feel better, admitting I'm a hypocrite."

He leads me to the car.

I settle into the passenger seat. "I want to feel good for a while." I take a deep breath. "Can we not fight or talk about my sister?"

He nods and starts the car.

The mall isn't any more crowded than normal. It's expensive enough that the usual crowd ignores bargains.

After an hour of window shopping, another round of caffeine, and lunch at the food court, I feel a little better.

Miles insists we do more window shopping. He holds my hand, guiding me through the outdoor mall. It's a beautiful day. The sky is bright blue. The sun is shining high. There are barely any clouds.

I move a little closer to Miles. We aren't saying much but we aren't fighting either.

That's something.

I stop at an independent boutique. It was one of Rosie's favorite stores.

The mannequin is wearing a hot pink dress. It

looks just like a dress Rosie used to wear. It's just long enough for work or school, just tight enough for clubs or dates. The neckline is wider, the waist is lower. Otherwise, it's a dead ringer for her favorite dress.

The rack of dresses is in the back of the store. It's in another color, black, something she never wore.

Miles wraps his arms around me. He pulls me into his chest and brings his mouth to my ear. "You're thinking something?"

"Just shopping."

He sucks on my earlobe. "You're not that good at hiding your feelings."

I step forward, breaking his hold. "Nothing important. Just thinking that if my sister was here, she would've made me buy that dress." I nod to the hot pink dress.

"It would look good on you."

"No. I can't wear bright colors."

"Why not?" He moves closer, wrapping his arms around me again.

I lean into him. "I'll stand out."

Miles laughs. "You stand out now. You're gorgeous."

My cheeks flush. "That's sweet of you to say, but it's not true. I'm too tall, too skinny, too flat-chested."

Miles takes my shoulders and turns me around so we're eye to eye. His expression gets mock serious. "One more negative word about your boobs, and I'm dragging you into that dressing room and forcing you to appreciate them."

This pang shoots straight to my sex. He's so good at making me forget everything but how much I want him.

"Maybe we should go to another store," I say.

He shakes his head. "Try on the dress."

"You want me to try on clothing?"

He presses his lips against mine. "I want to think about you naked in that tiny dressing room. Go." He steps away and plants on one of the boyfriend chairs just outside the dressing room.

He's not actually my boyfriend, but I guess the chair doesn't know that.

I take the dress in a few sizes and let myself into a fitting room. While I'm changing, I take in my reflection. I can almost see myself through his eyes, physically, at least. Tall and thin doesn't have to mean gawky. It can mean modelesque. And my boobs might be tiny, but they have a nice shape. He certainly seems to like them.

The dress is flattering. When I pull my hair behind my ears, the way my sister wore hers, I can see the resemblance. It's there in my dark features, my nose, the shape of my lips. She's gone from my parents' house, but she's still there in my face. I still look like her. Whatever they do, they can't take that away.

I step out of the dressing room to show off to Miles, but he's talking to someone else. A woman, around my age. She must be a fan. She has that starstruck look in her eyes.

"I love that song No Way in Hell," she says. "Is it really true it's about falling in love?"

Miles shrugs, effortlessly casual. "My lips are sealed."

My heart pounds. She thinks it's about love, too.

It's not just me.

I run through the lyrics in my head. Damn things are the only clue I have to what Miles feels and they're doing me no good.

His eyes turn to me. "I'm buying you that dress."

"That isn't necessary."

"Already picked out some things to go under it."

The fan blushes madly. She stares at us, dumbstruck, like she just caught Brad Pitt and Angelina Jolie having sex.

I collect my clothes in the dressing room and make my way back to Miles. I like the dress. I'm staying in it. About time I wear something bright.

The fangirl is still watching us, but I don't care. I sit next to Miles, lean in close, and whisper in his ear.

"Is it about falling in love?" I ask.

He stares straight into my eyes, steel expression giving nothing away. "It's about whatever you want it to be about."

"That's not an answer."

"It's the only one you're going to get."

CHAPTER TWENTY-EIGHT

Mom's jaw drops when I walk into the restaurant. Recognition flashes on her face. And then it's there—the pain of losing Rosie. I know how that feels. Some mornings I wake up and think of texting her only to realize I can't.

Some nights I toss and turn, desperate to ask my big sister for advice. But I can't. She's gone.

I know it's wrong to push Mom like this. I should let her grieve her own way, in her own time. But I can't take it anymore. I can't keep pretending.

We're all hiding. Miles hides behind his songs. My parents hide being their perfect image.

And I hide between my schoolwork. I drown myself in my studies in an attempt to escape the grief, but it only hurts worse when I resurface.

I take a seat across from my mother.

She nods a polite hello. "Your dress is lovely. New?"

"Found it today. It was a great deal."

She studies me. Her mouth opens like she's about to speak, but she says nothing. I guess that's a Smart family tradition. Words are always on the tips of our tongues, just barely failing us.

Miles glances at me like I'm a vase he's checking for cracks. His gaze turns back to my parents. "This is a lovely restaurant." Under the table, he takes my hand. "I'm afraid Meg and I need to leave after this."

"Oh?" Mom asks.

"She has a test Tuesday, and I have a deadline."

"What do you do, son?" My dad asks.

"I'm a songwriter." Miles skips over the rock star, sex god part. "Pop, mostly. The rules are strict, but I have fun with it."

"Anything I would know?" Dad asks.

Miles names another few songs. Different ones. Mom's gaze shoots to me. Her mood shifts now that she has something pleasant to latch on to. Her only daughter has a successful boyfriend. Only that's a lie, because I'm the one keeping up appearances.

I let Miles take the spotlight. He's effortlessly charming, begging my parents for stories about my childhood, asking if I was always such an adorable little nerd. He really sells it, really acts like my sweet, calm, loving boyfriend.

This restaurant serves expensive organic food. It usually tastes good, but not today. My tea has no flavor. Even my curry shrimp, a dish that's usually bursting with spice, has no flavor.

Finally, we finish eating. Miles insists on paying the check. My parents pretend to object. They look at me with pride. I've always been the good girl who didn't get into trouble. Future doctor. Perfect grades. Sweet boyfriend. I follow so well in their footsteps, keeping up these fraudulent appearances.

My parents invite us to join them at the wine bar across the street from the mall. We decline.

After some goodbyes and tense hugs, Miles and I leave.

We walk to the car in silence. We drive to my parents' house in silence. Our suitcases are already packed. I guess he thought of everything.

He really is a great boyfriend. Even if that's all a lie to please my parents.

I linger in Rosie's cleaned-out room. The spare room. It's completely transformed. There are no signs of her—no pop princess posters, no touches of bright purple, no ornamental vanity. There's nothing here but a bed and a dresser.

Maybe this is what moving on looks like. Would it be better to keep her room intact, a shrine to a girl who doesn't exist anymore? I don't know.

All I know is that this house is too expansive, too quiet. I'm going to suffocate.

I bring my suitcase downstairs. Miles is sitting on the edge of the couch. His eyes are on mine.

What does that look mean?

I don't know that either. But I do know something. I need to feel better. He's the only person who makes me feel better.

I takes his hands and pull him off the couch.

He leans closer. There's intention in his eyes. There are words on the tip of his tongue.

But he doesn't speak them. He kisses me.

I kiss back. Finally, I feel something. Finally, I taste something. Finally, I need something.

I grind my crotch against his. I dig my hands into his hair. I need him to wipe away everything that hurts.

He pulls back. His eyes find mine. They're filled with concern.

I run my fingertips along his neck. "Fuck me."

"I'm not your distraction."

"Please. I need to feel something good."

I press my lips into his. For a moment, he doesn't kiss back. Then something in him takes over, and his hands are on my ass. His tongue is in my mouth, sliding around mine like he can't bring himself to do anything but fuck me.

Miles breaks the kiss. "Look me in the eyes and tell me it's because you want me and not because you're miserable."

"I want you." Okay, no more playing around. I reach under my dress and slide my underwear to my knees. "I want you coming inside me."

All the resolve on his face fades away. I'm the one affecting him, making him bend to my will.

"What if your parents come home?" he asks.

"They won't. They hate it here as much as I do."

He moves closer, pressing his lips against my neck, his crotch against mine. "Say it again."

"I want you inside me." I lean into his kiss. "I want to feel you come."

He groans. His fingers dig into my hips. He can't control himself any longer. He wants this as badly as I do.

He pins me to the wall, kissing me hard and deep.

I close my eyes. This is a Miles I understand. Every place he touches is on fire, burning away everything that hurts.

His teeth sink into my neck. He unzips my dress and slides it down my shoulders. His hand slides over my bra. I groan and reach for his shoulders, but he grabs my wrists and pins them against the wall.

"Not yet," he growls.

He thrusts his hips into mine. I'm pressed firmly against the wall, no way of moving, nowhere to go, nothing to feel except this.

I turn into his embrace. I rock my body into his.

Miles bites me again. The sting sends waves of pleasure through my body. Everything he does feels so good. It's hard to believe he's ever caused me pain.

He pulls my bra out of the way, exposing my breasts. He groans, sinking his teeth into my neck again.

I push away everything that's been weighing me down until I'm light enough to float. This is my chance to feel good.

This is my chance to be his.

To have him be mine.

I make another move for his back, but his hands are on my wrists almost instantly.

He pins me to the wall again. I arch my back. I rock my hips into his. His erection is pressed against my stomach, and I want more of it. I want to feel him in my hands, my mouth, my sex.

He brings his hand to my chest and draws circles around my nipples, one at a time. I moan. I already need him so badly. He's the only thing that can free me.

"Miles, please."

"Mhmmm."

Every part of my body is begging for his touch, but his hands feel so good on my breasts. I'm an instrument, and I'm tuned to perfection. I lose track of everything but the pleasure. His touch is so light I can barely feel it. Somehow, that makes it more intense

Pleasure shoots through my body. I bite my lip. I rock my crotch into his.

"Please," I groan.

He slides one hand between my legs. Slowly, his fingertips skim my thigh. Then they're on me.

He lets out a low moan. "You're so fucking wet."

He brings his lips back to mine. His kiss is intense but steady. He strokes me again and again. I moan. I shake. I suck on his lips.

But he doesn't relent. My sex pangs. Almost.

I groan into his mouth, kissing him harder. I rock my hips to match his motions. Pleasure pools inside me. Almost. Yes, almost.

He rubs my nipple with his thumb. I can't do anything except moan and kiss him harder.

The pressure inside me builds. It's so much, so intense. I break away from his kiss to cry out.

"Miles," I groan.

An orgasm rushes through me. It's only good, only pleasure. I close my eyes and hold onto it as long as I can. My body is warm, relaxed, free.

My arms fall to my sides. He unhooks my bra and tosses it aside. Then it's my new dress. It's a heap on the floor.

His eyes find mine. They're heavy with lust like he's lost in this, too. Like he needs this as much as I do.

Somewhere deep inside, he hurts. For the next few minutes, I'll be the one to wipe it away.

I pull his shirt over his head and explore his body with my hands. Every inch of him is hard. His skin is warm, soft. It belongs against my fingers.

We belong together. Maybe our hearts and our heads are fucked, but our bodies are perfect together.

He undoes his jeans and kicks them to the floor. His boxers go with them.

He's naked. He's naked, and for now, he's mine.

Miles slides his hand under my thigh and wraps my leg around his waist. "I've never tried this before."

"You say that to all the girls you pin against the wall."

"No." He presses his lips against my neck. "Only you."

He takes my other thigh and wraps that leg around his waist. I'm airborne. I squeeze him with my thighs. I hug his shoulders.

His hands slide to my ass. He pulls me into position. My sex is hovering over his cock. Then we're there. His tip strains against me, teasing me.

I groan.

Is it really possible to need someone this much?

The world clicks into place as he enters me. Hard to believe I ever felt anything but bliss. Hard to believe I could belong anywhere but pressed against Miles.

He holds onto my ass and thrusts into me. He's deep already. He feels good already.

I hold him as tightly as I can, and I surrender to the ride. I press my back and head against the wall to give him leverage, and he thrusts deeper. Deeper.

His nails dig into my ass.

He groans against my mouth, holding me tighter.

"Harder," I breathe. I need more of him. I need all of him.

He moves harder, deeper. I close my eyes and rock my hips to meet him. I bite my lip. I turn my head, offering him my neck.

He runs his lips against my skin. Then it's his teeth. He bites me hard, like he's marking me, like he feels so good he can't help it.

I hug his shoulders. "Harder."

His grip around my hips tightens. He pins me to the wall and he fucks me. No illusions of making love. We're two broken people finding a way to feel good.

I close my eyes, soaking in every bit of pleasure and pain.

Almost. Almost. Almost. The knot inside me builds until I can't take it anymore.

An orgasm rushes through me. It's fast and intense. I have to scream to contain it.

His breath is strained. He grunts, lost in the sensation.

I'm almost there again.

I groan.

He slams my hips into the wall.

One more thrust and all that tension releases inside me. I gasp, clawing at his back, screaming his name over and over.

He holds me steady, rocking into me as I come. His breath gets heavier. His eyelids press together.

He pins me to the wall as he thrusts harder and harder. Then he's there. I can feel his cock pulsing inside me as he comes.

He holds me for a moment then unwraps my legs and sets my feet on the ground.

For a minute, everything is right. We kiss desperately, slowly, like we mean it. Then the kiss breaks and he steps back. We clean up and dress.

There's a shift in the mood. Neither one of us

wants to talk.

I roll my suitcase to the door.

"You ready to go back to L.A.?" he asks.

I shake my head. "No. There's somewhere else I want to go."

"Where?"

"To visit Rosie."

The grass is dry. There's no danger of slipping in my canvas sneakers. I squeeze Miles's hand and make my way to my sister's grave. Just left of the center line, sandwiched between a beloved grandmother and another girl who died way too young.

My hands are empty. No flowers, no trinkets, nothing to offer her. It's silly. I know she isn't here, that her spirit is off in some other plane of existence. But I can almost feel her. She would've hated it here, so dull and drab and totally average.

I sit, cross-legged, on the ground, no concern for the grass stains that might form on my dress. Miles kneels behind me. He wraps his arms around me and leans in close.

"Do you want some time alone?" he asks.

I shake my head. "No, I like your company. Even when you're driving me out of my mind."

"Meg, we're not"

"I know. It's just… you know how this feels. It hurts for such a long time. Then one day you wake up and it doesn't hurt quite as much, and you're not sure how you're supposed to deal with that."

He shifts, melting into me. His breath warms my neck but he says nothing.

I turn my attention to the tombstone. "Rosie

would've warned me about you."

"That right?"

"Absolutely." I play with a blade of grass. My shoulders tense. I roll them back and take a deep breath. It's a little easier. A little softer.

The last few months have been difficult between school and work and Miles making me lose track of which way is up and which way is down. But it doesn't hurt as much anymore. It's a dull ache instead of a crushing pain.

"I'm sorry," I say to someone, maybe Rosie, maybe myself. "I wish I'd stopped running sooner. I should never have let you get away with lying to me. But I understand now, how it starts. It's one lie, one temptation. Then it snowballs into something you can't control." I run my fingers over the tombstone, tracing the letters in her name. "I'm sorry. I love you, and I miss you, and mostly, I forgive you."

My exhale is long and deep. It's like there isn't an ounce of oxygen left in my body. I forgive my sister for lying to me. I forgive my parents for trying to cope. I forgive myself for missing all the signs she was drowning.

I forgive myself for running from the pain. But I'm done running.

The muscles of my back relax. I'm a puddle again, taking shape around Miles. He holds me close, the way he would if he really loved me.

We stay like that for minutes. It's calm, intimate.

Slowly, I push myself to my feet and walk back to the car.

He runs his fingers over my neck. "Hey."

"Hey."

"Look at me."

I turn so we're eye to eye.

"We still have those same terms—no lies?"

"Yeah."

His expression gets serious. "I have to ask you something."

Miles is reminding me about honesty? That's rich, but I guess I can entertain him. "What?"

"Do you have feelings for me?"

CHAPTER TWENTY-NINE

Do I have feelings for Miles? A few come to mind—frustration, confusion, lust. But that's not what he's asking.

He's asking if I love him. If I'm in love with him.

It's hard to breathe. I can't love Miles. He doesn't trust me. He doesn't respect me.

My inhale breaks up the tension in my throat. He plays everything casual. I can do the same.

"Mostly frustration," I say. "That what you mean?"

"You know what I'm asking."

He's staring at me, through me. It's enough to tear me in half. I look to the ground so I don't crumble. Of course I know what he's asking. But I can't answer.

I meet his gaze. "You know enough about my feelings."

"Meg."

"I know where we stand. We're friends who have sex. Nothing more, nothing less."

He studies my expression. Finally, he releases my gaze and gets into the car.

I follow suit.

There's something different about his posture, something serious. I blink and it's gone. He's back to that old Miles, the playful one who lives to tease me.

"I'm falling behind on breaking my orgasm records," he says. "Want to change that this weekend?"

There. The Miles I understand. I nod. "My place or yours?"

"Malibu is too far. I'm taking you to Hollywood." He starts the car. "There are a few places I want to mark as ours."

Tom fixes his gaze on me, eyebrows raised. He's the picture of concern.

Miles pushes the door shut. Shoots a passive aggressive nod in Tom's direction. "What are you doing here?"

"Pete's visiting Cindy in New York. Mom has a date. Says she doesn't want me cunt-blocking her."

Miles chuckles. "Your mom is a bad ass."

Tom nods. "I'm heading back tomorrow morning." His eyes narrow. "We need to speak. Now."

"Later. I have to put Meg to bed. She's very tired."

"No. Now." He offers me an apologetic glance. "We need a little privacy."

"Don't ask my guest to acquiesce to your bullshit."

"You don't want to have this conversation in front of her," Tom says.

The smile drops off Miles's face. He's not having

fun anymore, not playing around.

His voice drops. "Give us a minute."

Tom offers me an apologetic look. "We have cable. Any channel you want. Even the dirty ones."

"I'm good, thanks." The mental image of Tom watching porn on the couch is burned into my brain. Fantastic.

Miles avoids my gaze. His hands are clenched and his jaw is tight.

"My room or yours?" Tom asks.

"Yours."

They move up the stairs with heavy footsteps. Not a fun conversation, I take it. Probably about me. About that secret Tom wouldn't spill and how it spells trouble for my torrid relationship with Miles.

I bite my lip. How can this be so damn important? I take a seat on the couch, attempting to push their conversation out of mind.

It's impossible. I have to know what they're discussing.

I creep up the stairs. Light footsteps, but they still sound so fucking loud. All the doors in the hallway are closed, but there's sound and light coming from one of them. Must be Tom's room.

"It's casual. She understands that," Miles says.

"You just spent Thanksgiving with her."

"So?"

"Then you bring her here for the rest of the weekend." Tom sighs. "How is that casual?"

"Sorry you can't wrap your brain around hanging out with a girl after you've fucked her. I understand, though. Not like any girl ever gave you the chance."

"Get off it, asshole. At least I'm honest about things being no strings attached."

Someone pushes against the door. I shrink backwards. There's nowhere to hide, so I press myself against the wall.

There's no movement from the door. No one is leaving.

Miles starts. "I've got it under control. No spinning out, no relapsing, nothing. I'm as clean as... well, clean isn't your strong suit, so I can't find the perfect metaphor."

"You remember what happened last time you lost someone you cared about?"

"That was my uncle. Not some girl."

My heart thuds against my chest. My mind reels, trying to piece this together to come up with a proper response. I'm not some girl.

Does he really think that?

"You keeping running off, spending weekends by yourself. Or with her. I don't fucking know." Tom's voice is heavy. "She deserves to know what she's dealing with."

"There's no dealing. I've been fine for the last fucking year."

"Yeah? What about after that girl in Detroit?"

"What about her?" Miles snaps.

"Found you face down on your bed next to a half empty bottle of vodka and God, I don't even know what else you took. Only that it was enough you nearly went into a coma. Was that doing well?"

"She threatened to kill herself. That's a sensitive issue for me."

"Are you fucking blind? Even I see it. That girl is crazy about you. What happens when you fuck things up? What if she threatens to kill herself because she can't live without you?"

Relapse. Vodka. Enough drugs to go into a coma. Prescription opiates and alcohol are a dangerous combination.

The words rattle around my brain. Miles could be an alcoholic. A drug addict. But he's so casual about not drinking, and after what I said about Rosie... how much watching that hurt, how much I can't stand being around drugs... he would've told me.

That can't be right.

"Meg isn't like that," Miles says. "She doesn't even drink."

Tom makes that harrumph sound that usually means yeah right.

"It's just sex. That's how she wants it."

"You met her fucking parents!"

"And?"

"You need to tell her you're a drug addict."

"Recovering addict."

My stomach drops. Miles. Is. A. Drug. Addict. Recovering, sure, but still a drug addict. And he didn't fucking tell me.

"I'm not watching you relapse, Miles. I'm not going to spend my nights wondering if you're in some hotel room choking on your own vomit. I'm not going on tour with you in that self-destructive bullshit state."

"I won't."

"You want to be another 'Rock Star Dies of a Drug Overdose' tabloid headline?"

I lose track of their words. The same sentence keeps running through my brain. Miles is a recovering drug addict.

It's a lie of omission.

That night in Malibu, I was crying about my sister,

and he said nothing.

The next day, I asked if there was anything I needed to know, and he said nothing.

He had a million chances to tell me, and every time, he said nothing.

My legs wobble. I hit the floor with a thud. Shit. That's loud.

The door opens and Tom steps into the hall.

He offers his hand. His green eyes fill with a mix of sympathy and concern. "You hear everything?"

I nod. "I need to go home now."

Miles steps out. His face is filled with dread. It's an expression I've never seen on him before. Regret, anguish, something like that.

Maybe he's actually sorry.

"Wait." Miles reaches for me.

"Wait? What for? I'm 'some girl' and this is all casual. What does it matter to you if I leave?"

"Meg…"

"Don't 'Meg' me. We had one rule, and you broke it." I push myself to my feet and take a step back.

They're both staring at me, nervous, like I'm that girl in Detroit who threatened to kill herself.

I could promise my mental fortitude, but screw that, Miles deserves to worry. He deserves the same sinking feeling in his stomach that's in mine.

"Fuck you both," I say. "Don't call me again. And don't write any more songs about me!"

I don't wait for an explanation. There isn't one coming. I turn and rush down the stairs.

Damn. I miss a step. I grab onto the banister, only barely managing to catch my balance.

Someone runs after me. Maybe it's Miles. Maybe it's Tom. But I don't care. My suitcase is in his car.

Screw the suitcase.

I rush down the stairs, grab my purse, and get the hell out of there.

CHAPTER THIRTY

The bus takes forever. All I want to do is scream, but I'm surrounded by strangers. Screaming would get me a quick trip to the police station or maybe the psych ward.

I get off two stops early and walk to my apartment. It's dark. There's nothing around me to keep my attention off that asshole, so I cover my ears with headphones and listen to anything but rock music.

It's cold tonight, but I don't feel it. I'm hot all over. It's like my blood is really boiling. I knew there was bullshit to everything Miles said, but to listen to my story about Rosie and tell me I can talk to him, that I can trust him…

I'm too pissed to take the elevator. I storm up the stairs to my apartment, key in hand. I need to be somewhere else. The hallway is too small. It can't contain the anger welling up in my gut.

Fuck.

He's here. Miles is leaning against my door. At a glance, he's the picture of cool and contained—worn jeans, messy brown hair hanging in front of his piercing blue eyes, hands in the pockets of his leather jacket.

But there are signs of frustration on his face. In his furrowed brow, his heavy eyes, the purse of his lips.

It's not my problem. He had every chance to tell me this. He's the one who caused this frustration.

I hold my ground. "Get out of my way."

He doesn't. He grabs my shoulders and leans in close. "I'm going to explain."

I push past him, sliding my key into the lock. "Explain it to the door."

His grip tightens as he holds me in place. "Listen."

"No."

I reach for the doorknob. He grabs my wrist and holds on tightly.

My heartbeat picks up. My body is confused. It thinks this means he's about to throw me against the wall and rip off my panties. But that isn't happening.

That isn't happening ever again.

His expression is desperate. "I'm not leaving until I explain."

I consider kicking him. A swift knee to the balls would do wonders to push him off. But I can't bring myself to put him out of commission.

I fight his grip. "Let me go."

He does. But then he opens the door and steps inside.

He's in my apartment, like I'm the one who owes him something.

He pulls the door wider. "You coming in?"

"What if I don't?"

"I'll have to chase you wherever you go."

"That sounds annoying."

He motions for me to come inside. "You could save yourself some time here."

I bite my lip. Fine. It might be amusing to see him try and explain his way out of this.

I step inside.

Miles slams the door shut and presses me against it. "Sit down and listen."

"Hard to move when you're pinning me to the wall." I close my eyes. I'm not going down this road again.

"Fair enough." Miles takes a tiny step back. "But I'm not leaving until we discuss this."

"Did the definition of discuss change recently? 'Cause last time I checked, it involves two people exchanging opinions, not one person sitting down and listening."

"Meg."

"Miles." I do sit down, but I'm not necessarily going to listen. "You better make this good. I have to study."

He sighs. "I knew this would happen."

"You mean that lying would blow up in your face? How the hell did you guess that one?"

"That you'd overreact to my recovery."

Acid churns in my stomach. "Fuck you."

"I almost told you that night in Malibu, but I couldn't bring myself to add to your anger."

I stare at the window. There's nothing to see except the dark blue sky. "Take responsibility for your decisions. You didn't tell me because you wanted to fuck me again."

"I could have fucked you right there."

"Fine. Because you wanted this, whatever you call it, to continue."

"Meg."

"No lies, no secrets. That was our deal. But you still kept this a secret."

"I didn't want to upset you."

I try to stay calm. He's smarter than this. He must know he's full of shit.

I stare back at Miles. "You fucked that up. I'm upset."

He has no smart-ass response.

"You don't even respect me enough to admit you lied."

"It's not like that."

"Then look me in the eyes and apologize for keeping this from me."

"You would've ended things."

"That's not an apology." I turn away from him. "You should go."

"Meg—"

"You don't trust me. I don't trust you." My heart is in my throat. I take a deep breath, anything to keep my voice steady. "What the hell are we doing this for?"

His eyes turn towards mine. "I couldn't tell you. It still hurt too much." He slides his hands into his pockets.

"I'm sorry, Miles, but you were so clear yesterday. Today, too. I'm 'some girl' to you. And you want to deal with everything alone. Where the hell is there room for me in that?"

He sighs. "I guess you're right."

My stomach drops. He's not fighting this. Not at all. That's how little I mean to him.

Miles lowers his voice. "We should have ended this earlier. Now, feelings are getting involved."

"Excuse you?"

"Tom was right. The way you're looking at me—"

"Fuck off." I shift so I'm staring right into his eyes. "Feelings are getting involved? Feelings have been involved. What the hell do you call holding me all night? Or promising I can tell you anything? You insisted on meeting my parents. You promised you cared about me. You stared into my eyes and kissed me like you loved me. What the hell do you call that?"

"I didn't mean to lead you on."

He's still so fucking calm.

"Yes, you did," I say. "You get off on me caring about you."

"Meg."

"Do you love me?"

His lips curl into a frown. "I told you when this started—I don't do relationships."

"No, you just treat me like your girlfriend and act like my boyfriend and expect me to know the fucking difference!" I stare through him the way he stares through me. "It doesn't matter. You don't respect me. You throw away my feelings. You lie right to my face. You're nothing to me."

He folds his arms.

"I'm not putting up with it anymore. Go. Away. Now."

"Is that really what you want?"

No. I want him to apologize. To mean it. I want him to convince me he loves me and respects me.

That isn't going to happen. That means he needs to leave.

My breath is choppy, but I fight it. This is the last

thing I need to get out. "Yes."

"Fine." He pulls the door open and steps into the hallway.

And he's gone.

CHAPTER THIRTY-ONE

I spend the weekend staring at my textbooks. I make a hundred flash cards and go through them a hundred times. I rewrite all my notes with my favorite purple pen.

I absorb nothing.

I try to sleep, but whenever I close my eyes, I see Miles. I see that look on his face, that desperation and pain that he's so sure he wants to handle alone. He lied a million times and he's still the only thing I can think about.

This is the end. Miles and I are over, forever, the end. Hell, we were never anything worth discussing. Not really.

It's better this way. He can go bullshit some other girl. I can focus all my attention on medical school. A guy would only get in the way.

Miles would only get in the way.

"Honey, you look like hell." Kara plops in the seat next to mine. "But you know I've got you covered."

She pulls a can of green tea out of her purse.

Sweet, sweet caffeine. Class is going to start in five minutes, and I need every ounce of attention I have for the lecture.

I press the can against my chest. The aluminum is so cold, and I've been hot all weekend. I don't know if it's anger, frustration, or the damn flu.

"I'm guessing your parents were difficult," she says.

"They put everything in Rosie's room in storage."

"That sucks."

"And her trophies. The family pictures. It's all gone. Everything. It's like being in some stranger's house with some stranger's parents." I pop open the can and take a greedy sip. I've learned plenty about caffeine—it takes twenty minutes to absorb into the bloodstream—but I feel like it's going straight to my brain. "Thanks. How was your weekend?"

"Saw my mom. Ate some food. Nothing worth discussing." A frown creeps onto her face.

There's something worth discussing. "We could talk about it anyway."

Kara turns to me. She's about to say something when Professor Rivers walks into the room. All chatter ceases.

She whispers, "I'd rather talk about you and Miles."

I nod to the professor.

Kara shakes her head. She opens her notebook and scribbles a message: Something happened, something bad. I can tell from the look on your face. You don't have to pretend you're fine. Whatever it was, you don't have to deal with it yourself. I want to help, even if that means watching Star Wars fifty times.

I nod and mouth thank you. Kara raises her eyebrows, a real talk to me now dammit kind of look.

I motion to the professor.

"This is an elective for you," she says.

"And I need to maintain a good GPA."

"Your senior-year GPA won't factor into your med school apps."

"If I apply this year," I say.

"Since when are you even considering a gap year?"

The guy sitting next to me slaps my desk. He leans in towards Kara and me. "Could you two please shut up?"

Kara flips him off. I suppress a smile. She really is a great friend.

She picks up her pen and scribbles something else.

You can't keep dodging a conversation with me. What are you hiding from?

"Nothing," I say.

"Hey! Quiet," the guy says.

Kara turns the page, writes FUCK YOU, and holds it up to the guy.

"Want me to call Professor Rivers?" he asks.

She rolls her eyes.

"We can talk after class," I say.

"Then, after class, you say you need to study, and you disappear, and you cancel our brunch date to avoid this damn conversation."

"I won't do that."

The guy leans in. "Would you please shut your big mouths?"

Kara snaps. "Hey! My best friend and I are going

through something. So why don't you mind your own damn business?"

A few students around us turn. Even the professor notices. His eyes go straight to Kara.

"I know it's tough to come back after a break, but let's get our eyes on the screen, huh?" He presses a button to change to the next slide.

Kara tears a sheet of paper from her notebook. She fishes through her bag, pulls out a pen, and slams it on my desk.

Write it down if you have to, but tell me why you look like hell. It's not just about your parents and your sister. It's more than that.

She mouths now.

I scribble on the paper: I don't want to talk about it.

She writes: At least tell me what happened with Miles.

Fine. I write two words: It's over.

"More than that," she whispers.

"That's it."

"That's obviously not it, but fine. This is the friendship you want to have—that's what we'll have."

The annoying guy leans in, but she cuts him off.

"I'm fucking leaving, okay?" Kara shoves her things into her bag, pushes out of her seat, and makes for the door.

She's leaving ten minutes into class.

Screw it. I shove my stuff into my bag and follow Kara out the door.

There are a few students in the hallway, staring at their books, but it's otherwise empty.

I follow Kara towards the front door. "I don't want to talk about Miles, but we can still talk about other stuff."

She pushes the door open and plops on the nearest bench.

I sit next to her, resting my head on her shoulder. "I don't want to fight."

"Me either," she says.

"I'm sorry I've been distant."

"It's okay," she says. "I have a lot of stuff to deal with the next two weeks. Then it's finals. We can meet up after that and watch some dumb movie and eat too much popcorn." Kara shifts so she's looking at me. "If you want to talk, I'm here. Any time, day or night, okay?"

I nod.

"Is there any chance you're going to call me?"

"It's possible."

Kara squeezes me. "Promise anyway."

"I promise."

By the weekend, my concentration is back. I spend all day Saturday studying. It's about time for a break when there's a knock on the door.

My heart thuds against my chest. For a split second, I'm face to face with that awful feeling—hope.

I push it away. There's no way it's Miles.

I get up and open the door. It's Kara.

She brandishes a takeout bag. "I brought sushi. I know it's not as good as a hot, rock star boyfriend, but there are about four orders of salmon sashimi." She sets the bag on the counter and fixes two plates.

"What are you doing here?" I ask.

"You're my best friend. I need a break. You're

moping. Adds up to us going out." She looks at me. "Did you eat dinner?"

"It's still early."

"It's almost ten." She sets a can of green tea on the counter and motions to it. "You have soy sauce?"

"In the fridge. But you know I eat my sashimi plain."

"Yes, but I'm not as hardcore as you are." She grabs soy sauce and drowns her sushi in it.

"Shouldn't we talk or something?"

"You want to talk about Miles?"

I pick up a piece of salmon sashimi with my chopsticks. "Not really."

"Do you want to think about him?"

"Never again."

She smiles. "I was hoping you'd say that." She grabs a fork and stabs a California roll. "Because I have the perfect way to turn off your brain cells. Alcohol optional."

"I'm terrified."

"You'll like it. Promise."

"Are you going to tell me?"

"Agree to do it first." She stares me right in the eyes. "You need to feel better."

I take a deep breath. I really do trust Kara, and I really don't want to think about Miles. "Okay."

Her eyes light up. "We're going dancing."

"I hate dancing."

"You think you hate dancing because you sit in the corner by yourself." She takes a long sip of her tea. "But tonight, you're going to grab the hottest guy you can find, and you're going to get back in touch with what your body wants."

"I'm not screwing some random guy."

"Just dancing. It's a great release."

"I don't know." A release sounds amazing. And I love the idea of house music drowning out every thought in my head. But I'm not keen on random guys in clubs. "I don't want a stranger touching me."

"Then dance with me." She scoops sashimi on my plate and motions eat. "But I'm not leaving you alone tonight. You need to let off some steam, and I need to make sure my best friend is okay."

"Drew didn't take my place?"

"In his dreams."

CHAPTER THIRTY-TWO

The club is packed to the brim. There must be two hundred people on the dance floor. It's a mix of tourists and locals, celebrities and ordinary people, the barely legal and the pushing forty.

The crowd has one thing in common—amazing style. The guys are in suits. The women are in tight cocktail dresses and shiny heels.

Kara locks arms with me. "Let's start with a drink. If you want."

My shoulders tense. I roll them back, but it does nothing to relax them. Deep breath. I'm twenty-one. Drinking is normal. Fun. Maybe the only way I'll actually allow myself to dance with a stranger. "Yeah. I do."

"You sure?"

"Positive."

Kara leans over the bar, squeezing her arms together to highlight her cleavage. The bartender notices instantly.

"What are you drinking?" He stares at her chest.

"A paloma for my friend. Actually, two palomas." She turns to me. "It's like a grapefruit margarita. You'll adore it."

My heart flutters. "Okay."

I scan the room. There's a VIP area in one corner. I can just make out a few famous faces—a singer known for her outlandish costumes and the stars of this awful teen soap I totally never, ever watche

"Here you go, ladies." The bartender offers up our drinks.

Kara pays and she drags me to a velvet booth. It's plush and soft and there's a curtain in front. I pull the curtain closed, and suddenly we're hidden from view. It goes to just past our knees and it blocks out the rest of the club.

They're sex curtains.

Kara pulls the curtain wide open. "Don't get any ideas." She sips her frothy pink drink. "Shit, you really are going to love this."

I take a sip. It's amazing—tart and sweet with the faint taste of alcohol. My face flushes. I already feel more relaxed.

"I want fifty of these," I say.

"Going from zero to drunk pretty fast there." She slides her arm around my shoulder. "But I get it. You don't want to think about that asshole, but not all your brain cells are cooperating."

"They can either assimilate or be destroyed."

Kara laughs. "I missed this Meg."

"Me too."

She downs half her drink. She looks at me like she's reading a gauge. "I see a few hot guys, and they look lonely. Want to fix that?"

I polish off my drink, stand, and smooth my dress. "Well, we can't have lonely, hot guys."

We move to the dance floor.

There's barely any wiggle room. I've never been a big dancer, but there's something intoxicating about the thumping music and the soft blue-purple lighting. I throw my arms over my head and sway my hips in time with the beat.

Kara laughs. She drags me farther into the fray. We dance like we're the only two people here. I look around the club. It's built just like the place where Sinful Serenade had their secret show, only with a smaller stage and more room to sit.

The music fades into the next song. I circle my hips and roll my shoulders. Usually, I feel so insecure about my dancing. But tonight, anything goes.

A cute guy comes up to me. He's wearing a gray suit, and he's a little stiff. A total Business Guy. He motions as if to ask me to dance. I look back to Kara. She mouths go for it. So I do.

I press my back against his chest. He grabs my hips, holding my body against his. I close my eyes, trying to inhale the sensation, but there's nothing there. It doesn't hold a candle to Miles.

I turn around so I'm facing Business Guy. He's cute. Nice eyes, clean haircut. I slide my arms around his shoulders. He moves his hands to my waist.

He really is handsome. And he smells good. His body is hard. Not his cock—I'm not that close—but his arms and his chest.

He's safe, comfortable. I'm not going to fall in love with him. It could be one easy night.

He leans closer, his mouth a few inches below my ear. He's quite a bit shorter than I am, and I'm wearing three-inch heels.

"Can I buy you a drink?" he asks.

"Yeah." I wave goodbye to Kara—she's already dancing with a jock—and follow Business Guy to the bar.

He slides his hand around my waist and over my hip. It's a little much so soon, but there's something nice about his touch. Not electrifying. Just nice.

"I'm Johnathan," he says.

"Meg."

"What are you drinking, Meg?"

"Paloma."

He signals the bartender and orders our drinks. Whiskey on the rocks for him. Paloma for me. Figures I'm drinking something girly and pink.

I take another look at Business Guy. Johnathan. He is cute. And he seems nice enough. He probably owns his own house. Not a mansion in Malibu, but a modest house somewhere nice. He'd probably take me to breakfast in the morning then never call me again.

The bartender arrives. Drinks are ready. Johnathan hands the pink one to me and raises his glass to toast.

Whatever. I'll toast. To all the lonely people in the club.

He scans my body. It's sexy when Miles looks me over, but this is awkward. I pull my arm over my chest. I don't want Johnathan picturing me naked.

"Do you go to school around here?" he asks.

"UCLA."

"Let me guess your major."

Oh, lord. I take a long sip of my drink and nod politely. He bought me this amazing grapefruit concoction. I'll entertain his guessing game.

"Sure," I say.

He scratches his chin. "There's something intellectual about you."

Yeah, I look really intellectual in this tight silver dress. Does he use this line on every girl he meets, or just the ones who strike him as gullible?

I take another sip. It's perfection. I guess I can entertain him for another thirty seconds. "Is there?"

"Yeah... I can see you curled up in bed with a good book."

"What kind of book?"

He smiles. "History."

My drink is empty, but the good news is that my head is spinning. There's something amusing about Johnathan. It's been a while since I've been tipsy, but I'm sure it's the alcohol talking.

"Excuse me." A familiar voice cuts through the room.

And Miles steps in between me and Business Guy. Johnathan. What the hell is Miles doing here?

"You mind, buddy?" Johnathan says.

"I do, actually." Miles plants his hand on my hip. "Since when do you drink?"

"Since tonight." I swat him away like my body isn't humming from his touch. "I'm having a conversation."

"You don't seem interested," Miles says.

"None of your business what I seem anymore. Excuse me." I step away from Miles and lean over the bar the same way Kara did. "Another paloma please!"

"How many have you had?" Miles asks.

"Oh, let me check. Hmmm. That's also not your business."

"I'm talking to the lady," Johnathan says.

Miles turns and glares like he's going to deck Johnathan right in the mouth. It works.

Johnathan steps back. He mutters something under his breath and disappears into the crowd.

Miles brings my attention back to me. "What the hell are you doing?"

"You're the one who followed me here. What, did Kara rat me out to you?"

"Drew."

"Asshole acted like he could keep a secret." I shake my head. "Did he at least tell you to apologize?"

Miles nods. "Threatened to break my jaw if I broke your heart."

"I knew there was something I liked about him."

Miles reaches for my hand.

I take a step back. "Last time I checked, we're nothing. So what the hell are you doing following me to clubs?"

"I wanted to see you."

"To what—screw with me one last time? Leave me alone."

He leans closer, until his chest is pressed against my back. "I can't."

"Sure you can. It's called self-control. You made yourself clear a hundred times. You don't do boyfriend. You don't fall in love. Hell, you want to be alone. You didn't have any right to scare that guy off."

"You'd rather he be the one pressed against you?"

I bite my tongue. "Doesn't matter. We're nothing."

His mouth hovers over my ear. "I miss you."

"You miss fucking me."

"No, I miss you." He digs his fingers into my hips and pulls my body closer. "Let's talk somewhere private."

"Oh, you want to talk now that you can't have me." I press my palms against his hips. I mean to push him away, but my hands like his hips so much they linger there. "You had a million chances to talk. I'm not interested in talking to you anymore."

"But you'd fuck me."

I stare into Miles's eyes. As usual, he's unflinching. Staring through me like he's untouchable.

Heat surges inside me. I'd certainly like to fuck him. His body already feels so damn good.

"Yes," I say. "I'd do it right here."

"Are you drunk?"

"Not yet."

Right on cue, the bartender drops off my drink. Miles pulls a twenty from his wallet, slams it on the bar, and waves the bartender away.

I grab my drink and make a move for the booths. Miles follows, but I ignore him.

I take a seat and wrap my lips around the straw. It's just as sweet and tart as my first drink, but this time I'm much more desperate for the release from my inhibitions. There's this nasty bit of politeness in my brain keeping me from telling Miles exactly what an asshole he is.

Miles sits next to me. He's wearing Converse, jeans, and a t-shirt. Even his clothes are cool and casual.

I down half my drink. "Can I help you somehow?"

"I should have told you about my recovery."

"Hmm, so close to an apology, yet something is missing."

His eyes find mine. "I'm sorry I kept that from you."

I finish my drink and slam it on the table. "I

appreciate the apology, but it's not enough."

"Meg." His voice is low, desperate. He pulls the curtain closed so we're hidden from view.

"You're playing a game, but nothing has changed. You don't respect me. You don't love me. You don't trust me."

He pushes a stray hair behind my ear. "I respect you."

"And the other two?"

"I don't know." He traces the outline of my collarbone. "I've never done the other two before."

His fingertips skim the neckline of my dress. My body buzzes with want. He feels so much better than Business Guy. He feels so much better than anything.

"Let me take you somewhere quiet," he says.

I squeeze my thighs together. "I don't want to talk."

He pulls the strap of my dress aside and slips his hand into my bra. "I do."

I bite my lip. "You're not exactly encouraging conversation."

He rubs my nipple. "Is this really all you want from me?"

His eyes meet mine. There's a desperation in his expression. He means this. He wants more from me, more than sex.

But I'm not so sure.

His hand works its magic on my breast. Damn, he's good at this. Want builds in my core.

I need Miles. Now.

His eyes light up. He knows he's driving me out of my fucking mind.

"Will someone see?" I ask.

"No." He rubs me with his thumb. "Would you

care if they did?"

Right now, I don't care about anything but him touching me. I only barely manage to shake my head.

Miles leans closer. "Answer me. Please. Is this really all you want from me?"

His lips are inches from mine. I close my eyes and kiss him. He's soft and warm, and he tastes like Miles. Like coming home.

"No," I breathe. "But I'm never going to get what I want from you."

"What makes you so sure?"

I copy his words, the ones he used to explain why he was so sure he'd never fall in love. "I just know."

He drags his thumb over my nipple, sending pangs of lust to ever corner of my body.

My breath hitches in my throat. "There must be two hundred people here."

"I know." He slides his hand between my thighs. "But I'm not leaving until I hear you come."

"Miles." A groan escapes my lips.

"That's a start." He unhooks my bra.

Then his hands are on my panties. He doesn't waste any time. He pulls them to my knees and runs his fingertips over my clit.

I bite my lip to keep from screaming. God, I missed this. I missed him. I missed everything.

I press my lips into Miles's. He kisses back hard like he's claiming me as his. My head is swimming. This is wrong, this is dangerous, but this is so fucking good.

He pulls me onto his lap. I plant my knees on the bench, straddling him.

I sink into his body. He's hard. I need that.

I tug at his t-shirt. "Let's go someplace quiet. Like

you said."

His breath is warm on my neck. His fingertips are light on my thighs. "Hmm… Let me check. Have I heard you come yet?"

I shake my head.

He smiles. "Then I'm not leaving yet."

With the curtain closed, we're out of view. Still, it feels naughty and dangerous, undressing in public.

It's exciting.

All those awful you shouldn't do this thoughts swirl around my brain, but in my inebriated state, they simply fly away. This is far from my best idea. Someone might see. Miles might think I forgive him. That this means I'm his.

I still don't know if I can be his for the long haul. But for tonight, it's perfect.

His touch is gentle as he strokes me. I kiss him hard, digging my nails into his shoulders.

The noise around us fades. I'm on top of the fucking world.

This is easy.

Life is easy.

Being with him is easy.

My body fills with pleasure. It spreads from my core all the way to my fingers and toes.

He strokes me with an even rhythm. Again, and again, and again. An orgasm wells up inside me. It's so tight, so tense, so fucking amazing.

I bring my mouth to his ear and moan his name again and again. A wave of pleasure washes over me. Every bit of tension in my body releases.

It feels so fucking good.

He kisses me. I sink into him, my chest against him, my thighs against his. I can still feel him—hard through his jeans.

I grind my crotch against his. "Fuck me. Please."

His eyes are heavy with desire. "I fucking missed you." He tugs at my dress, exposing my breasts. He flings my bra aside. "I'm been going out of my mind thinking about you."

"Like this?"

He pulls my dress lower. "Like everything." He grabs my hips and lifts me. "This is going to be quicker than I'd like."

"I don't care." I shift closer to him. "As long as you're inside me."

"Mhmm." He unzips his jeans, shoves his boxers aside, and wraps his hand around his cock.

Yes, please. I shift my hips so I'm hovering over him. He grabs me, bringing me down hard.

I gasp as Miles enters me. It's like coming home, like I'm exactly where I need to be. I grab his shoulders and shift over him, pushing him deeper.

He sinks his nails into my ass, guiding me. His eyes find mine. He's staring at me, through me. Before, it was too much. But it feels right. I see him, everything inside him. He's not honest yet, not mine yet, but maybe we can get there.

He presses his palm against my back, bringing my breasts to his mouth. His lips close around my nipple.

Pleasure floods my body. He's so much better than I remembered. He's perfect.

He sucks on me as he fucks me. I squeeze my thighs, pressing my hands against his shoulders for leverage. My body screams. I never want this to end. Never.

I dig my hands into his hair, holding him close. Everything else about this relationship is a mess, but this is perfect.

Here, we're perfect.

I groan, arching my back to push him deeper. My heart thuds. My breath is strained. Pleasure wells up inside me again. It's so tense, so tight, so much.

Miles sinks his teeth into my nipple, a tiny hint of pain. Then his eyes are on mine. He's looking at me like he loves me. I almost believe him.

I arch until he's deeper, until he's as deep as he'll go. One more thrust, one more tug at the knot inside me, and an orgasm washes over me. It's harder, more intense, and it takes everything I have to resist screaming his name.

Miles claws at my back. He holds my body against his as he thrusts into me.

He lets out a heavy moan.

He groans and shakes and scrapes his nails against my skin.

He's about to come. I can feel it in his body, hear it in his voice. Pressure wells up in me again. I'm making him come. I'm bringing him all this pleasure.

"Mhmm."

He holds me against him as he fucks me. It's hard and fast. I have to squeeze his shoulders to stay upright.

Then he's there. His cock pulses, filling me.

He collapses, sinking into the bench seat.

His eyes find mine. His lips part like he's going to speak, but he says nothing.

I shift off him, find my underwear, and pull it on. There's no way to clean up. This will have to do.

There's no sign of my bra. Oh well. It was nothing special.

He reaches for my wrist. "Come home with me."

"That's not a good idea."

"Then tell me what this was."

"I don't know." I find my purse and slide it over my shoulder. "But I enjoyed it."

"Go somewhere with me."

My heart flutters. "Where?"

"It's a surprise." He runs his fingertips over my wrist. "I'll fuck you there. If you're still in the mood."

"That's not a good idea, either."

He stares right into my eyes. "There has to be some way I can convince you."

That look cuts straight to my soul. No matter what I do, I can't fight it. I still want to take all his pain away.

I swallow hard. "Okay. I'll go."

CHAPTER THIRTY-THREE

The night air rushes around me. Damn, that cold has bite. Southern California afternoons are sunny and warm. It's easy to forget the temperature plummets on winter nights.

Goosebumps spread across my arms. I shiver and hug my chest. A cocktail dress isn't the warmest attire.

Miles slides his leather jacket off and slings it around my shoulders. He pulls me closer. "I guess that means your buzz is wearing off."

I don't laugh. I don't know what that's supposed to mean.

Or what the hell this trip is supposed to mean.

My high heels poke tiny holes in the grass. I try my best to lean forward, weight on my toes, but one of the heels gets stuck. I trip.

Miles catches me. He saves me from scraping my knee on one of the grey tombstones.

Yes, we're at the cemetery, the one in Ladera Heights. It's too dark to see most of the place, but I still make out a large stone crucifix and a statue of the Virgin Mary.

It's funny. There's a mall four blocks away. To my left is the somber remembrance of death. To my right, there's a Target and a Forever 21 and a parking lot with bright white lights.

Miles kneels down next to me and gingerly unhooks my shoes, one at a time. He pulls them off my feet, his fingertips lingering on my ankle.

It should be criminal for anything to feel this good. Especially in a place where everything usually feels so bad.

"You okay?" he asks.

"Not really dressed for mourning."

"I disagree." He takes my shoes with one hand and holds me close with the other. "You're celebrating life. Death is just another part of that cycle." His eyes find mine. "You know that tattoo on my chest."

"I'd love to be reminded."

He pulls his t-shirt down, exposing his gorgeous, perfect pectoral muscles. There it is—be brave, live—in thick black letters.

"I always that it was a little new age for you," I say.

"It's a recovery thing. A reminder to experience life instead of trying to numb myself to anything that might hurt."

It's a nice sentiment, but I don't see how it's relevant to the discussion at hand. If there's even a discussion. This is more like show and tell. Miles shows, and Miles tells, and I can take it or leave it.

He studies my reaction. Runs his fingers over my cheek to my chin, tilting me so we're eye to eye. Those blue eyes of his are so damn earnest.

"I know you hate when people are cryptic," he

says.

"Accurate."

"But give me a minute." He brings his hand to my lower back and leads me down another row.

We walk for a few more moments and Miles stops in front of a plain gray tombstone. Damon Webb. Father, Uncle, Friend. He died last year, just like Miles said.

"He adopted me legally after my mom died. I took his name instead of my dad's," Miles explains. He sets my shoes on the ground, turns to face me, and takes my hands. "The quote. It's cheesy. But it was something my uncle always said when I started causing trouble. He saw right through my bullshit. When I got suspended for getting into a fight, he'd sit me down on that leather couch and toss a bag of frozen peas in my hands. Then he'd kneel next to me, stare into my eyes, and he'd tell me that if I wanted to run, I'd be running forever."

"Yeah?"

"Yeah, he was a smart guy. Self-made fortune, knew all the business stuff that bored me to tears. He knew how I felt losing my mom, especially to suicide. It hurt him, too. He was angry, too. But I got into fights every week. I got suspended fifteen times. I broke all my guitars."

I suck in a deep breath. I want to trust Miles but I'm not sure I'm ready to let my guard down again. Not yet.

Still, we were friends, or something close to that. I want to be there for him right now. Maybe not tomorrow, or next week, but right now.

He squeezes my hands. "After my twentieth fight, we made a deal. He'd buy me one more guitar if I agreed to be brave and confront how much it hurt to lose my mom. I could wail on that guitar all day. I could scream my lungs out, write a song that was nothing but 'Fuck Simon.' That was my father's name. But if I got in trouble, even one more time, that was it. I was going to boarding school."

"And?"

"And that was it. I wrote a song about it. I felt a little better. Every time I wanted to hit someone, I wrote a song instead."

I hug my chest. "How did you start doing drugs?"

"It wasn't a problem at first. Or at least I didn't think it was. I liked the way it relaxed me. Made me calm. Made me feel like I didn't have to take on the world. But it became a habit. Tom confronted me. I slowed down enough that I could hide it. But when Damon got cancer... I freaked. Ran from it. I couldn't go five minutes sober. Couldn't deal with those thoughts." He rubs my shoulders. "That's how I know you're strong, Meg. You confront your pain headfirst. You never come close to buckling."

"I can't say that anyone has ever complimented me for not doing drugs before." I laugh.

"I really do love your laugh."

"I love yours too." I really do.

He shifts back to the serious tone. "I only stopped because Tom threatened to kick me out of the band, and I didn't want my uncle to die thinking I was that same stupid kid who kept running away."

My heart pounds against my chest. Miles went through so much.

Be brave, live.

This isn't the kind of pain that goes away with a few hugs and kisses. I can't take away his. He can't take away mine. We're both stuck until we find our way out.

He lowers his voice to a whisper. "I was in rehab when he died. That was the part that hurt the most, that he was alone because I was kept stewing in self-pity."

"But you weren't stewing anymore. You were confronting it head on."

"Yeah. Maybe." He slides a hand through his hair. "I'm sorry I didn't tell you about my recovery. At first, I didn't think this would be serious enough it would matter. By the time I realized how much you hurt, how much you've been through, I wasn't afraid I'd lose you if I told you."

I hug myself a little tighter. "Okay."

"It's not a good excuse. I was wrong. And I really am sorry."

"Thank you." I stare into Miles's eyes, at all the pain I can't take away. I want to forgive him, I do. But my heart isn't there yet.

"I like you, Meg. I really do. And I'm pretty sure you like me, too."

"I do, but—"

"No but." He takes my hands and pulls my body into his. "That's all we need to know."

He's warm, and it feels damn good being pressed against him. But that tension is still in my chest.

I take a step backwards. "I'm sorry. I understand why you lied, but I'm not sure I'm ready to trust you yet. I want to. But it's not there right now. I don't feel it."

"Could you?"

"I don't know. But Miles, I want to be with someone who loves me, who wants to share his feelings with me because he loves me and trusts me, and not because it's the only way he can win me over."

He considers my words like they're poetry. "I can do that."

"Maybe. But it doesn't feel like it to me." I pull the jacket tight around my chest. The neighboring street is wide and clean and completely empty. "Can you take me home?"

"Yeah." He presses his palm into the small of my back. "I really am sorry."

"Me too."

In more ways than one.

Miles still has my suitcase in his trunk. He brings it all the way to my apartment door.

"I'd like to come in," he says.

I shake my head. "I'm not up for that... any of that right now." I fiddle with my key. "Finals start Monday. I've got to turn everything off so I can study."

He nods. "When are you done?"

"The twelfth."

"I'll see you on the twelfth."

He slides his hands around my waist, pulls my body into his, and kisses me. Heat floods my body. It's sweet and hot and delicate all at once.

I slide his leather jacket off my arms and try to hand it over.

He waves it away. "I want you to keep it."

I nod.

"Bye, Meg."

"Bye."

I don't breathe properly until I hear the elevator doors shut behind him.

CHAPTER THIRTY-FOUR

Finals fly by in a sticky mess of anxiety. After our last test, Kara and I crash on her couch and take turns picking movies to marathon. Sometime around midnight, I turn my phone on.

It's been a week since I've seen anything but my school email.

The screen flashes on. Those little bars appear next to the connection icon. Notifications pop up—a dozen new text messages and one voicemail.

I check the texts. Mostly little things—one from my mom about vacation, one from Kara, a bunch from the people in my study group.

The voicemail is from Miles.

Kara can read the look on my face. "Put it on speaker?"

"Okay." I'm going to need someone to talk me down.

I tap the play button. There's a burst of static, then it's Miles.

"Hey, Meg. I know you asked me, well screamed at me as you were rushing out of the house, not to write any more songs about you. But I couldn't abide by those terms. This might not make it on the album, but the single is going live Tuesday. It will be everywhere. This is the acoustic version. Drew would cringe if he heard my attempt at his guitar solo, but you'll get the idea."

My heart collects in my throat. A song. He wrote another song about me.

It's what he does when he doesn't want to run away from his feelings.

There's the strum of a guitar. It's a pleasant melody, but it stirs up something inside of me. Something uncomfortable. I go to delete the message, but Kara grabs the phone.

"No chance." She climbs on top of the couch to hold the phone over my head.

It's all over.
I'm ga-ga out of my head,
one of those idiots
I always made fun of.

Everyone said, "boy can't you see
that girl is crazy about you."
Just shook my head.
"No way, not her, she's even
as the number two."

His voice is heavy, but there's something sweet about it, too.

It's all over.

That flutter in my chest.
Love, funny word,
what the hell does it mean?

Everyone said, "boy can't you see
that girl is crazy about you."
Just shook my head
"No way, not her, she's even
as the number two."

Air escapes my lungs. It's perfect.

It's all over.
I surrender.
First time I ever have.

"Holy shit." Kara's jaw drops. "I was waiting to show you this." She jumps to her computer and pulls up a gossip site. "In case you never wanted to hear another word about him."

She turns the screen so it's facing me. Sinful Serenade Singer Gets Hot New Tattoo. There's a picture of Miles beneath it, shirtless, of course, and right above his chest, opposite Be Brave, Live, reads Megara.

Holy shit.

I try a deep breath. Nothing is happening. My stomach flip-flops. I'm queasy. He got my name as a tattoo. He got my name as a tattoo. My name. Tattoo.

"There's more." Kara points to the middle of the article.

When reached for comment, Miles Webb had one of his trademark cheeky replies.

"I made a deal with this friend of mine that if I

ever fell in love with someone, I'd get her name tattooed on my chest. What can I say? I'm a man of my word."

We asked how he felt this would affect his reputation for extracurricular activities (let's face it— the man is a slut!) and he laughed right in our faces, well, right into our cell phones.

"I doubt it will be any harder to take home women. I mean, look at me. But I don't care about other women. The only woman I want is Meg. If she won't have me, then I'll be alone. No one else could ever compare to her."

Kara grabs my shoulders, turning me so we're face to face. "You okay? You want me to beat him up and smash every computer that ever saw a fragment of the MP3 of that song?"

I shake my head.

"Talk to me, sweetie."

"He loves me."

"Yeah, I'm pretty sure he does," she says.

"He's so… how the hell do I respond to this?"

She smiles. "I have an idea."

CHAPTER THIRTY-FIVE

Kara presses her phone to her ear. She paces around the apartment shaking her head. She's totally frantic.

"How are you not freaking out?" she asks.

"It's a lot to take in. I'm not sure how I feel."

She shakes her head and throws her phone onto the couch. "Drew isn't picking up. But they're probably at the house."

"It's almost one a.m."

"And the guy you love sent you a declaration. This is no time to wait!" She grabs her backpack and nearly tears it apart in search of her keys and wallet. "You okay wearing that?"

I look at my finals outfit. It's jeans and a t-shirt, not the thing of romantic declarations. I should throw on a princess dress and heels, something that would look as dramatic as this feels.

"Fuck it, wear that or I'm dressing you. You have five seconds to decide," she says.

"Will it be slutty?"

"Three seconds."

"Okay, dress me. No. It doesn't matter. Let's just go."

"Good thinking." She lunges for her phone, wraps her hand around my wrist, and nearly drags me outside. "I wish you could drive stick. I'm so nervous for you."

My heart thuds against my chest. My head is still swimming. Miles loves me. He trusts me. He respects me. This is everything I want.

"I'm so nervous for me," I say.

She fumbles with the lock. Checks the door twice. Then she drags me to her car.

Kara drives like a maniac. She breezes through yellow lights on her way to the freeway. She's at seventy, eighty, almost ninety.

"I'd rather get there alive," I say.

She slows down, but her fingers are tight around the wheel. She's almost more nervous than I am, but I don't think that's technically possible.

My stomach is tied up in knots. My heart is thumping against my chest like it's the freaking Jaws theme. And my breath—it's physically impossible, but I'm pretty sure I haven't taken a breath since I heard the song.

Kara pulls off the freeway. The Sinful mansion is way up in the Hollywood Hills. It's still another ten minutes to their place. Breathing would go a long way towards arriving alive.

I force myself to inhale, but it only heightens the tingling sensation in my body. The song might not mean he wants me. It might be an apology or an admission that ends in sorry, but it's over.

I close my eyes and force myself to exhale. Kara is

here. Whatever happens, I'll survive.

But I'd much rather survive with Miles.

We turn onto one of the local streets, and we drive up, up, up the winding roads into the hills. The lights are on in the house, and Miles's car is in the driveway. His bike is there, too.

He must be here.

Kara parks and jumps out of the car. She's back to bouncing around, ready to knock down anything in her way. She's on my side this time. Thank God. I need the ally.

I climb out of the car. My feet feel wobbly. I'm in sneakers, but I can barely stand. Jelly. My legs are jelly. I press my palm against the car to stay upright.

What if he asks me to get lost? What if I misinterpreted everything?

"Come on." Kara grabs my hand and pulls me up the stone steps.

Somehow, I don't slip. I make it all the way to the oversized front door. Knock. I need to knock. I curl my fingers into a fist and tap it against the door. It barely makes a sound.

"I think I'm going to faint," I whisper.

Kara shakes her head. "You've got this." She presses the doorbell.

Ding. Dong. It really does make that sound, like the game we played when we were kids where we'd press the neighbor's doorbell, run away, and watch to see if they came out.

Ding Dong Ditch. And it sounds like a fantastic idea. Run away, never face Miles, never get the crushing news that he doesn't love me.

The door opens. Damn. That means we lose the game. It's Tom, and he's halfway undressed. Jeans.

315

No t-shirt, no shoes. There's giggling in the background. Ah, there's a half-naked woman in the kitchen. His conquest of the day.

Or Miles's conquest of the day.

My heart thuds. If it keeps beating this fast and hard, it's going to burst right out of my chest.

"Jesus, what did he do now?" Tom asks.

Kara sticks her tongue out and steps inside.

"Come in, please." He rolls his eyes. "Should I call him? I don't even know where to start."

Kara rolls her eyes. "I'm more than happy to storm up to Miles's room and drag him down here."

"Give me a minute," Tom says. He makes some kind of signal to the half-naked woman then turns back to us. His lips purse and he exhales in a dramatic sigh. "He's fucking devastated, you know."

"Just get him," I say.

"You want to tell me what this is about?"

"Meg needs to speak with Miles. Get him or I will," Kara says.

"What do they need to speak about?" Tom folds his arms.

She glares at him like he's the source of all evil in the universe. "They're in love."

Tom raises an eyebrow. He looks at me as if to ask is this shit true?

I nod. As far as I know.

He finally drops the pout. "I hope you're right. But I'm going to do this the old-fashioned way." He pulls out his phone and dials Miles.

There's the faint sound of a ring. A door opens. Footsteps.

Miles appears at the top of the stairs. "You can't walk one fucking flight, Tom?" His eyes find mine, and the irritated scowl drops off his face.

He looks nervous. Miles, the rock star sex god, is nervous because of me.

"Meg. Hey." He clutches the banister on his way down the stairs. "Everything okay?"

I open my mouth, but no sounds come out. Deep breath. "I heard your song."

His lips curl into the tiniest smile. "Yeah?"

"Yeah." I press my fingers against my hips. "That one about me, too?"

He reaches the bottom of the stairs. "I haven't fallen in love with any other girls this year."

My breath catches in my throat. He said... he must mean... he must...

I'm dizzy. My legs are wobbly. "You, um, did you mean what you said?"

"Every word." He takes a step towards me. "Though, technically, I sang them."

"Technically."

Miles sends Tom the evil eye. "A little privacy, maybe?"

"Hell no." He raises his voice. "Drew, Pete, you fuckers here to see this?"

"It's okay," I say. "They can stay."

Miles is five feet away. "I usually write songs to avoid these kinds of declarations."

"You're screwed now. You have an audience and expectations."

He smirks. "If there's anything I know how to do, it's put on a show."

"All I want is the truth."

One more step. He's six inches from me. He brushes my hair behind my ear. "I love you, Meg. I had something perfect right under my nose, and it took me forever to realize it. But I realize it now."

Tom' voice booms. "YOU FUCKERS ARE MISSING OUT!"

A bedroom door slams and Pete appears at the top of the stairs. He spots Miles. "He's out of his room?"

Miles shakes his head. "They're really ruining the moment."

"No, it's perfect."

He slides his hand around my waist. "I'm not good at this relationship thing, but I want to do it with you."

"You sure?"

"Positive." He pulls me closer. "If you're willing to forgive me for being an utter idiot."

"Yeah." I lean into him. "The biggest idiot."

"I'll take that as a yes." He presses his lips into mine.

All of our other kisses were amazing. All of our other kisses set my body on fire. But this one is on another level. It's like every bit of need in him is pouring into me, like he's prying himself open for me and showing me all the ways he hurts.

The kiss breaks, and I pull back. I stare into his gorgeous eyes. "I love you, too."

And I swear to God, he melts.

The world is spinning around me. There's clapping. It's Tom, I think. Then it's Kara, and Pete. I look around the room, and Drew is there, too.

They're clapping, but it's not like this is silly. It's like they mean it.

Miles leans a little closer. "Assholes were convinced I'd die miserable and alone."

"Utter assholes."

"I'd say let's give them a free show, but I want you

all to myself."

He presses his lips against mine again. It's as sweet as the first kiss of the night, but it's hotter. It's so hot, I'm pretty sure I'm going to ignite.

"Okay, I think that's my cue," Kara says. "You're taking her home tomorrow."

"Stay," Pete calls out. "We're going to have to blast a movie if we want to hear anything besides Miles screaming in ecstasy." He laughs. "Though, Meg, you're free to make as much noise as you want."

"That's my girlfriend, asshole," Miles says. "If that's okay with you."

My body fills with warmth. "Absolutely."

"You're lucky I'm preoccupied, or I'd kick your ass." Miles leads me up the stairs. "Tom, berate Pete about the loud phone sex."

"Any time." Tom sends us a salute.

We pass Drew and Pete. My cheeks burn. I mouth thank you, though I'm not sure who I'm thanking. Everyone, I guess.

They're all happy for us.

Pete winks at me. I'm pretty sure Miles sees it, but I don't think he cares.

We're going to be preoccupied for the rest of the night.

EPILOGUE

Miles squeezes my hand. "You ready?"

Deep breath. Almost. Yeah. I think I am. No, I absolutely am. I nod. "Yes."

"Do the honors." He takes my hand and places it on the computer mouse.

Eyes open. The cursor hovers over "Submit Application." Okay. I can do this. I press my finger down until the mouse clicks.

Submitting…

Thank you for submitting to Harvard Medical School. Check your email for a submission confirmation.

I let out something suspiciously close to a scream. "Oh my God." I throw my arms around Miles and kiss him like the goddamn ship is going down.

His body relaxes into mine. He digs his hands into my hair and pulls our lips apart. "Honey, you have six of these to go. I can't take the blue balls if you do this every time."

"Too bad."

"Your parents will hear."

"Too bad for them."

"Oh yeah?" He slides his hand under my wool skirt and runs his fingers over the seam of my tights. "Better get these off."

"Okay, point taken." I navigate to the next page. Yale. Aim high, right? We spent the morning filling these out. Now there's nothing left to do but submit them.

I squeeze Miles with one hand and with the other...

Click!

Submitting...

Thank you for submitting to Yale Medical School.

Miles presses his lips into my neck. "You're such a little nerd."

"Jealous?"

"Hey! I'm a rock star. Have some respect." He finds the top of my tights and tugs them down ever so gently. "Or else I'll force you to respect me."

"We have five to go."

"You can go while you come."

"Okay, I don't want my parents to hear," I say. "They were very hospitable accepting a last-minute guest. And a depraved rock star no less."

"Your parents love me more than you do."

I kiss him on the forehead. "That's not possible."

It's the day after Christmas, and Miles has been here, in my parents' Newport Beach place, for a week. Things between me and my parents were strained at first, but I had a heart-to-heart with Mom and Dad. We sat at the dining-room table until midnight, crying and laughing, and trading stories about Rosie and how much we missed her. Mom even put one of the family pictures back up.

"Well, we both know you'll never manage to be quiet," he says.

"So you'll have to live with blue balls."

"No, I'll have to invent some kind of catastrophe so your parents are called to the hospital and we have the place to ourselves."

"They're going out to dinner tonight," I say.

"That's hours away."

He slides his arms around my waist, pulling me closer. My ass is presses against his erection. Yes, it would feel amazing to fuck Miles again, but I'm a little preoccupied.

"In due time," I say. "You're supposed to be supporting me."

He grabs the mouse and navigates to the next page. UCSF. "You want me to do the honors?"

"Yes, please."

Click.

Submitting…

Thank you for submitting to UCSF!

"Why are you leaving tomorrow?" I ask. "Does Sinful Serenade really need its singer that badly?"

"Desperately." He runs his hands over my shoulders. "Why don't you come with me?"

Next application. Stanford. Click. Submitting… Done.

"I can't," I say. "I have school. And work."

"You're off work until your semester starts. It's an international tour. Our first international tour. You can be a part of history." He presses his lips to my neck. "And it ends the second day of school."

Next application. UCLA. Click. Submitting…

Done.

"You want to take me to Tokyo and Osaka and Madrid and London?" I ask.

"And Paris and Berlin and a few other cities I don't remember." He turns me around so we're face to face. "Come. We can hang out backstage every night and tour fantastic cities every day."

"Are you sure?"

"Positive." He rubs my shoulders. "I want you to come. And to tour with me."

A million excuses pop into my brain, but none of them matter. Traveling the world with my hot rock-star boyfriend—I'd be a fool to say no.

"Okay," I say.

"That's it—okay?"

"Hell to the yes! Better?"

"Much."

I turn back around so I'm facing the computer. One more application. The one I was dreading for a million years.

UCI.

I don't know where I'll be this time next year, but wherever I am, I won't be running from anything.

Click. Submitting… Done.

Miles sucks on my earlobe. "You know we have to celebrate."

"When my parents leave."

"Now." He pulls my tights to my knees. "And when your parents leave."

I can live with that.

EXCERPT FROM STRUM YOUR HEART OUT
Kara + Drew

A buxom fan saunters in my direction. But she's not interested in me. I am invisible to her.

Her eyes are on Drew. She smiles. She shoves her hand in his face like I'm not here. "Oh my gosh. You must be Drew Denton. I'm such a big fan. "

He shakes her hand, no signs of interest on his face. "I am."

She drags her fake red fingernails over Drew's forearm and thrusts her chest at him. "I love Sinful Serenade, " she slurs. "You're soooooo good with your hands."

The worst part about having a rock star guitarist friend is hearing that line over and over and over.

Drew's lips curl into a smile. A smug expression creeps onto his face. "That's what I'm told."

And there's the second-worst part——hearing him give that same flirty response to every fan who is too rude to acknowledge the girl sitting next to him. Is it that obvious we're just friends or is she too desperate to care?"

"Do you think... Oh, gosh. Could you sign my, um..." She giggles. "My chest?"

His eyes dart to said chest. It's hard to blame him when her top is cut down to her belly button. No judgment. I've worn far sluttier things. Hell, my current getup could go toe-to-toe with this girl's in a who is showing the most boob competition.

A girl has to do what she can to get what she wants.

Apparently, this girl wants Drew's attention on her cans.

It's working. His eyes are wide. His mouth is open. He's staring like he's thinking about burying his face between her boobs.

Not that it bothers me or anything. Not like I want him to look at me that way. Not anything like that.

I adjust my bustier top for maximum cleavage potential and push myself up from my seat. Drew looks at me for a second then his attention goes right back to the fangirl.

She drags those red fingernails up his biceps. "How do you stay so... fit on tour?"

He smiles. "On the floor."

She gasps like she's not at all familiar with the concept of pushups. He smiles, all cocky and smug and totally cool.

He never flirts like this.

Never.

It shouldn't bother me. He's my friend and he can flirt with anyone he wants.

Doesn't mean I have to watch it.

I make my way to the dance floor. Through the

horde of twentysomething beautiful people here for the scene and not the music.

It's a pulsating, throbbing, electronic thing. Perfect. I step onto the vinyl. Eyes closed. Arms over my head. I shift my hips back and forth. No fancy moves. Just instinct.

The fangirl's hyena laugh cuts through the room. I must be imagining things. There's no way she's louder than the music.

Drew is still talking with the fangirl. Not so much flirting with her. But certainly staring at her cans.

This tension builds in between my shoulder blades. It's all wrong. My body is loose and free when I dance. Tension is not part of the equation. And Drew is my friend. He's flirting with a floozy. So what? He's a rock star. He flirts with lots of floozies.

He probably fucks them too.

My nostrils flare. I shake my head and press my eyelids together. No. I refuse to feel this right now. I refuse to feel anything except the music.

I throw myself into dancing. The world melts away, one piece at a time. The rest of the club. The hyena laugh. Drew's wide-eyed, lust-filled smile as the fangirl mauls him.

It's not even on my mind.

I move closer to the speakers. They drown out every other thought inside my brain. I'm only a vessel for the music. My hips move of their own accord. My chest shifts. My arms sway.

I'm free.

And then there are hands on my hips. Strong hands. A guy's hands. It's a normal part of clubbing. Usually one I enjoy.

But this feels off. I take a step forward to break

free of the hands, so it's nothing but me and the music. Better. That tension between my shoulder blades relaxes. I drift into bliss…

The damn hands are back! I turn to face this guy. He's tall. Broad. He looks like a TV actor—handsome but not out-of-this-world hot. Any other night, I'd welcome him as a dance partner.

I throw my arms above my head and match his movements. He's a good dancer—perfectly in time with the rhythm. It's not altogether awful.

He takes a step towards me so he's pressed up against me. Those hands go to my hips again. No more bliss. I'm utterly on edge—tense and strained in all the wrong places.

"Excuse me." I make my way to the bar. Some area free of guys with too few manners to ask permission.

The guy follows me. "Can I buy you a drink?"

"No thank you."

"Come on. It will be fun." He grabs my wrist. The left. Right above my silver watch.

I pull my hand into my chest. Manners be damned, next time he does that, I'm slapping him.

I offer my most polite smile and shake my head. "No, thank you. I'm here with someone."

"Who?"

Fine. I hate using this line, but it's the only thing that works on guys like this. "My boyfriend."

The guy takes a long, hard look at me. At my cleavage, mostly. That awkward, awful tension builds between my shoulder blades again.

What the hell? This is supposed to feel good. A hot guy is checking me out. A hot guy wants to press his body up against mine in time with the music.

"Your boyfriend lets you go out like that?" he asks.

"Believe it or not, I have this funny thing called free will." I step backwards. "And I don't let guys tell me what to wear."

"Your boyfriend sounds like a pussy."

"I'll let him know your feelings." Okay. The bar thing isn't working. Time for the nuclear option. I make my way to the women's restroom.

The guy follows. "I only want to talk."

"And I don't."

I take a quick step but even with my heels, I've got short legs and this guy is all kinds of tall. He's faster than I am.

He grabs my wrist. The right. I shake it off. No slapping necessary. Yet.

"You don't have to be so rude," he says.

Obviously, I do, 'cause he's not taking the hint. I turn so I'm facing the asshole. Anger flares in my gut. I manage to hold my tongue. There are merits to telling this guy what he can do with that grabby hand, but it seems silly to cause a scene. It's easier to slip away with a careful excuse. No conflict necessary.

"Excuse me, ladies room," I say.

He reaches for me again. Left wrist this time. Okay, that's it. I pull my hand free and go to slap him.

But someone stops me. His hand closes around my triceps. There's something right about it. Something magical.

It's Drew. Drew's hand is tight around my arm. Drew is touching me.

He looks at the asshole guy. "Can I help you?"

The guy looks at me with disbelief. "This your boyfriend?"

I throw Drew a please play along look. "Yes. And

we're very busy tonight."

"Is this guy bothering you?" Drew asks.

"It's fine."

"It doesn't look fine." Drew's eyes narrow. He stares down the guy. "You followed her across the dance floor."

He was watching me?

"We were having a conversation," the guy says.

"You grabbed her. Do it again and it will be the last time you ever touch anyone or anything beautiful," Drew says.

The guy holds Drew's stare. Trying out some kind of intimidation and failing miserably. I almost feel bad for him. Idiot has no clue what he's in for.

The guy takes a step back. He mutters under his breath. "She's not even that hot."

"We both know that's not true." Drew slides his hand around my waist.

But the guy is still staring at us.

"If you don't leave in the next ten seconds, my first is going to make contact with your face. And I'm gonna to make hitting you worth it. Means I won't be able to pick up my guitar tomorrow." Drew glares at the guy.

"Drew, honey," I try my best we're totally a couple voice. "Don't. He's not worth it." I turn to Drew. I slide my arm around his neck to sell the whole we're clearly a couple thing.

But the guy is still staring at me.

Drew stares back at him. "You have five seconds left."

It does nothing to scare the guy off.

I grab Drew's arm and squeeze as hard as I can. No way I'm going to be responsible for the kind of fight that will get all three of us kicked out of the club.

Drew turns back to me. He takes my hand and places it on his shoulder. It's like he's promising this won't get out of hand.

His eyes find mine. He mouths you trust me?

I nod. Yes. Of course.

His palm presses into my lower back, pushing my body into his. He leans closer. His eyes close.

Mine do the same. Pure reflex. I rise to my tiptoes.

His lips brush against mine. A quick kiss to start. Then it's more. He sucks on my lower lip. He digs his other hand into my hair.

My heart picks up until it's going so fast I can't keep track. I'm aware of every inch of my body. The light feeling in my chest and stomach. The strain of my calves. The flutter building between my legs.

This is why I dance.

Drew releases me. He steps back and looks as if to check that the coast is clear. His demeanor shifts. No longer my fake boyfriend. Just my best friend. "You okay?"

"Yeah."

His arm goes back to his side. His body moves away from mine. My heart is still racing. My chest is still light. I'm still acutely aware of every place that stretches or strains, of every flutter or rush or buzz of electricity.

Drew kissed me.

For show, but still.

Drew kissed me and my entire body is in overdrive.

Drew. Kissed. Me.

And God, I want him to kiss me again.

Printed in Great Britain
by Amazon